D0232602

Deadly Stakes

Deadly Stakes

H. Fred Wiser

Walker and Company
New York

All the characters and events portrayed in this story are fictitious.

First published in the United States of America in 1989
by Walker Publishing Company, Inc.

Published simultaneously in Canada by Thomas Allen & Son
Canada, Limited, Markham, Ontario.

Library of Congress Cataloging-in-Publication Data

H. Fred Wiser
Deadly stakes.

I. Title.
PS3556.R518D44 1989 813'.54 88-37878
ISBN 0-8027-5732-4

Printed in the United States of America

10 9 8 7 6 5 4 3 2 1

This is for our parents,
and for men and women of valor everywhere.

Deadly Stakes

1

THE ASSEMBLYWOMANPERSON SHIFTED her butt around uncomfortably on our new white-plastic and chrome client's chair. White for purity shows our faith in human nature.

It was only a few moments earlier, when thoughts of homemade porn, blackmail, and political intrigue were furthest from our minds, that she had walked unannounced into our tiny second-floor office, looking to throw a little business toward one of her favorite former students. That would be my partner, Jessica Munroe. I was never anyone's favorite student.

It was pretty nervy of her to walk in just like that off the street, no call or anything. I mean, how could she know we'd be sitting there twiddling our thumbs, waiting for business to walk our way? I yawned.

She was having trouble coming out with the reason for her visit. Her light hazel eyes shifted from me to Jessica, to me again—then to the book-size, brown-wrapped package in her lap. Her gaze finally settled on Jessica, though there was still the occasional glance darted toward my side of the room. It was a little bit like watching a game of table tennis in stereo. I fiddled with the Monday-morning mail on my desk blotter—bills mostly.

She swallowed hard and tried again. "I thought you worked alone, Ms. Munroe."

"Sorry to disappoint you, Professor Walters."

"It's Mrs. Walters now."

She stopped short of saying, "It always was," but

Jessica and I already knew that she had been a lecturer rather than a professor when we took her political science course at Brooklyn College some years ago. Elite colleges like Brooklyn don't give a teacher professional rank without a Ph.D. in hand.

"Ms. Walters, then. Jason Reddy and I have been teamed up for more than a year now. You remember Mr. Reddy, don't you?"

The ping-pong balls darted to my side of the room again. Sure, she remembered me. One thing I know about teachers is that they remember the best students and the troublemakers. Let's just say I wasn't among the former.

Her eyes bounced back to focus on Jessica, who was saying, "I've known him for a very long time, and needless to say, he's completely trustworthy."

My, my. I'll have to get reluctant clients in here more often.

By now, the bills on my desk were arranged in two neat piles—Pay and Wait. I tried hard to look trustworthy. It must have worked because she started pouring out her story to Jessica.

With the ping-pong game temporarily suspended, I had a chance to observe her with a professional eye. After all, I already had more than a year of full-time detective work, not counting that bit of time I spent on covert commando operations along the Ho Chi Minh Trail—a period that never did count for much.

The brown paper package was still sitting on our potential client's lap. She fingered it gingerly from time to time, like a hot iron.

Althea Walters had been elected to the state assembly by the discriminating voters of Bay Ridge. She was an attractive, middle-aged woman with well-defined features and an air of strength and competence. Her shoulder-length hair, combed away from her forehead, was mostly brown, but if you looked hard enough you could find a strand or two of just about any color, including gray. Her dress was plain, black, and short-sleeved—a straight up-and-down shapeless piece of summer-weight material that made me wonder what was underneath.

She was maybe a couple of years older than me, which was another reason we didn't get along back in my college days. I had been older than most of the other students. My tour of duty over, I was in college courtesy of Uncle Sam. I guess she was a couple of years older than me even back then, but I'd recently been to hell and lived to tell the tale, and I felt older than Moses himself. Who knows, maybe I was. I was also a bit of a wiseass.

She looked like a woman who would be more comfortable giving orders than sitting meekly in someone else's office with a small package hurting her lap. The way her fingers gripped that package, I didn't think she'd ever be able to let go, but it seemed she would have to. It seemed that package was crucial to the story she was telling Jessica.

"It came in the regular mail. A tape—a videocassette."

"Did you play it?" Jessica always asks the bright questions.

Walters had absentmindedly ripped off a narrow strip of the brown-paper wrapping and was now working that strip into little shreds. "It was awful. It was me." The small brown-paper shreddings piled up in her lap. "But it wasn't me. I never did it."

"Are we talking blackmail here?" Jessica asked.

"Blackmail?"

"You're saying there's something incriminating on that videotape, right?"

"Yes, dammit."

"Well, was there a blackmail demand with the tape?"

"No. I don't think so."

"No note?"
"No."
"No telephone call?"
"No."
"Any idea who sent it?"
"No."
Jessica reached under her desk for a ten-pound dumbbell. Some people chew gum when they tense up, or smoke a cigarette, or make coffee. Jessica works out—anywhere. She started doing curls. Five times on the right arm, then five on the left—and so on. It helps her think.
"Ms. Walters, we're going to have to see that tape."
I think it was the "we" that got to Ms. Walters. As she turned to look at me, her face and neck went so white that I checked the floor under her seat, half expecting to see a pool of blood. I couldn't think of anywhere else it could have gone.
After some debate back and forth, during which that look of hers made me feel like a leering piece of turd, the tape was finally on Jessica's desk along with a two-hundred-dollar retainer and a signed contract. A copy of the contract found its way into the assemblyperson's handbag as well.
"I don't want to see that tape again," she said. She shook her head violently from side to side. "I never in my life did anything like that. I know it's me on the tape, but I don't know how it happened. Do I have to see it again?"
"Not right now," Jessica comforted her. "But we may need your help with it at some other time."
A perceptible shiver ran through our client.
Jessica patted her reassuringly on the back. "Don't worry, Ms. Walters. We'll find out who's behind this."
She didn't seem terribly reassured. "Why would someone—? Why would anyone—?"

"We'll know that when we find them." Jessica patted her again and ushered her out the door. "We'll call you tonight, Ms. Walters."

When she was safely out of earshot, I asked, "Where did she hear that you're in private investigations now, Munroe? And, uh, how come she didn't know you had a partner?"

Jessica waited a moment before answering, "I see her over at the Women's Club from time to time. But not since you and I teamed up."

I made a face. Jessica knows how I feel about *women's lib*. "That dyke place?"

"It's not a dyke place at all, Jason Reddy."

"Oh, yeah? Well then, tell me," I said, triumphantly, "how come none of the women who hang out there wanted to go to bed with me?"

A smile played on her lips. "Did you ever think," she asked, "that maybe it's because they're *not* dykes?"

"Ooh. Low blow."

"But well aimed. Want to see a movie?"

It was a VHS videocassette, and our Panasonic could handle it. We shut the blinds on our only window, doused the fluorescent light, and put the office into near darkness. The room was now lit only by our oversized television screen on which were projected flesh-toned images against a blue background, and not much else. Although we could both see the screen perfectly from our respective desks, Jessica took her weights to the floor and ran through one of her workouts while the tape played.

Walters had been right when she said that it was her and it wasn't her. The image on the screen was undoubtedly our favorite assemblyperson in the flesh. No way was that a double. However, she was acting more like an alter ego of the woman who had, just moments before, occupied the spiffy white chair. Our client was reserved and had even appeared a bit matronly. The woman on the screen was outgoing, boisterous, and totally uninhibited. Totally. Also, my keen detective's curiosity was satisfied that the black dress she had been wearing today was more shapeless than she.

It was clear that a man and a woman were romping along with her, although it was impossible to determine who they were. They wore animal masks or, rather, the heads of animal costumes, which lent to the whole thing an air of pucklike unreality. He was the donkey, she the rabbit. Our Ms. Walters was not similarly disguised.

The donkey, the rabbit, and the assemblywoman were busily engaged in such diverse social perversions as pseudobestiality, multiple-partner orgy, and mutual humiliation—all over that big blue bed. At least, I think it was a bed. There was no frame visible, only the mattress, and no pillows or covers. The unpatterned walls were the same blue color so that they melded with the bed and nothing detracted from the show on center stage.

I slumped low in my chair, sipped cold coffee from a cardboard container, and watched as the fleshy scene worked its way to conclusion.

Jessica watched from the floor while she worked on thighs and abdomen. At one point she stopped in midgrunt to stare at the screen and, after a few seconds, resumed her routine. Every once in a while I groaned a bit in sympathetic muscle strain. The screen went dark just as Jessica completed three cleansing breaths. She rose from the floor in one graceful motion and went over to the controls.

"What do you think?"

"Tasteless, amateurish, and disgusting," I said. "I was shocked. Play it again."

Before she had a chance to oblige, we both realized there was more. This time there were no players, no bed, just a white background with dark green, glowing lettering in big block letters.

"Recognize someone?" it said. "We don't want much. Just a friendly vote now and again. We'll let you know specifics. You be our friend, we'll be yours. Remember who your friends are."

We watched the tape again, all the way through. It seemed likely that Walters had shut the thing off too quickly to get to the friendly message. All in all, that afternoon, we played the darn thing about a dozen times, sometimes fast, sometimes slow, sometimes advancing, sometimes going back, sometimes pausing for a still pose. What were we looking for? Clues, which were about as plentiful in that film as cabs on a rainy day—though there were a couple of things.

"She has green eyes," I said.

"She?"

"The rabbit, not the client."

"I didn't think you were exactly focusing on her eyes."

"I always notice eyes."

I thought of the frantic ping-pong match. Jessica had probably missed it. She frequently ignores details.

"What color were his eyes?"

"Black—or brown. Something dark."

She was grinning.

"Okay, okay. So I didn't spend too much time on the guy. Anyway, what did you think of him, Bigmouth?"

"I thought he looked like an ass."

"So with me it's her eyes, with you it's his—"

"What about her hands?"

Surprised, I said, "Hands help a lot."

"At least as much as eyes."

"Okay, tell me about hands."

"Her fingers are small and dainty. She has long, painted nails and she knows how to handle them."

"What do you mean, handle them?"

"She held up her own neatly manicured fingernails to

me. They were very short. "If I would paste nails on, or even grow them from time to time, I would have a hell of a time doing the things I normally do with my hands. I would always be compensating for the extra length and probably keep forgetting myself and breaking the nails and scratching up people and pets."

"You don't have any pets."

"Hypothetical pets. Anyhow," she continued, "the nails are no big deal. It just means that she's very used to them and I'd be surprised to ever find her without them."

"How about his fingers?"

"Long. Bony."

Oh, boy. "All eleven of them?"

She laughed. "You said it, I didn't."

"Yeah, but you were thinking it."

We had a hell of a time judging their height, but we figured the donkey for somewhere in the area of five-nine to six-one and the rabbit for five feet to five-four.

Meanwhile, I was pessimistic about the job. "Think we can pull it off, Munroe?" She looked at me. "I mean, find the blackmailer, person or persons, and destroy the tape or retrieve it or whatever?"

Jessica shrugged. "It's what we do," she said.

I shrugged back, then busied myself making a few flat still images from the film. They were, naturally, of pretty poor quality. Six of them were of the animal heads from various positions, a few were full-length body shots, one was of the rabbit's bottom—not so much for lascivious purposes, as for the small, indistinct, lavenderish spot on the lower part of her left buttock. I thought it might be a clue. Well, all right, maybe I am a little lascivious.

Jessica called our client to set up a meeting for the following morning. "What time would you prefer?" Jessica said to the phone. "That's fine. We'll see you then."

I raised my eyebrows at my partner.

"Seven o'clock," she said.

"Oh?" I didn't like the cruel gleam in her eye—which she, no doubt, would have called a mischievous twinkle. "I thought you said morning."

"That's right. Tomorrow morning."

"There is no seven o'clock in the morning."

"Oh, come on, Red."

I was incredulous. "You mean there actually are two seven o'clocks in a day?"

"I'll tell you what. You can stay over at my place tonight instead of taking the subway all the way to the city." When you live or work in Brooklyn, Manhattan is always called "the city," even though Brooklyn hasn't been exactly a suburban haven for about sixty years. "But you have to promise to behave yourself."

"Why?" I raised my eyebrow again. It was the one muscle that I exercised and she didn't.

"And Jason, tomorrow when our honorable client returns, let me do the talking, okay?"

"Didn't I behave like a good boy today, Mommy?"

"You were great today. You kept quiet and gave me a chance to gain her confidence. On the other hand, sometimes your so-called wit can be offensive to certain people—women, for instance."

"Not to you, I trust."

"This is a very strange case, Jason. We have virtually no information. Not even a concrete blackmail demand. I don't want you to get so frustrated that you take it out on our client and give her the third degree, or get belligerent."

"Belligerent? You mean like yell at a client? You mean like strike a partner?"

"Don't take it the wrong way, Red. I'm telling you this for the good of the firm."

"I won't say a word, Munroe," I said as I crossed my fingers behind my back.

Later, over dinner at our favorite neighborhood spot, we both ignored the case for a while. We frequently eat at a gourmet health food restaurant called Food for Thought, which is on Flatbush Avenue, a very short walk from our office. Jessica likes it because she can keep her body healthy. I like it because the food is actually good and they serve more than just minute portions of salad and flaked fish. They'll even fix you a nice-sized broiled steak, as long as you present a note from your doctor attesting to a severe cholesterol deficiency.

Jessica ordered the macrobiotic special, right out of yogi heaven. Brown rice, stir-fried bean curd, and steamed fresh vegetables topped with sprouts. Wow.

I bravely ordered my favorite pasta dish with extra meat.

We kept the discussion casual as long as the banana cake, my decaf, and Jessica's carrot juice lasted. Jessica dug her fork into the last bite of banana cake.

"I'm glad to see you have a healthy appetite," she said. "Human beings weren't meant to subsist on computer manuals."

"What's wrong with computer manuals?"

She rolled her eyes. "Sometimes it seems like all you think about are bytes and memory boards and input devices. Then you say something fairly intelligent and I remember that you really do have a splendid human brain."

"Thanks, I think. Anyway"—I pointed to my head—"we call it analog."

"What?"

"That's the difference between a digital computer, such as the tiny one in our office, and an analog computer which operates by voltage measurements. . . ."

I saw the heavy curtains go down in front of her eyes.

My chosen field bores her into polite, living death. I changed the subject.

"Got a date with what's-his-name tonight?"

"Hmm. You?"

"Had." I nodded. "A late date—which I'll have to cancel, thanks to you and your seven A.M. appointment."

"Gloria?"

"That was over days ago," I said. Jessica grinned in spite of herself. "Doris."

"Ah, another intellectual?"

"Don't be a snob. Besides," I said, "your friend Sardine is no great catch."

"Sandy."

"Get it? Sardine?"

"You know perfectly well his name is Sandy."

"Sandy? Oh, no." I ran a hand affectedly through my hair and grinned, widely exposing all my teeth. "Sanford Douglas Foxworth, Junior," I intoned, moving my mouth as little as possible while I did so.

Jessica rolled her eyes. Sanford Douglas Foxworth, Junior—also known as Sandy to his friends, if he had any—is a local real estate salesman. You've met him, I'm sure. His hair is colored, waved, and styled. His teeth are perfectly straight and white—exactly as if they were capped. He wears a gold chain under his shirt, and two chains on top of it, and three rings on the fingers of one hand, and one on the other hand. His suits cost five hundred dollars apiece. His shirts are custom-fit and monogrammed. A pair of shoes sets him back two hundred dollars. This is not classified information. It's the first thing he tells you after hello.

"Where's he taking you?"

"Don't know." She colored slightly. "We'll probably just watch TV at his place."

"Uh-huh." I quietly finished my desert.

Jessica giggled. That surprised me. I hadn't heard her giggle since college. I had a momentary this-is-your-life type of mental flashback. I was back in our college days, after we had become friends. We'd go into a bar—sometimes it was the College Pub, the students' favorite watering hole—where I would set up an arm-wrestling match for Jessica. I'd pick out a real tough guy and announce to the other patrons that an ordinary woman could beat him at arm wrestling. The bets would mount. Then Jessica did her stuff. This went on for about two years. Only one guy ever beat Jessica in all that time. It generally went like this:

Jessica sits facing her opponent over the table in the College Pub. His huge frame is full of beer and five times the size of hers. They clasp hands, elbow to elbow. Jessica silently wills her tough little arm past the point of resistance. Her opponent is red-faced and short of breath, his beefy forearm bulging with surprised muscles and veins. He tries to get some leverage by placing his left hand on the table. Just moments earlier, I had easily hustled him into arm wrestling with a *broad*—for fun—and a nice cash ante from the rest of the youthful patrons in the bar. Like taking candy.

Afterwards she would giggle, while her hand trembled slightly as she swept the bills off the table.

"I haven't heard you giggle since college."

"I was thinking of college," she said. "Remember what the kids used to call Professor Walters? Old Stony-Face Walters?"

"We're taking her money, Munroe. We should at least treat her with a little respect. Anyway, she's Ms. Walters now—or The Honorable Ms.—not Professor. And, as you and I have recently observed—on film, no less—she's not as stony-faced as poli sci made her appear."

"Everyone has lapses, now and then."
"Not you," I sighed. "At least, not with me."
"We're not talking about me."
"Maybe later," I added hopefully.
"Not even later. But it's true, you know. Every human being has at some time done something to be ashamed of in the morning."
"Everyone doesn't do it with a donkey and a rabbit."

We didn't do it at all that night and so had nothing to be ashamed of in the morning.

I did stay over at Jessica's. She has a fairly large house. I've visited often enough over the last ten years or so to know it pretty well. When I first met her she was living with an elderly maiden aunt. After a while, the house became an inheritance and Jessica lived there alone.

It was a large old house on Ocean Parkway, in one of Brooklyn's classier neighborhoods. The downstairs had a formal living room and dining room that were practically bare, a large kitchen and a den that shared a common fireplace. I bunked on the couch in the den. A maid's quarters had long ago been converted into some kind of laundry room. Upstairs was Jessica's bedroom, an empty room, and a study, both of which had once been guest rooms.

Shortly after midnight she returned from her date with Sandy. I had already made myself comfortable on the couch in the den, but I still had the light on. I was reading the latest selection of our own private book club: *The Women's Room* by Marilyn French. Where does she find these books?

I heard her lock and bolt the front door and walk to the kitchen. Heard the refrigerator door open, heard it close. Heard the clink of glass. Then she was in the den carrying a Miller and a Perrier. The Miller was for me.

Give me a hearty, nutritious ale over phony French seltzer water any day.

We drank in silence for a while, each lost in private thoughts. Jessica was parked on an armchair close to my head, her legs crossed and stretched out in front of her, feet resting on my couch. I couldn't begin to guess what she was thinking.

"You ever consider settling down, Red?"

So that was it. "Are you proposing, Munroe?" I put on my most alluring smile.

"Oh, come on—"

"Propositioning?"

She stood up abruptly and started out of the room. I just managed to pull her back and almost spilled her drink. She sat down on the edge of the couch, pressed close against my chest. My arms circled her waist as I steadied her—or steadied me.

I peered into her brown eyes. "Sanford Douglas Foxworth, Junior, has asked for your hand?"

"Mmm," she nodded, miserably. At least it seemed that way to me.

"And the rest of you, too, I suppose."

She examined her hands. "Do you know how old I am?"

"Ancient."

"Twenty-nine."

I shook my head. "In dog years, maybe."

"Old enough to have a kid. To have a man who's, you know, there. To have someone buy me flowers."

"I'm there."

She smirked. "Are you going to buy me flowers?"

I matched her, smirk for smirk. "You dead?"

There didn't seem to be much to say after that, but the tension had eased. Jessica went to bed. I punched up my pillow and finished my drink. My friend-partner has always fascinated me, even before I was her partner, even before she was my friend. Jessica is probably the coolest dude I know. We don't always see eye-to-eye, but when you've been friends as long as we have you don't let a little disagreement get in the way of that friendship.

I lay there for a while, trying to characterize our relationship. I suppose, since we've teamed up to battle crime in the big, nasty metropolis, we're something of a Mr. and Mrs. North of the eighties—except for not being married—and except for not sleeping together. Actually, it has never been proven that Mr. and Mrs. North slept together either, so maybe there's more of a similarity than I thought.

After a while, I fell asleep.

2

"WHAT DO YOU mean, you don't know where the film was shot? Were you there or weren't you?"

Assemblywoman Walters, sharply dressed in a pastel-blue, lightweight suit, had eschewed the chair in favor of pacing hither and thither across our modest office. And that was Jessica badgering the client, not me. I said nothing. Instead, I bit my tongue to keep my mouth straight.

On a piece of yellow, self-stick notepaper, I wrote, "Let's not overdo it with the soft and sweet routine. She might think we want her for her money. P.S. I'm stuck on you."

I attached the note to one of Jessica's ten-pound dumbbells, parked it on top of her desk, and felt duly revenged for the patronizing and critical tone she had taken the day before.

Jessica read the note, drew in her breath, and let it out again. "Ms. Walters," she said with a straight face, "my colleague has just reminded me of a very important engagement I have in the building. I won't be long. In the meantime, please try to remember something that would have a bearing on your problem. Otherwise, I don't know if we will be able to help you."

That Jessica had an important engagement in the building was news to me. As she left I noticed that she took the ladies' room key along, but no dumbbells. There's a limit, I guess, to the number of places where one can work out.

I was still quiet, although I didn't plan to stay that way for long. I was considering various approaches and openings. I'm basically an honest guy and she's a politician. What could I say to a person whose chosen profession was diametrically opposed to so many of my firmest beliefs? Part of the friction between us in college, I recalled, had been due to the fact that I felt I had learned more about politics and politicians in Vietnam than I would ever learn in her political science course. Now, however, she was my client. It was time to get to know her on a different level.

Meanwhile, Walters stood, half turned from the window—the one cleverly designed to keep our office in shadow for the better part of the day—staring at me the way one stares at a person who is known to be disturbed. You can't be certain when he'll do something crazy, and you don't want your back turned when he does.

Luckily, we were both distracted by a double beep from my terminal. I had mail. Electronic mail, that is. Due to the wonder of miniature integrated circuits and miles of telephone cabling, anyone with a remote terminal setup can send electronic messages to me via one of the several services to which I subscribe.

I swiveled to the blinking screen, brought up the message and, without even looking, transferred it into a file in memory to be checked later.

"Did you study computers in college?" Walters had found the opening herself.

"A bit." I'd majored in it. I sure as hell didn't major in poli sci. "This isn't only a computer, Ms. Walters. It's also set up as an intelligent remote terminal."

She looked confused. I might have said, "This isn't just a computer. It's also a spaceship navigation unit. There's a little green Martian inside of it."

"Oh."

We used a few more single-syllable words on each

other and I tried pulling some information out of her, but that wasn't getting us anywhere. I decided to take a different tack, that of reporting to a client. I relayed to her what little information we had put together from the videotape—especially the crucial part at the end which she had apparently missed.

"I have to admit I shut it off in the middle." She made a sour face. "I didn't want to see any more."

"You did watch some of it?"

"Well, yes."

"Was there anything familiar about the two other participants?"

"I already told you I don't remember ever making that video or doing those things."

"I mean, did you recognize them when you viewed the tape?"

"No."

"Nothing? You're sure?" I prodded her memory gently. "How about their body language, the way they moved? Anything you can remember seeing before?"

"I never saw them before in my life!"

"How can you be so sure? They were wearing masks."

Her eyes opened wide. "I guess you're right. I can't be absolutely certain I don't know them."

"All right. Let's forget the people for a moment. Did you ever see the masks before? Do masks mean anything special to someone you know?"

A brief shake of her head answered no to all my questions at once. Maybe to all the questions I would ever ask.

I felt like I was losing her again. For several seconds she sat quite still. Only her lips moved. They were pressed tightly together in a thin horizontal line, and she kept pressing them tighter still. I couldn't help feeling that the lower part of her face would soon be suctioned right into her mouth.

She managed somehow to relax a little and go on. "Jason." With the panic of yesterday still in her eyes, she said, "Tell me the truth. Is there anything we can do?"

I think it was the "we" that got me—plus the fact that we still had her two hundred in the office safe and I didn't want to return it to her.

"Ms. Walters," I began, then considered for a moment. "Am I old enough now to call you Althea?"

She laughed—a very short laugh, barely more than a grin really, but it helped. Suddenly she seemed human again. Suddenly I felt human again.

"Nobody's old enough to use that name, Jason. With the sole exception, perhaps, of my mother, and she's been dead for eight years." The shadow of a smile was still on her face and her eyes had softened. "My friends call me Allie. Why don't you?"

By the time Jessica returned from her urgent engagement, Allie and I were deeply engrossed in avid discussion of the intricacies of the blackmail scheme and approaching a healthy level of mutual confidence. Given the arctic coolness of the scene Jessica had left not that long ago, I imagine the state of affairs upon her return made her feel like she'd taken the wrong door out of the Twilight Zone.

Allie and I grinned complacently at her. Jessica quietly resumed her place behind her desk. On second thought, maybe she felt like she had just crossed *into* the Twilight Zone.

I began again. "Allie, I think you ought to begin by telling us about yourself."

"What do you need to know?"

"Anything. Everything. You can never tell where a

piece of information might lead. Start with your daily routine—work habits, acquaintances, family, whatever."

"Won't that take a long time?"

I glanced at my watch. Brief memories of bed and an all-too-early awakening flashed through my mind. "Allie," I sighed, "my day hasn't even started yet."

Jessica and I filled page after page in our notebooks that morning. Most of it, of course, would prove useless in the long run, but at least we all felt we were doing something. Actually, there were a couple of things I could think of that I'd rather be doing, but then I'd have to give the two hundred back.

As it turned out, Althea "Allie" Walters was a fairly private individual, even if she did work in the public arena. Her late husband, Arthur, an investment banker, had left her a comfortable, if young, widow. Her daughter, Veronica, nineteen, would enter her sophomore year at Yale in September and was currently spending her summer vacation touring through Europe. Assemblyperson Walters was a true-blue representative of the Bay Ridge area, having lived there all her life. Her father still lived there as well. She enjoyed her work and was politically ambitious.

Her platform was strong, conservative, law-and-order, but she favored such rehabilitative efforts as community-service programs. She backed welfare reform, opposed legalization of marijuana and other drugs, championed aid to the elderly, opposed legalized gambling and legalized prostitution. She was a member of MADD, Mothers Against Drunk Driving, and CCCC, the Citizen's Committee to Crack down on Crack. She attended church regularly—Episcopal.

Along about two dozen pages into my green-lined spiral notebook, we hit pay dirt, I was sure. Call it intuition. Call it a detective's hunch. Call it the blank, startled look in her hazel eyes and the small "Oh!" that leaked out of her mouth.

She'd been talking about the parties that local political figures are invited to. The strange thing about this particular party was that she had lost time. She had somehow become drunk. She did not remember passing out, but she woke up on the couch in her own living room without any recollection of having gotten there.

"I was surprised, at the time. I had never been drunk before, never passed out or lost time before. I'd heard about this happening to other people and it scared me. I telephoned the host the following morning to ask him if anything unusual had happened at the party. He assured me that it ended at a reasonable hour and was conducted with the utmost decorum. I asked him about the drinks that were served. He said the bartender was known to him personally and his guests were served nothing but the finest." She sighed. "Since then I haven't had more than a few sips at one sitting."

"How long ago was this party?"

"A few weeks, maybe a month ago."

I nodded. "Long enough so you wouldn't remember too many details. How much did you have to drink?

"Two or three glasses of white wine. It was something new, something imported."

I raised my eyebrows at Jessica. She shrugged.

I said, "That doesn't seem like nearly enough to get a person drunk."

"I agree. That's why I was worried. I thought there might be something wrong with my metabolism."

"Have you had that much alcohol on other occasions?"

"Certainly."

"Were you on medication at the time?"

"No." She smiled. "And to answer your next question, I don't take drugs."

"That's an interesting subject," I said. "There are drugs that can make people black out, and drugs that encourage people to do things they wouldn't ordinarily."

Our client's face flushed pink. "They lose their inhibitions." Her voice sounded thin and strangled and we lost eye contact.

"How much time can't you account for?"

"A couple of hours."

Jessica stopped writing. "We're going to follow this up, Allie, and see if it leads us anywhere. Tell us everything you can remember about that party."

It had been on a Friday night, in a big house at 704 Willow Place—that's in Brooklyn Heights, a classy section of Brooklyn overlooking the East River. The party wasn't a social event as such, but part of her job, really. The gathering was hosted by a real estate tycoon named Matthew Taylor, who dabbled in politics in the sense that he prided himself on knowing everything and everybody of importance to the real estate industry. Although himself a member of the Democratic Club, his philanthropy to Republican and Democratic candidates alike was legendary. His parties had a reputation for good food, good drinks, and wealthy guests like himself—a politician's dream.

Mr. Matthew Andrew Taylor was in his early fifties, divorced, living alone, and had a great tan and graying sideburns. He didn't have much to say at his parties besides, "Call me Matt, ha-ha," as he greeted acquaintances old and new. A good host, he always left most of the conversation to his distinguished guests.

Jessica listened with her usual nonchalance to Allie's recitation of these particulars. Jessica's feet were propped up on her desk. She wore her entire summer wardrobe—jeans, tee shirt, and running shoes—and twirled a lock of her curly, dark auburn hair with the index finger of her right hand. People sometimes made the mistake of assuming that she wasn't paying attention, but I knew that her brain was soaking up every scrap of information that might be even remotely important. She didn't miss a thing.

She looked up suddenly and asked, "Can anyone get into these bashes?"

"You need an invitation, but there are always a few floating around the office. They're formal and engraved, but not personally addressed."

"Can you get us a couple?"

"Sure." She bit her lip. "Ms. Munroe." Pause. "Jessica."

Jessica touched her arm in a sisterly way. "Allie. Don't worry. We'll find the people who did this to you, and we'll get that tape back."

"It's just that"—her eyes started to water—"oh, Jessica. I'm so grateful for your help. I'm also grateful that my Veronica is out of the country for a while."

Jessica nodded. "When is she returning to the States?"

"At the end of the summer. If she should—"

"She won't. We'll get you off the hook, Allie." Jessica ushered her out of the office. "And if you remember anything else, be sure to give us a call. Reporting works both ways, you know."

Walters went off to work. The digital clock in the corner of my green monitor flashed 10:22. I said to Jessica, "Planning on partying, are we?"

She shrugged. "Just buying insurance."

"Good thing," I nodded. "You never know when you might feel like stepping out and have nowhere to go."

We decided to split the rest of the day's work, since none of what we had to do was more than a one-person job. Jessica left to check out 704 Willow Place and the gracious host of the suspicious party. I was to follow up on the stills I had taken from the videotape.

At the moment, however, I was standing at our northwest window—our only window—appraising the midmorning hustle and bustle of the junction below. Brooklyn College was only one small block away, and even now, I could see a number of summer students amid the morning shoppers. They clustered together in front of the college bookstores, the ice cream store, the fast food stores, and at the bus stops.

I took the photos from the drawer in my desk where I had stashed them the day before and laid them across the top of my worn and crusty green blotter. They weren't very good, due to the amateur manner in which they were shot. It is extremely difficult to take a decent still photograph off of videotaped material, even with a very good camera, since what you see is actually a sequence of images that change about thirty times a second. Consequently, you couldn't use these pictures for identification, but for my needs they were adequate.

I separated the ones of the animal heads to one side. They wouldn't tell me much about the performers in that video classic. I examined the full-body shots. The disguise was perfect. Even if the resolution had been better, I would be hard put to pick either one out of a lineup. I tossed the photos aside. The only one left was the picture of Ms. Rabbit's buttocks. I examined it more closely. I was hot on the tail of this case.

The small, lavenderish spot was still there.

I put the photograph in my shirt pocket, got the videotape out of the safe, and went off to visit a local photographer that we work with from time to time. Barbara Crenshaw's studio was located on Nostrand Avenue north of Farragut Road, which meant that she didn't get very much walk-in business, but then, she didn't need it. Besides being a super photographer, she is up to date on all the latest advances in cameras, development processes, and video technology. She has enough equipment in her place to put NASA to shame. Not to mention on her person.

I found her studying some large color prints in the far corner. She was looking great as usual in her starched, white lab coat and dark blond hair pulled severely back into a ponytail. There was no one else in the studio. I leaned over and kissed her on the neck. She smelled great as she whirled around.

"Jason, you old rake. What brings you here, business or pleasure?"

"That depends, Barb," I replied. "How much do you charge?"

She put down the print she'd been looking at. "More than you could ever afford, Jason," she said.

I took the photo out of my pocket. "Spare a few minutes?" She locked the front door and put the "CLOSED" sign out.

"What did you try to do? Take a picture from a television screen or something stupid like that?"

"Something like that."

She mumbled something about the superiority of digital techniques that bypass electronic noise and distortion. "Looks like you were watching something interesting."

I handed the videotape over to her. "Do I have to say that this is classified and confidential?"

"It always is, isn't it?"

Barbara was somehow able to produce a perfect image of the frame containing the best shot of the spot I was interested in. She used her Polaroid FreezeFrame video-image recorder. It was brand-new, and she was glad to have an opportunity to try it out. The finished picture and slide that she handed me were far superior in quality and resolution to my feeble attempt at direct-screen photography. She had enlarged the shot to ten times its original size. That was fine, but enlarging doesn't make an image easier to distinguish. What we did notice, however, was that the spot in question wasn't lavender at all, but a close arrangement of pink and blue areas.

"Any ideas?" I asked.

Barbara had her nose up against the slide as she held it up to the light. "That depends," she said. "What do you think?"

"At first I thought that was some sort of birthmark. But now I don't know. I don't think birthmarks come two-tone."

"Tattoo?"

"You may have something there. And I know just how I'm going to get a better look at it." I grabbed the pictures from her, stashed the videotape back in my pocket. Before I was out the door, I called over my shoulder, "Thanks a lot, Barbara. Send us a bill."

"Darn right I'll send you a bill," I heard her muttering as I left.

I beelined for the office. A while back I had purchased a new peripheral for my computer. It wasn't even hooked up yet. I hauled out the small carton in which it was packed and assembled the unit and its cable, somehow finding a place for it among the modem and disk-storage units. One of these days I was definitely going to have to find a way to organize the clutter of machinery and instruction manuals that made clear to every visitor which side of the office was mine.

The unit I was interested in at the moment was a digitizer, and somewhere in my assortment of floppy disks was one that held a program I would need. I soon found that, too. My lucky day.

When everything was operational, keeping one eye on the instruction manual, I got a digitized image of the photograph on my color monitor. After a few false moves and unproductive trials, I had it. The digitized image on the screen had been filled in to produce the most likely pattern. I struck a few keys and pressed a few buttons, and the image was reproduced on the four-color laser jet printer.

It was a tattoo, all right. A tiny, delicate, intricately drawn tulip. In pink and blue.

I had an idea. I got my workstation into communication mode and dialed an X-rated bulletin board I had heard about. I left a message giving physical descriptions, necessarily sketchy, of the two performers, paying special attention to that tulip tattoo. I was working under the assumption that the two had worked as a team before, probably in some porno flicks. If so, my anonymous electronic friends would very probably have seen them. If not, well . . . I tried not to think about that.

While waiting for some pervert hacker to read my message and leave a reply, I got busy on the phone. Out of some fifty costumers in Manhattan and Brooklyn, only eleven could recall carrying masks or heads of the type I described. Of these, four hadn't stocked them in more than two years. The remaining seven were at various Manhattan locations. I wrote the addresses in my notebook, though I didn't really have much hope for success in that avenue. Once I was through with Manhattan, there would still be the other boroughs, and New Jersey, and Connecticut, and just about anyplace.

I checked on my bulletin-board message. No reply yet. I checked my watch. It was 12:09. Considering my early rising, that made it a good time for lunch. My stomach had been telling me as much, but I hadn't paid it any attention till now. I had a sandwich, coffee, and pie in the coffee shop downstairs and felt much better. Being a crack detective can take a lot out of you.

When I returned, there was, indeed, a reply to my query on the computer. In fact, there were several. Some listed the names of the movies the two had been in. One offered to send me a copy of one at a severely reduced rate. Some knew their names—Tulip Sensuous and Big Jake Strong. I don't know why, but I had the feeling these were not the names on their birth certificates. To find out their real names, I called a friend of mine who works for the *Village Voice*.

"I need some information, buddy."

"Only if it's a quickie, Jason. We're pushing hard at deadline today."

"Can anyone there get me the real names and addresses of two porno-ers?" I gave him the names I had.

"Piece of cake. We keep a file. Hold a sec."

There was no musak, so I hummed a tune to myself till Tom was back on the line.

"I've got it, Jason. They're shacking up together, if this info is still current." He gave me the information, Marie Selby and Vince Hartle and a West 80th Street address. "You get anything really happening, you give me a call, hey?"

I entered the names and address into my notebook and told him I didn't think the two lovebirds would be happening for a while yet. He agreed.

The day was balmy and pleasant and, considering that this long-time New York City resident recognizes a balmy Tuesday in July as nothing less than a small miracle, I took the subway from Brooklyn to a couple of stops short of my destination and walked through Central Park, past stone walls, cultivated greenery, and large patches of seemingly unkempt foliage growing wild.

There was life everywhere—the growing kind and the four-legged and two-legged varieties. A young family on summer holiday fed their picnic remains to a couple of grateful and greedy squirrels and a great flapping of gray park pigeons. A few paces off their grassy knoll, a couple of park bums watched the heart-warming family scene with envy. They were probably jealous of the squirrels.

Before I turned away from the park, I caught a glimpse

of another man, sitting with his back against the stone wall which kept the park in and the city out. His knees were drawn up against his body, as if for warmth. He wore pants which were torn and ragged and a coat with no buttons and no shirt on underneath. His face was bordered top and bottom by shaggy and matted, thick, black hair and beard. One shoe flapped open obscenely; the other, a tennis shoe, was taped up in a haphazard fashion. He was talking calmly and quietly and quite rationally, to himself.

As I turned away from the park, two artsy types—a bearded, one-earringed man and a skinny, long-haired woman—with serious-looking cameras were considering angles and looking through their viewers at the portrait of a man in tattered rags against a stone wall. He didn't even notice them. For their part, they didn't seem to care whether he did or not. It was, perhaps, the ultimate violation, possible only when there was nothing else left to take.

The West 80th Street address turned out to be a high-rise, probably condos. V. Hartle and M. Selby lived in number 14G on the fourteenth floor. Neither of the entranceways was locked, so I walked on through and up.

I knocked carefully on the nice, new shiny door. It opened slightly, and I positioned my left shoe in the crack. Jessica can't do that. She always wears sneakers.

"Yeah? Whattayawant?" The face that peered out at me was clean shaven with brown eyes, a fine straight nose, and a soft jaw, all framed by golden, Prince Valiant locks.

"You Big Jake?" I asked in my most disarming voice.

"Who wants to know?" Surly.

"Name's Reddy." I flipped open the plastic case that held a copy of my license. "I'm a private detective. I'd like to ask you some questions about 704 Willow Place."

To which he obligingly responded, "Go to hell."

My foot in the door came in handy now.

"If you don't take your friggin' foot outta my door, I'll smash it, private dick-face."

He applied force—a surprising amount considering his good looks—but as any ten year old is wise enough to know, get your foot into a good strong shoe and put it in a door and you're almost home. I slid my foot forward slightly to meet the added pressure.

"That's it," said my eloquent companion. "You're dead meat, mister."

He stepped back, letting the door swing open, and inertia catapulted me a few feet into the room. That's when I realized his good looks didn't stop at his face. What hadn't been apparent in the videotape was the muscular development of his upper body. He was working with these muscles now and it was definitely apparent. And he knew it. I got the feeling that he would have preferred a mirrored room.

The next feeling I got was in my shoulder, where his punch landed after I sidestepped it. A lot of people look at my size and make the mistake of thinking I move slowly. I threw a punch to his gut. It met its mark. Hartle doubled over for a few seconds, then came back at me swinging with both fists.

I felt sorry for him. He'd built up his muscles but he didn't know how to use them. I outskilled him by a mile. I blocked his swings with my left while I punched him in the belly with my right. Then I used my left fist and applied it to the side of his jaw. The sound of the impact told me I'd done it right. What I hadn't counted on was a hysterical actor.

He doubled over, put both his hands over his face and screamed, "Stay away from my face!" Loud. Again, "Stay away from my face, you creep! Not my face!" Very loud. I wondered if we were alone in the apartment.

I didn't have much time for wondering. He dipped his left hand into his pocket and came out with a switchblade, open. His right hand was still covering his precious face.

"You hit me in my face and you're gonna pay, mister." He came slowly toward me, flicking the knife menacingly as he approached. "You know what I'm gonna do?" Rhetorical question? "I'm gonna cut your balls off. How do you like that?" Definitely, a rhetorical question.

When he got close enough, I pivoted on my left foot and, with my right, side-kicked the hand holding the knife. My Special Forces training came in handy once again. The switchblade dropped to the floor. While he was still wincing from the pain in his hand, I stepped back and kicked him easily in the groin. I'm such a nice guy.

He was sitting on the floor, his knees up, his hands pressed against his crotch for dear life. Then, all of a sudden, he fell dead away to the floor, probably from fright. I made certain he was breathing, then I picked up the switchblade and looked around.

The apartment was furnished in Early Yucchy. Everything was gaudy and in the most garish colors and contrasts. There were mirrors everywhere. The bathroom had neither walls nor ceiling, just mirrors. A zillion me's were everywhere. I looked at the toilet and decided to wait.

She was in the bedroom, stretched out naked on an oversized bed atop a red lacquer and gold-leaf spread, staring vacantly at the mirrored ceiling. The bed didn't seem solid, so I felt it. She didn't move. Not a waterbed, I decided, more like jelly.

She was part Oriental, part something else, with bright green eyes, long, silky, black hair, and long, red nails. Her body was fine, but then I already knew that. She had good color, but she was so darn still. I knew she was probably just doped up, but I felt her throat for a pulse anyway. She was alive, at least in some sense. If she knew I was in the room, she gave no sign. Gently, I turned her slightly onto her right side and took a peek.

There it was—a pink and blue tulip tattoo.

I went back to the front room. He was up, but I had the knife now. I held it against the side of his face, just under his soft brown, terrified eyes.

I said, "You've got five seconds to start talking and talking civilly. If you don't tell me everything I want to know, I'll fix your face so the only movies you'll be able to star in are horror films."

"Okay." He took a deep breath. I could tell it hurt. "Look man, I don't do that scam no more, but I'll tell you what you want to know. Just don't hurt my face. Please."

He told me what I wanted to know. It didn't amount to much. He and his partner had some ten gigs, all told, at the big house in Brooklyn over the last year or so. They were paid twenty-five-hundred dollars each for their nocturnal shenanigans and for their silence. The payment was made to them by Matthew Taylor himself.

The victim was sometimes a man, sometimes a woman, always somewhat dopey. "Under the influence" was Hartle's term for it. Somehow, he and his pal managed to lead the victim through the routine for the benefit of the camera. A man was naturally more difficult than a woman.

"Who were these people?" I asked. "Did you know any of them?"

"Nah. Just regular people. Real nerds."

"Did these nerds have names?"

Small beads of perspiration slid down the side of his face. "Mr. Taylor don't like nobody to use names. He even made us wear these masks—man, were they hot—

so no one would know who we were. We just did what we was told to do and got out."

I muttered under my breath, "The old Nuremberg defense, eh?"

"What's that? I didn't hear you good."

"Tell me about the nerds. If you didn't know their names, what did they look like?"

"Regular people, you know."

I rested the cold, flat blade against his upper lip. "No, I don't know, Hartle. Describe them."

"Hell, I was never good with descriptions."

I wasn't too surprised at the answer. I just didn't know if it was an honest one. "Hartle, a great creative artist like you ought to be able to do better than that. Did you ever see any of them on TV?"

"No."

"How many were men?"

He considered. "Six. No, seven."

We went on at it for a while. Even with my encouragement, I managed to shake only two meager descriptions from his underused memory banks—a very tall, thin, blond-haired woman and an extremely short, fat man with a pointed, dark brown beard. The only reason he managed to remember even those was because of their unusual appearances and proportions.

I balanced the knife in my right hand and drew a business card out of my pocket with my left. I tossed the card onto a nearby writing desk. "You remember anything else, give me a call. I might be able to make it worth your while."

"Sure. Whatever you say."

"Anyone else ever do the same work for Taylor as you and Tulip?"

"Nah. Mr. Taylor said we're the best." His tone was confidential, yet proud. "We've got plenty of experience. We're both on the way up."

"On the way up? Didn't you ever wonder what exactly you were involved in?"

He laughed. "Some kind of joke." A sly, crooked, half-hearted laugh. "Right, man?"

The hand holding the knife was feeling itchy. "A joke?" Suddenly I was yelling at him. "You and your partner clear five thou having group sex with a zonked-out pigeon, and it's all for a joke? What kind of idiot do you think I am?" I pulled his sweaty hair back with my free hand, placed my knee square on his middle, and adjusted the knife under his nose, blade up.

"N—n—no. Don't. It was no joke."

"What, then?"

"A blackmail scam. A big one, I figure, cause, like you said, of the five thou and all."

I pulled his hair tighter. "And what happened when you told Taylor you wanted a piece of the action?"

His eyes opened wide. "I didn't tell you that."

I'm not psychic, just experienced. "What happened? He didn't cut you in, did he?"

"He laughed and said I'm lucky to be alive with both my legs working. I don't mess with that kind of rough stuff, but I was afraid to quit."

"Tulip too?"

He didn't miss a beat. "I don't know. I guess so. She can do what she damn well wants. I told you everything I know."

I folded the switchblade shut. He jumped up valiantly and tried to wrestle it away from me.

"C'mon Vinnie," I said. "We went through this already. Be a good boy and back off so I can leave without hurting you."

"You really burn me up. I've a mind to call—"

I raised one eyebrow. "Who?"

"Never mind. You just be careful. One of these days you'll be walking alone at night and someone will—"

"Someone will what?"

The sly, crooked smile was back. "Just you take care, Detective."

I smiled and tossed the switchblade at him. "Thanks for the tip, buddy."

As the door swung shut behind me, I thought I could just make out the sound of the touch-tone telephone. I wondered if I should be worried.

When I returned to the office, Jessica was at her desk, fingers tapping. As usual, she wore no makeup. She didn't want to poison her soft, olive-tone skin, which didn't need any makeup anyway. Her thick, auburn hair fell into short, lively curls that framed her face, which was now glistening with sweat. I had noticed her bicycle as I entered the building and guessed that she had cycled over from Ocean Parkway. My second guess was that she had been using the bike to get around all day.

Jessica straightened some papers on her desk. "I went over to the house today—"

"The one on Willow Place?"

"Isn't that the house we're talking about?"

"On your bike?"

She took a Kleenex from her desk and wiped the sweat off her face. "It was no big deal, Red."

I whistled in admiration. "I've got to hand it to you, Jess. Not very many people can do that." Or, want to.

"Coming from you I suspect that's not as much of a compliment as it seems. But anyway, that address is definitely in a very posh Brooklyn Heights neighborhood. To live in this area you've got to have dough."

"If I wanted to buy that house?"

"You would have to plunk down at least two hundred thousand cash and still sell your soul to the bank for life."

"What's the setup?"

"It's a pretty big house. Dark blue shingle, new windows. It seems to be a single dwelling—One entrance, one bell, one mail slot. Two levels plus an attic. A driveway and a garage, unusual for a neighborhood like that where land is at a premium. The house appears to be older than the others around it but has been well taken care of and will probably outlast them. The place is professionally landscaped in front. There didn't seem to be anyone at home, but it didn't look exactly deserted either. Taylor was probably at the office."

"Security?"

"To the hilt." She narrowed her eyes slightly. "Breaking and/or entering is definitely not advisable."

I smiled. "Yeah. We don't want to embarrass any of your old buddies at the precinct. Imagine one of their own being picked up for a B and E."

With a wave of her hand, she conveyed the insignificance of those six years of her life, then singled out one of the sheets of paper from her desk. "I cycled over to Borough Hall and found out that the house is, in fact, owned by a Mr. Matthew A. Taylor."

"You think we can get inside?"

"You want to look for a blue room?"

"Uh-huh. And a video camera. And, if we're real lucky, some hot tapes."

"Judging by the looks of the house, I'd say it was certainly alarmed or booby-trapped somehow. It would be better to talk our way in."

I looked at my watch. Five o'clock. "Better wait till evening."

"There's an alternative."

"The insurance you mentioned?"

"That's it. When I got back here, there was a message on the answering machine. Our client called to say that she has two tickets for us to Taylor's next party."

"When is it?"

"Saturday night."

"This weekend? Already?"

"Just our luck," Jessica said. "A chance to boogie with the rich and powerful."

"Munroe, I think boogie is just a little outdated."

"Twist?" she asked innocently. "Cha-cha?"

"Did you find out anything else about this Taylor fellow?"

"I called Jerry Cosnick at the *Journal*. He didn't have to do much digging. He spent a little time in research and talked to some of his contacts at Dun & Bradstreet. Afterwards, I contacted Sandy. He'd heard of Taylor, naturally, but couldn't tell me more than I already knew."

"And?"

"And we're taking Jerry out to dinner tonight. Mr. Matthew Andrew Taylor is, indeed, a real estate tycoon. Not altogether a self-made man, there was some money on his mother's side, but he built his reputation pretty much on his own. Some of his bigger deals went sour a short while back. He was overextended and close to bankruptcy, but he obviously found someone to help him out in the form of a business loan. He has always donated a lot of money to important political candidates. According to Jerry, in order to survive in the real estate business in New York, that's the only practical way to go. Everything a real estate tycoon could possibly be interested in is legislated, from zoning laws to rent increases, to condominium conversions. Taylor is known as a big fundraiser for various candidates. His parties occur frequently, an average of once a month, with hordes of public servants crawling out of the woodwork and into party clothes. It seems that when a rich guy throws a party other rich people come, and that brings out the politicians. Nowadays it's called networking."

I let out a sigh. "That's what makes our country great. Want to hear about my day?"

"Sure." She started on her stretching exercises. "How'd the hunt go? Find any big bad donkeys or little bitty bunny rabbits?"

"I didn't have much success in the animal department. I narrowed the source down to a couple of customers on Broadway. They sell a lot of them, not as masks or heads but as full costumes. Our friend Taylor obviously just didn't see fit to use the bottom part. The only way we'll come up with anything useful from that angle is if we get the cops involved. They can get a warrant to look at the receipts over the last couple of years, but that's sort of like the old needle in the old haystack."

I pulled out my notebook and the reconstructed tulip. "This is what appeared to be a fuzzy, lavender birthmark on Rabbit's bottom."

"How did you manage to blow it up into such a clear picture? I didn't think that was possible."

"Remember that little doodad I purchased for the computer a while back?"

Jessica rolled her eyes. "Which one, Red? You get doodads for that money-eating monster on average twice a week."

"I had Barbara develop an enlarged photo from the tape, then I got a digitized image of the mark, and there's this little program I had, it uses artificial intelligence—"

"That's okay, Red. I believe you." Jessica denies that she is totally bored with anything remotely involving computers. She insists that it's just that when a computer expert starts talking about his field, no real human being can understand him. "But how can you be so sure that it came out right?" she asked.

"I had the opportunity to check that out later on."

"You've been a busy boy, haven't you? Want to tell me about it?"

"Sure, Jess." I paused for effect. "Oh, by the way.

Guess what? I located the players in the blackmail tape.'' Gosh, I'm cute.

''I sort of had that idea.''

I told her about Hartle and Selby, and the information I had obtained from Hartle, which wasn't much considering what I'd gone through to get it.

She was frowning. ''Taylor seems to be involved up to his earlobes in our client's problem. Do you think he's working alone?''

''Why not? The information you got from Jerry seems to point that way. He needed money badly. Saw that he could use his parties as a cover for dirty doings that would tide his business over during the rough times.''

''There's one problem with that.''

''What's that?''

''He didn't ask Walters for any money.''

''Yet.''

Jessica gave a small grunt. She was trying out some new isometric exercises. ''Why the delay?''

''I dunno, Munroe. But he held on to the tape for nearly a month before sending it.''

''That was to ensure that the details of that night were hazy in the victim's mind. Maybe he's working out a collection procedure that wouldn't implicate him. For all he knows, Althea Walters is still his best friend. He has no way of knowing we've dug into his mess. For that matter, we can't be completely certain the night of the party was when the film was shot.''

She was coming to the end of a set of exercises. Good thing. I was exhausted.

''Funny thing,'' I said. ''You know how a punk acts who thinks he's connected but doesn't know how really low on the totem pole he is?''

''You mean like swaggers and winks and I-know-the-big-boys talk?''

''Yeah.''

"So?"

"Hartle had some of that. I mean at first he kept begging me to stay away from his lousy face. He was literally on the floor, begging—"

"One of your prouder moments, I'm sure."

"And later, when I was leaving, he threatened me. Said something to the effect that I'd be sorry for what I'd done."

"For scaring him half to death?"

"That's what I mean. Threatening, yet childish. The sort of behavior you'd expect from low-grade cons who never make it to the top."

"Or to tomorrow."

"Yeah, well, " I sighed. "One day at a time."

Jessica was straightening her desktop, getting ready to close up shop for the day. "Don't forget about our dinner date. I'm going to cycle home and change. We'll meet at the Steak 'n Brew. You know where that is?"

I licked my lips. "Do I ever. But I've got a heavy date of my own tonight. I'll have to leave you to Jerry Cosnick's sweet embraces."

She laughed. "Jerry Cosnick would prefer *your* sweet embraces, if you'd only let him get close enough." She put her sweatband on her forehead and picked up the leather gloves she uses even in July so that her hands don't slip off the handlebars. "Well, have a very stimulating evening."

"Oh, I intend to. In fact we're going to discuss that book you said I should read."

"So Big?"

"Uh-huh."

"Will wonders never cease? You're actually going out with a woman who reads?"

"Oh, no. She didn't actually read the book." I winked. "I told her it was the story of my sex life."

3

THE HOUSE WAS on fire. Red-hot flames were on every side of me as I attempted to make good my escape through the narrow window. I tried to attract someone's attention. I yelled, "Help!" several times, but no one paid any attention. I was six flights up. Below, people walked calmly back and forth about their business. "Help!" I cried. Maybe I wasn't calling loud enough. My voice sounded muffled, even to me. Fire engines seemed to be getting closer, their sirens ringing. Ringing. Ringing . . .

It wasn't sirens, it was the telephone. And the night had turned hot and New York-humid. The bedsheets were sweated through.

I dragged the receiver to my ear. "Minute," I mumbled.

I got up, turned on the air conditioner, and shut the window. It was light outside. I forced myself to do a dozen jumping jacks, then took the telephone in hand once again and blared into it, "Do you know what time it is?" The clock on the dresser said six twenty-five.

"Morning, Red."

"Sure, Munroe. I should've known it'd be you. Did you wake the birds up, too?"

"The birds have been up for hours. Don't you have any in Manhattan?"

I sighed and sat down on the edge of the bed. "Just the one jaded old-timer I can see from my window at night. He's got a tiny little drink in one wing and a cigarette butt dangling from his beak."

"Something's happened, Red."

I felt my heartbeat quicken. "You okay, Munroe?"

"I heard it on the radio a short while ago. A lover's leap several flights up from an apartment building on the Upper West Side."

"It wasn't me, Jess." I lifted a corner of the cover just to be sure. Doris was sleeping comfortably, the way I should've been. "I live around Gramercy Park."

"Reddy, are you still asleep? Where were you yesterday?"

"West 80th Street. But that doesn't mean anything, Jessica."

"The bulletin said that the couple had starred in some grade B movies and weren't too well-known."

"Lots of people knew these guys."

"Look. I'm at a pay phone. I'm on my way over to pick you up. Get ready. We're going over there."

"I am Reddy. Always have been."

She hung up. Doris nuzzled down into the pillow. The air-conditioning was starting to make the room livable again. I stayed a good half hour under the shower, making the water as hot as I could stand it. I always do that in the summertime so that when I get out of the steamed-up bathroom I feel relatively cool. I toweled myself roughly to help the wake-up process and padded naked to the tiny kitchen area, where I had already started the coffee brewing before washing up.

The coffeemaker had turned itself off automatically. Clever little gadget. I tossed four slices of whole-grain bread into the toaster oven, cracked six eggs perfectly into a hot Silverstone pan, got a can of frozen orange juice concentrate out of the freezer, threw out the old orange juice that was in the fridge, and made some fresh. All the while I made believe I hadn't noticed her sitting on one of my padded stools at the breakfast bar. Grinning.

Jessica laughed out loud. "Take care not to spill anything hot on yourself."

"Shh," I said, pointing in the direction of the bedroom. "Doris would be shocked if she saw us like this. She thinks I'm a one-woman guy."

"Aren't you?"

"Sure," I said. "One woman at a time."

I expertly split the sunny-side up eggs in two equal parts and slid them onto two plates. Two more plates for the toast, and, with a flourish, breakfast for two was served.

"Eaten yet?" I asked.

She looked in surprise at the meal on the counter in front of her, then back at me. "What about Doris?"

I sat down and began munching on my toast. "Let her get her own breakfast."

By the time we arrived at the West 80th Street address, I had all my clothes on and we both felt better with some breakfast inside of us. Jessica had returned my house key to her wallet, where she kept it for emergencies—or whatever. When we first joined forces, we decided to exchange house keys in case a dangerous situation should ever call for speedy action. Of course, the reality is that we spend most of our time on relatively peaceful pursuits, such as investigating retail fraud and looking for youngsters who don't want to be found.

I was wide-awake by now. The three cups of coffee I had with breakfast helped. Jessica never touched the stuff—or tea or chocolate or colas or tobacco or alcohol. She claims she'll live longer. As they used to say on the Borscht Belt, you call that living?

There were three police cars out front. This was the place, after all. The two unmarked cars were just pulling away as we arrived. One of them vacated a spot directly across the street from the building I had visited yesterday. We pulled in gratefully. The ambulance and reporters and most of the idly curious were obviously long gone. I made a mental note to buy the *New York Post,* the only paper that would give a story like this the coverage it didn't deserve. There was still a handful of people milling around, probably because of the empty patrol car parked at the fire hydrant a few feet down.

We sat in Jessica's car for a few minutes, watching the building. I asked, "Think they stationed a uniform in there?"

Jessica was the expert on NYPD procedure due to her six long years on the force. She'd been a good cop at a time when it was tough to be a woman or a cop, let alone both.

"No reason to. Radio said suicide." She leaned over to turn the radio on again to WINS. "Probably sealing up the apartment, just in case, or until next of kin settles with the landlord."

We listened to the radio at a low volume and watched the front of the building waiting for the blue uniforms to emerge. Ten minutes of this told us the important news of the day. A well-known, well-loved jet set couple whose names meant nothing to me were happily off on their honeymoon, President Reagan was definitely continuing with his Strategic Defense Initiative, and there hadn't been another New York City political corruption scandal in at least a month. Those were the headline stories. You'd think the world was at peace, people weren't murdering each other in Afghanistan and Lebanon and South America and the Persian Gulf and South Africa, the African famine was over, prisons were successfully transforming maladjusted, malcontent dopers into citizens of conscience, there was no violent crime in the streets.

I said as much to Jessica, who was doing leg lifts, to a count of ten. With her usual practical slant, she responded, "If those things were really true, Reddy, they would be news."

Now our story was on the air. I turned the volume up slightly. It wasn't much different from the one we'd heard earlier, on the way over from my apartment downtown. Two out-of-work actors, a couple in love, had thrown themselves out of the window of the fourteenth-floor apartment that they had shared for two years on Manhattan's Upper West Side. A suicide love pact at three A.M. Neighbors heard no shrieks, just the sound of impact. Police were called to the scene at five o'clock by the building maintenance man, who noticed the mess when he went to transfer the huge pile of trash bags to the curb for regular sanitation pickup.

Upon investigation of the lovers' apartment, police had found a small assortment of drugs and a suicide note—no mention of whether the note was addressed to anyone in particular. The bodies, or what was left of them, were rushed to Roosevelt Hospital, where they were pronounced dead on arrival. The pair had acted in numerous grade B and pornographic films but were not working on anything currently. Names were being withheld from the public pending notification of next of kin. When asked whether he thought there was anything suspicious about the early-morning double death, Lieutenant Leonard Starky of the 20th Precinct had obligingly responded, "No comment."

Two uniformed police officers came through the huge double glass doors. One was laughing at whatever joke he had just told and got a friendly punch in the shoulder for his trouble. They went to their car and leaned on the hood scribbling notes for their report.

WINS had switched to a celebrity poll. Some bright person in radio news had asked Joan Collins, O.J. Simpson, and Cheryl Tiegs their opinions on who would be the next Democratic presidential nominee. In this country, entertainment and sports personalities are supposed to know about everything. It's a good thing Mickey Mouse and Donald Duck are cartoon characters or they'd be questioned on animal rights.

The cops finally drove away, and I turned the radio off. We locked the doors to the Chevy but left the two front windows open a half inch. It was turning into a real scorcher.

With the exit of the blue and white patrol car, the street was once again the picture of a typical New York City summer morning. A kid passed by attached by various straps and chains to a great dane, two schnauzers, and a dachshund, who were walking him as much as they were being walked by him. People of all sorts hurried in all directions, on their way to the various desks, taxis, diners, studios, and clubs. The same area in the middle of the night when deserted and littered with foul-smelling trash is similar in appearance to a long-deserted combat zone. Thirty or forty huge black trash bags were taped neatly closed and stacked high at the edge of the sidewalk. They had probably been hauled out through a walkway at the side of the building that was too small to be a driveway.

The pavement there looked as if a couple of buckets of dark paint had splashed or been kicked over. The reddish brown stuff had splattered over the brick walls of the two buildings and even over some of the ground-floor windowpanes. It's a long way to the ground from the fourteenth floor. I looked up, trying to spot Hartle's and Selby's apartment window. It was impossible. The angle was too steep to see anything higher than the fifth floor.

Jessica waved to someone behind one of the blood-stained windows, bright with floral kitchen-type curtains.

I smiled. Jessica favors the direct approach. She never just lurks. I tensed as the window opened as far as it would go, which was halfway. You never know what will come out of a window in this city.

A fortyish woman with warm brown skin and dark eyes leaned most of her plentiful upper body against work-weary arms that she rested on the spotless window sill. She clasped together large-boned hands and returned Jessica's smile. "Some mess, hey?" There was a trace of the Islands in her voice.

Jessica agreed. "Someone's sure going to have a time of it cleaning this up."

"Not me, honey. I got all I want with this." She pointed to the window and made a face. "You don't look like reporters."

Jessica shrugged. "We're not. We were just walking by and"—she gave a sheepish grin—"I got curious. I'm sorry if we bothered you."

"No bother't all. You look like a nice enough girl, but believe me you shouldn't be botherin' with the likes of those two." She nodded her head at the largest pool of color on the pavement.

Jessica brightened. "Did you know them then?"

The woman nodded sagely. "I surely did. Everyone in the building knew what they were. Good riddance to bad rubbish, I say."

She nodded her head again, with finality. We stood around a little longer, not saying anything, just looking curious—Officer Munroe's technique in interrogating friendly witnesses. Pretty soon, the woman started to speak again.

"I heard it, you know," she confided. "It was 'bout three o'clock, just like I told the police officers." We were suitably impressed and told her so. "I couldn't sleep much last night, it being so hot an' all. I heard a very big sound, like a heavy, heavy package hit the ground right outside my window." She pointed to the next window down. It must have been her bedroom. " 'Fore I could even finish getting out o' bed, what do I hear but another one just like the first." She wiped the sweat from her forehead with a dish towel. "I didn't know what it was an' I didn't want to know, bein' as I was sleepin' here all alone last night. The Sandersons, they're out of the country for the week," she added by way of explanation. "I just locked up the windows and door real good and parked myself in the big chair front of the TV and waited for daylight. My word," she said, talking to herself now, shaking her head slowly from side to side.

Finally, after reluctantly declining her offer of some cold fruit punch, we walked around the corner of the building and through the glass doors. Today the inner door was locked. We glanced around the small cubicle. To the left was a massive array of buzzers attached to nameplates, and a speaker for the intercom system. A fictional private detective like Lew Archer would simply ring a few bells and wait to be let in. We didn't think that would work so soon after the police had left. Mike Hammer would probably take out his gun and shoot the lock off. We didn't think that was too cool, either. Anyway, it was just a simple credit-card lock, not even worth the effort it cost to pull the door closed. My VISA card did the trick.

The large lobby was deserted. The place had been crawling with cops just a short while ago and I guessed that nobody was anxious to open doors to a possible further grilling. We took the elevator up to the fourteenth floor. I expected to see a seal plastered on the door to 14G, but there was nothing.

"Didn't you say something about the police department sealing the apartment?" I asked. "You know, for evidence."

Jessica shrugged. "Lots of times they just change the lock to keep a low profile."

"Low profile?"

She laughed. "I know. It doesn't sound like the department we both know and love. The thing is, sometimes a seal is taken as an invitation to burglars and other undesirables."

"Ah," I nodded. "An empty apartment shouting, I'm here, come and get me."

"The neighbors probably like it better this way."

I showed Jessica scratches along the side of the heavy wooden door where it met the door frame.

"Every door in New York City has marks like that."

"Except for the new ones, Jess. Yesterday this door was shiny and gorgeous."

I used my six-foot-two-inch, two-hundred-pound frame to block Jessica while she worked the locks with a pick she took from her jacket pocket. We slid quietly inside, and I gave Jessica a quick tour of the apartment. She liked the furnishings as much as I had, maybe even less.

I told her, "Maybe we could pick this stuff up real cheap. They might auction it off. We could fill up some of the empty rooms in that big house of yours real fast, Jess."

"I'd rather die first." The gaudy bedspread was crumpled on the floor. She reached down to feel the texture of it. "Now I know why they jumped."

I moved over to one of the bedroom windows. It overlooked the alley, but was not quite in the right position to be *the one*. I walked around the unmade bed to look at the other window. That was more like it.

"Come here, Munroe."

"This looks like the window they jumped from," she agreed.

"See this?" I pointed to where a small, thin piece of

wood had been ripped from the window sash and a few splinters were still sticking up. "Think that's recent?" I asked.

Jessica peered closely at the damage, then examined the rest of the window. "The window is old, Jason, but I'll tell you. The way the rest of this place looks, I can't believe damage like this would last more than a day here without getting lacquer over it."

"Yeah," I grinned. "The exposed wood looks pretty fresh, too. Tell me," I posed a question, "when someone jumps, do they generally hold onto the window frame so tightly that they scratch off some of the wood?"

"Suicide isn't holding up too well as a means of death here, is it?"

"Radio news," I asserted. "They can't get anything right."

We made a quick, careful search of the apartment, not really expecting to discover anything new. Most of what we found was clothing—good stuff, too, in every drawer and closet, on chairs, in boxes. Imelda Marcos had nothing on these two. It was pretty funny, actually, for a couple of actors who spent most of their time without any clothes on. Surprisingly, we didn't find any drugs.

"The department takes stuff like that, Red. There'll be a description in the case file of everything taken out of this apartment."

"Is that what happened to the suicide note, too?"

Jessica nodded. "If there really was one."

There was a small, elegant writing desk in the corner of the living room, with a portable typewriter incongruously balanced on the glass writing surface. Four delicate drawers held the usual stuff people tend to throw into their desk drawers, plus several boxes of engraved notepaper—deep tan for him with his stage name at the top, pastel pink for her, with her name in small delicate blue script—and near it, a blue tulip. I thought of the last time

I had seen an engraved tulip and wondered if there was anything left of it. My stomach churned, and I reached for the door.

"Let's go, Munroe."

We got to the stairway and off the fourteenth floor as quickly as we could.

Panting slightly, I asked, "Isn't breaking and entering a misdemeanor?"

Jessica grinned. "Felony, Red."

I raised my eyebrows. Leaning over, I put my mouth close to her ear and whispered, "You broke a rule, Jess."

She poked me in the ribs, not too softly. "Sometimes my halo slips. Want to try talking to some of the neighbors?"

"We might as well see if anyone knows anything. I have a hunch this was no suicide."

She nodded. "Let's go."

We didn't have much luck with the neighbors in Yuppieville. If you can afford an apartment in a building like that on Manhattan's West Side, chances are that on a Wednesday morning you'll be hard at work in some corporation, shuffling papers, meeting the right people, and always looking over your shoulder. There were some servants at home who were day workers and had no information regarding the previous night's excitement. They all told us the same thing as the woman at the alley window—the pair would not be greatly missed.

Of the regular residents, we were able to question only two. One, on the third floor, was either an out-of-work insurance agent or a full-time writer. He couldn't make up his mind which. I suspected that sometimes he was one, and other times he was the other. He answered the door wearing slippers and a lightweight checkered robe over an old tee shirt and I couldn't tell what else. He'd been up late working and once asleep didn't hear anything loud enough to wake him up. He didn't have much to say about the suicide except that it was a sad loss to the art world. From what I could tell, he was trying to write the kind of stuff that kept great actors like our late friends in business.

The woman in 15G was home from her regular job selling hi-tech products because her maid-babysitter had a case of acute bursitis and, ingrate that she was, had called to say that she would not be coming in to work that day. Hard to get good help and all that. Maybe it was for the best. She'd wanted for a while now to get someone a little more intelligent who would play educational games with the child and help him to realize his potential as a young overachiever. In a bright playpen in the middle of the front room, a seven-month-old infant in a designer stretchie drooled on an oversized plastic key. I immediately felt sorry for him.

The room was furnished expensively, with a thick, mauve, wool wall-to-wall carpet, several pieces of a sectional couch in white-on-white upholstery, three glass-topped endtables, a large book of art prints with a fine layer of dust on the dustcover, a baby grand piano, and bookshelves bearing several sets of books with matching covers. We started to sit on the cozy white couch, but she motioned us to some wooden folding chairs she had considerately set out for us.

Oh, boy.

What we learned from her was something we already knew—how little people know or care about their neighbors. Hartle and Selby meant nothing to her. Although their apartment was directly below hers, she never heard any noise of any kind. Their long fall from grace the previous night hadn't even disturbed her sleep. When the police showed her pictures of the two actors, she hadn't been able to identify them for certain as residents of the building. Had they, she wanted to know, been well-known celebrities or stars of important foreign films? We allowed that they had not.

The baby continued to drool in his playpen prison, and I wondered to myself about the advantages of being born into a privileged environment.

4

IT WAS PAST noon by the time we got back to the office. Tossing aside the *New York Post,* I scooped up the mail and glanced through it while Jessica checked in with our answering service.

Bill. Bill. Check. Bill. Circular. Circular. Circular. Check. Not bad. I filed two of the bills in the pending drawer of Jessica's desk and got out the checkbook to see if we could cover the others, which were a couple of weeks overdue.

My stomach told me that lunch was also overdue. I pulled the Smirnoff out of my bottom drawer and swallowed some neat, like a trooper. My stomach growled back. It can't be fooled.

Jessica was scribbling on her notepad. There were messages. Nice to be popular. I started writing out checks and stuffing them into envelopes.

Jessica consulted her notes. "Your friend Tom Reager from the *Voice* checked in."

"Uh-oh."

"You guessed it. He wants to know if you have anything for his paper about the double suicide this morning."

"Newspaper reporters get itchy if you ask questions about people just before they make it into the news. Do I have anything for him?"

"No." She glared at me. "You definitely do not have anything for him."

"You're right. What could he do with a pornographic blackmail tape and a double murder?"

I finished the checks and began browsing through the *Post*.

"Boris also called this morning. He wants to see us. Business, he said."

I looked up from the paper. "That's odd. It's usually the other way around."

Boris Radovich is a guy we met the day we called a car service to take us to the airport. He was driving. We call him in when we need a couple of extra hands on a case. He's a hard guy to describe. Probably, if you wanted to build someone who did not look anything like Robert Redford, you would build Boris. He stands about five-eleven and weighs maybe two-twenty-five. He has not an ounce of fat on him, but his face is round. That, together with his build, usually makes people think of him as fat, but he's not. His hair is dark, Ukrainian brown and he wears his black, bushy mustache like a protective shield. He manages to smile anyway. Underneath his gruff exterior—if he happens to let you in—is one hell of a warm, funny guy. He's extremely strong though and, while Jess and I are no slouches in that department, we bring him in sometimes for guard duty—body or property.

"Wonder what he wants," I mused.

Jessica smiled, as she dialed his number. "Last time I saw him, his big goal in life was to become a U.S. citizen."

"Must be close to it now."

Boris emigrated from the Soviet Union during the Carter administration. In Russia, he was an electrical engineer. Here, he drives for a car service. He still has a way to go in his English lessons, but he happens to be an all-around electronics genius and an intellectual. It was the latter that got him into trouble. He's one-fourth Jewish and his passport is stamped Jew.

One day, acting on a tip, the KGB found a Jewish Bible and other religious books in his house. Funny thing is, he wasn't a religious guy. After all, he'd taken the atheism courses along with everyone else. He was just an intellectual who liked to read. He lost his job over that, and one thing led to another. When a few neighborhood toughs set on him because he was a "dirty Jew," he took care of them with his usual lack of finesse.

He claims Siberia was an enriching experience. For one thing, New York winters now seem balmy. For another, he came into contact with many great minds and other intellectuals like himself.

Jessica left messages for Boris on the answering machine at his Brighton Beach apartment and with the dispatcher at the local car service. He has his own car and keeps his own hours. Nobody can accuse him of coming to America to make a lot of money. He says he just likes being free. Brooklyn's Brighton Beach is known as Little Odessa to the thousands of Russian immigrants who live there. "Russian spoken here" is the catchphrase of many of the shops and places of worship.

Meanwhile, my stomach was becoming a real problem. Jessica was responding to another message. I called the health food restaurant and ordered thick salmon sandwiches on seven-grain bread, plenty of salad, and a six-pack. The beer was for me. I put through a call to Tom Reager at the *Village Voice* and managed to convince him that the Hartle-Selby suicide was unrelated to my previous inquiry. Then I put a little more Smirnoff down my throat to keep the first shot from getting lonely until some real food arrived.

I tried to read the scratches on Jessica's notepad to see who she was talking to. Above a mess of doodles, she rewrote the name neatly—Slaker. Great.

Jonah Slaker is an unlikely name for a cop. He was Jessica's reluctant partner when she was on the force and has since made it to sergeant. He likes Jessica better now that he's not teamed up with her anymore, but he gets a little nervous at the thought of her tearing all over the city to solve crimes. Also, he doesn't like her current partner much. He thinks I look at the New York City streets as my personal My Lai. He has said as much to me on numerous occasions. From listening to Jessica's side of the conversation, I could tell that he had been working on the Hartle-Selby deaths and something had led him to us. Goody.

The other line on the phone lit up. I got it at my desk. It was Boris. "Hellaw, Rreddy?"

Good thing U.S. citizenship doesn't depend on losing your foreign accent; he'd never make it. I try to get him to use my first name, but he always says it "Chase-on" and it breaks me up.

"Rreddy. I must to see you and Munroe. I can to come overr now?"

I looked at Jessica who was deep in conversation about the suicides. "I don't know, Boris. We're kind of in the middle of something here. Can it wait a few days?"

"Is—how you say"—Boris paused, searching for the right word—"heffy." Heavy would do. "Is family."

"Sure, Boris," I relented. He was after all a good friend who has helped us out more than a few times. "Come on over. You eat lunch yet?"

"Oh, no. But who can eat who has such prroblems? In tventy minutes I be therre."

The restaurant hadn't sent out our order yet. Since Boris wasn't hungry, I only ordered four sandwiches for him. He would protest, saying he really couldn't eat a thing, but in the end, I knew, he would manage to munch through all four with hardly any effort. Jessica hung up.

I gave her the news about our appointment with Boris and about lunch.

"What was Slaker so anxious about?" I asked. "Didn't you finally tell him that I absolutely refuse to move in with him?"

She smiled. "He wants to know who's paying us to investigate a cut-and-dried uptown suicide."

"Oh, ho. So that's the way it is, is it?"

"It seems his captain is working with the twentieth on this and he doesn't want us tramping around ruining evidence."

"Or maybe finding it before he does?"

"I asked him why he cares what we do, if it's being investigated as a suicide anyway."

"What did he say to that?"

"He said that nothing points to anything other than suicide, and he doesn't want us making a lot of noise that's going to make trouble for the department. He says the deceased were scum anyway, and nobody would be interested in them at all if not for us."

"Did you find out anything from him about our scum?"

"Oh," she said, "just a few minor details the papers haven't gotten yet."

"The *Post* says the note was typewritten and not addressed to anyone in particular. That's all. Did he tell you what it said?"

" 'Life stinks.' "

"Tell me about it." I grinned. "But what did the note say?"

She shrugged. "They were high."

" 'Life stinks'? That's it?"

"Not their usual articulate selves."

I fiddled with a cigarette—one of the few passions I succumb to only rarely—and finally ended up by putting it out in my ashtray. I thought I saw Jessica breathe a sigh of relief.

"I don't know, Jess," I said. "You just don't wake up at three in the morning and decide to commit suicide. Especially not with a friend."

"How do you know they hadn't planned it for a long time?"

"Jess, when I was there earlier in the day, the bed was made properly and neatly. This morning the bed had been slept in and there were fresh clothes for the next day laid out on the dresser." The sandwiches arrived. I cleared a space on my desk for Boris's lunch. "When I was there yesterday," I continued, "the door was new, so new I noticed that it was new. Today, it was tampered with."

"I asked Slaker if he noticed that," Jessica said. "What do you think his response was?"

"That this is New York City, and doors come that way from the lumber yard."

She nodded. "And, since the door was locked when the cops arrived, there's nothing that says it wasn't suicide. You know he can always come up with answers to questions like that, Red."

"Oh? Also to the one about the broken window sash? And what about the lovely good-bye note?"

"What about it?"

"Typewritten? Do you believe those two jerks would use a typewriter just to say that 'Life stinks'? Anyone could have typed that note, then locked the door on the way out." Boris came in without knocking. "Anyway, to me, the broken sash suggests to me that they were forced out the window. It was not a graceful exit."

Jessica said, "It wasn't even really a lover's leap. Any suicide pact I ever heard of, the lovers jump together." I pointed Boris to the chair I had placed near my desk and the food that was laid out. She continued, "That way neither one had a chance for a change of heart. These two jumped in sequence, according to our earwitness. I don't know how you feel about it, Red, but I think it was murder and we better figure out if it's related to our case."

I munched on a sandwich. "I think it's gotta be mob."

"The connections Hartle was bragging about yesterday?"

I nodded. "I'm sure I heard him calling someone when I left."

"If that's what did it, then it is related to our case."

"Good chance of it, anyway." I picked my head up. "I just thought of something." She looked a question. "Did Slaker say how he knew we were there?"

"Sure, it was no big secret. The folks in the building told him."

"He didn't mention finding my business card on the desk in the front room?"

She shook her head. "Uh-uh. Did you leave it there?"

"That's where Hartle put it." I said. "Then, this morning, it wasn't there anymore."

"Do you think we should worry about it?"

"Shucks," I smiled. "It's advertising. Maybe we'll get ourselves a client or two."

Boris looked down at his empty plate in surprise. He'd gone through his four sandwiches and then some. My stomach still rumbled. I finally lit a cigarette. I generally smoke three or four cigarettes a week, which is pretty good considering that I used to zip through a couple of packs each day without any trouble. I carefully blew some of the smoke in Jessica's direction. Why should I die first and leave her a going business?

"You see, Rreddy." Boris took us both in with a single glance. "Jessica." Chessica. "I must to do something about these hoodlooms in Brrighton. Is not something to do alone. I must to have yourr help." Actually, I didn't see. There was plenty of crime in this city and some of it was bound to get to Brighton Beach.

He had one stubby finger up in the air. "They frrighten the merrchants." Two fingers. "Some of the storrekeep-errs they beat op." Three. "They rreally enchoy to hurrt people"—he winced—"to hurrt vomen." Four. "They poot much dope on street and they poot it in the school. The choints, the coke, the crrack, the ludes, the angel doost." Five. "They drrive theirr carrs like crrazy people in mittle the night. Sometimes chust to botherr."

I interjected before he could start on his left hand. "Are they the only ones selling dope in the neighborhood?"

"Oh, no. But they arre bad, verry bad."

"Okay."

I got up and started to pace. I noticed that Jessica was surreptitiously doing some isometric exercises at her desk. She likes Boris as much as I do, and I guess we were both wondering why he wanted to take on an entire gang all by himself. Or, almost all by himself.

I said, "Sounds to me like one of the things they're pulling is the old protection scam."

Boris looked inquiringly at me, then at Jessica. He was confused. "They don't prrotect anybody," he said.

"No, no," she replied. "The word 'protection' is a euphemism." Boris looked confused, but he let her continue. "Tell me if this is the way it happens. They tell the shopkeeper that for a fee they will watch over his store to make sure that nothing bad happens to it. The shopkeeper says something like 'What can happen that I don't already know about? I've been in business twenty years.' The punk says his window might get smashed. The storekeeper sends him packing. That night, the store's show window is smashed and looted, and next day the punk is on the guy's payroll. How'm I doing?"

"Is it exoctly, Chessica. They make pay one hundrred dollars everry month. Is it hoppen usual?"

She was noncommittal. "It happens."

"Some merrchants, they werre tough. They thought mebbe they vait long time, the gang leave Brrighton Beach and everrything go back to how it vas. Theirr businesses werre rruined. Firres, rrobbing. Then they werre beaten op. One man go to hospital, a good man. He was in hospital fourrteen days. He didn't carre about brroken bones, but fourrteen days in hospital his storre vas closed. He has not mit vhat to feed his family."

"What about the police?" I asked.

Boris shook his head. "No one vill go to police. Everryone too scared. I think even cops afrraid. Anyvay, vheneverr some of gang charrged mit crrime, they get fife otherrs to give them alibi. Then, whomeverr brrought charrges is in hospital. Sometimes, his vife and childrren too."

"Are these guys from the neighborhood, Radovich?"

"Oh, no. Nobody know vherre they arre frrom. They live in little house nearr Brrighton Beach Avenue. It is not theirr house, city own it. City trry auction it but nobody buys. Is verry old and everrything starrting to rrot. They chost stay in dot house and light mit candles and parrk theirr carrs in yarrd. Mebbe one day it burrn down," he muttered to himself.

Jessica said, "If these guys are major drug suppliers, you can get the vice squad in on it. They don't scare easy."

"Mebbe." Boris stood up and walked around the small office. He ended up at the window overlooking Flatbush Avenue and stood there, his back to us, looking out for what seemed to be a very long time. I thought the back of his neck, the exposed part over the collar of his blue cotton shirt, was uncharacteristically red and flushed. I looked a question at Jessica. She shrugged. We waited. Jessica finished her set. I smoked another cigarette.

Finally, Jessica went over to Boris and stood next to him silently for a while, the two of them side by side staring out of our office window. Then she gently laid a hand on his shoulder. "It's personal, isn't it?" she asked.

"The merrchants arre my frriends, yes," he replied. "They ask me to do something, to help them, I don't know vhat to do. I thought . . ." He took a breath; I noticed his hands clenched at his sides. "I thought they go avay afterr a vhile." He turned to face us. "Now, I am angrry also. Also, ashamed dot I not help my frriends. You underrstant?" He said to Jessica, "Is true vhat you said. Is perrsonal. My niece—"

He choked a little. I held out the last can of beer to him. He eyed it cautiously, then came over to sit down. He took the can, pulled off the tab, and took a long drink. He appeared glad to have something to do.

"My niece, Nadia, she is fifteen," he began. "Verry sensitive," he smiled, "not like oncle. But maybe, yes, like oncle vhen he vas fifteen. One day, she vas coming home frrom Brrighton Beach Avenue, carrrying packages fooll grrocerries forr herr mama. My sisterr. Two of those animals stopped herr—they arre twins, identical. They call herr filthy names, and they tell her vhy she not do bad things?" He flushed. "She no say anything. She trry run avay. They grrab her, all herr packages fall down. They poot hands underr herr clothing. One of them took out his"—Boris's face colored here—"and made herr kiss. She no rrememberr after that. Doctorr says prrobably she faint, thanks God."

"When did this happen, Boris?"

"One week. Rright now, she in herr rroom, all time in herr rroom. She no go out, she no talk to frriends. But she no sleep good anyvay. Also," he sighed, "she take showerr all the time.'' He paused for breath. That little speech had taken a lot out of him. He went on, in a different vein. ''I love this countrry, you know dot,'' he said. ''To be frree is most imporrtant thing forr me. But vhat good is forr me be free if my little Nadia must sits locked in herr rroom?''

He reached into his pocket and pulled out an envelope. ''I vant to do it rright. They arre going to get out of Brrighton Beach and they arre going to get vhat is coming to them and they arre neverr going to come back.'' He tossed the envelope vehemently onto Jessica's desk. ''My family, everrybody give something, vhat they could.'' He slid the envelope toward Jessica.

She pushed it right back to him again. ''Of course we'll help, Boris. But no money. You're our family, too. And your family is our family.''

Boris used one thick hand to rub his face. He pushed the envelope back again. ''You take. Is perrsonal forr me. But forr you, business. These people arre dangerous, yes. But is yourr job so I ask forr help frrom you.''

Before Jessica had a chance to push the damn envelope back again, I jumped up and reached for it. I pocketed it after first looking inside. There was $189 in tens, fives, and ones. It was enough to break your heart. I solemnly made out a receipt for the cash and signed it. Boris nodded and put the receipt carefully in his wallet.

''I vill show my sisterr,'' he said. ''She vill be happy.''

We decided to go into Brighton that very evening, which left us with several hours in which to formulate a plan. It was a damn good plan, too, if I say so myself.

We arrived at the location around seven, so it was still pretty light out, sunset being about an hour off. Jessica and I disembarked from Boris's gray van when it was still some blocks away. We walked slowly and in a roundabout route to the gang's headquarters. We were dressed in our best, conservative, middle-America, apple-pie clothing. IBM would have been proud of us.

In that neighborhood, there were a few semideserted blocks that winos and junkies affectionately called home, and this was one of them. We held hands as we walked and kept our eyes directly in front of us mainly since we didn't dare look at Boris who, at that moment, was lying in a doorway across the street, clutching a bottle of muscatel to his chest. He stank of cheap wine, urine, and stale clothing. His attire was old and creased and tattered in places where we had earlier tattered it. The stale odor came from my sweat suit, which he wore underneath and would now be stretched out of all proportion to its original owner. The urine smell was his own doing.

We picked our way through a walk overgrown with tall weeds and knocked politely on the door with professional, loving smiles fixed on our faces. The door was opened finally by someone who could never be considered small. In fact, obese would be a compliment. He was six-foot-two or -three, about four hundred pounds. His belly hung so far over his belt that I felt like asking him when the baby was due. His beard looked like a neglected overgrowth or a maggot's den. To say that he was a filthy slob would be an injustice to true filthy slobs everywhere. Let's just say he made Boris look good.

We went into our pitch. I smiled and nodded politely and said, "Good evening, Brother."

Jessica matched my smile and said, "If you have a few minutes, we'd really like to talk with you about the Messiah."

I said, "Do you believe in the Messiah?"

Bigbelly responded in what I considered an incredibly insightful and profound manner. He rumbled, to me, "Turdface, if you're not off my property in five seconds,

I will personally tear your balls off and stuff them in your whore's mouth." Then he belched.

Lesser emissaries of the Lord might have turned and fled, but not us. We stood our ground. I said, "Let us pray, Brother. Prayer will make you feel fulfilled as a human being." I thought for sure I was getting somewhere.

He responded, "In two seconds, you will have to squat to piss." Does Billy Graham have these problems?

Jessica picked up the thread. "The Bible teaches us to love our fellow man. Now, I know you're not much of a man, but I suppose we have to love you anyway."

For some reason, he came after me.

I backed up a bit and said, "Don't ignore the little girl. What if she puts you away and you have to explain it to your buddies?"

He was obviously confused. He turned sideways to look at Jessica, who had stood her ground and was all sweetness and soft femininity. He shook his head at my obviously dumb ploy and came wholeheartedly after me, saying, "That's it, wiseass, you're dead."

The door he had been standing in was still wide open. I backed away some more and made him come after me until Jessica was squarely behind him. She raised her hand and delivered a powerful chop to the back of his neck. As he fell, I jumped and came down on him with a knee drop to his rib cage. There was an audible crack. Another blasphemer taught to turn the other cheek. Before I was altogether on my feet, Boris had joined us. We grabbed the overgrown punk, deftly gagged and tied him, and carried him a few feet to the van. The whole operation took less than a few minutes.

Boris had told us that there were seven members in the gang altogether. We were hoping to find the other six in the house, resting up in preparation for a hard night's work—or snorting up. The door gaped open like a silent invitation to anyone who might happen by. We walked right in. All six were there, and it looked like they were, indeed, already stoned. The room was unlit, but a brightly colored glow came from a television and video hookup at the far end of the room. The six were sprawled around the set with their backs to us. How does one watch television in an abandoned building whose power was shut off months before? Probably they had spliced into one of their neighbor's lines.

The video they were watching was a porno flick. Something along the line of *Snow White and the Seven Horny Midgets*. Summertime in the big city and these guys were sitting here getting educated. I felt a new respect for them.

We quietly closed the door behind us. Boris, Jessica, and I spread out across the room. I asked no one in particular, "Is this where Armpits Anonymous meets?" The six, in various stages of stupor, began to rouse themselves and look around. Lions surprised in their own lair, probably for the first time. "Androids Anonymous?" I inquired. "Assholes Anonymous?"

The fight didn't last long. They kept coming at us. We kept at it. Within ten minutes, my cohorts and I were surrounded by an assortment of broken ribs, smashed noses, and missing teeth. Of course, we had all the advantages—we had surprised them, we were sober, we were in better shape, and we had Jessica. Talk about your secret weapons. She was something to watch, when I had a moment to watch. She was in street fighting mode, which included side kicks, back kicks, kicks to the knee, kicks to the groin, fingers in the eyes. Considering that our opponents were overweight, out of shape, stoned, and had probably never had serious opposition before, it was no contest.

We managed to bind and gag the hoodlums with tape and twine and cotton balls. They watched helplessly as we searched their place for hidden caches of accumulated goodies. The lions' den. The holy of holies. We found thousands of dollars worth of drugs—marijuana, cocaine, crack, pills, heroin—and drug paraphernalia. A drugstore for bozos. We discovered the cash hidden away neatly in a box on the kitchen table, also in the freezer—altogether, some ten thousand dollars' worth. I pulled off eight thousand dollars and gave it to Boris in a small envelope together with the tens, fives, and ones that he had given us. Boris would present it to his niece later. The way I figured it, if she could get a fair shake in court, she'd get that much for mental anguish alone. The rest I stashed in another pocket. We'd find a use for it later.

The weapons we found were another thing entirely. These guys did not believe in kids' stuff. Two shotguns, three submachine guns. I recognized an Uzi and a Swedish Kulspruta. About two dozen automatics, some of them very expensive—several Italian Berettas, a German Walther PPK, a few Lugers, a few Belgian 9mm. Brownings, and some American-made automatics as well. No Saturday night specials for these guys. Ten hand grenades.

Some of the stuff we uncovered during our search would be useful later on. We got it ready to take with us. Some of it I packed into a small duffel bag that I found on the floor of a closet.

Jessica and I got a few cans of kerosene from the van and proceeded to soak the furnishings and a good portion of the floor surrounding the trussed-up gang members. Former gang members. Their eyes were huge, round, scared pennies. And not a little glassy, considering we obligingly helped them to some of their own supplies. Once we explained the great, permanent, allover tan we were going to give them free of charge, they graciously pointed us to their car keys. And to their three cars.

Boris had gone out and he presently returned with a

couple of his acquaintances. These he set to the task of bringing two of the cars to a local "chop" shop, a business enterprise that specialized in taking cars apart for the parts. Being familiar with your home neighborhood is one thing, but where does Boris get his information—and his acquaintances?

We found out later that the double operation netted Boris five thousand dollars. Maybe we had misjudged this gang. After all, once their religious lesson sank in, they apparently saw the error of their ways and coughed up thirteen thousand dollars to help Boris's niece. I was truly impressed. Of course, there was that one fellow whose gag came loose and he kept shouting that we would be dead meat when he was through with us. Maybe he needed some more religion.

We got the gang outside before the fire started. We weren't happy about starting a fire in a residential neighborhood, but we had to make certain they would never come back. We consoled ourselves that the house would probably have caught fire on its own one day, probably from the candles and the borrowed electrical lines. Anyway, we were certainly going to alert the fire department as soon as we had disposed of the gang. Boris drove away in the van and took five of the gang along with him. Jessica and I were left with the twins. We had special plans for them, although what Boris was about to do with the other five was nothing to sneeze at.

He was going for a drive in the country. New Jersey was only about forty-five minutes or so from New York City, and the long stretches of lonely highway were perfect for his plans. Once he got far enough—beginning, say, in Freehold—he would pull over every twenty miles or so and give one of the bums a debilitating good-bye present—one that would require subsequent hospitalization—and a warning to stay the hell out of Brooklyn. By that time, I would guess the warning was unnecessary.

Then, Boris would throw the bum out of the van onto the side of the road. Another twenty miles down, the next bum, and so on.

While Boris was getting ready to dump trash illegally along the highway sides of New Jersey, Jessica and I took the twins, maneuvered them into the front seat of the last remaining car, and tapped them lightly on the back of the head with an automatic. The light tap was sufficient to knock them out since they were already pretty well stoned. We made certain they were out and untied them. Drugs, weapons, and the two thousand dollars went in the back seat.

There's a small, twenty-four-hour restaurant on a corner of Brighton Beach Avenue, the part that's under the elevated train. It's fairly dark there at night, but the patrons of Aunt Angelina's don't mind. The food is so good that there's always at least one NYPD patrol car parked out front. The place is a favorite of cops in three precincts. That night, we passed by—I was driving and Jessica was in the back—and we saw one police car out front and one double-parked at the corner halfway into the intersection. Two cops were at the counter and two were eating at a table in the window. Perfect.

I drove around the block and hit the accelerator when we were about a block from the restaurant. We smashed into the police car at about forty miles per hour. That'll teach 'em to double-park. To add to the confusion, Jessica fired a few rounds at the restaurant window, just below where the cops were sitting. While Jessica tossed the gun into the front seat, I slid one of the guys over to the driver's side and grabbed the small package I had prepared for myself. I left my door open and hoped that the fresh salty night air wafting in from the nearby Atlantic would wake them up enough to take the rap.

After three or four blocks, we stopped running. Our

gloves ended up in a huge trash bin out front of a fruit and vegetable store. We took the D train to Avenue H after calling the fire department from a pay phone on the subway platform, and walked the rest of the way to Jessica's house to wait for a call from Boris.

Since the cops were on the scene pretty quickly, it didn't take long to find out what we wanted to know. By the time we finished preparing a little midnight supper of ice cream, lime Perrier, and vodka for me, radio news had the ball and was running with it.

"Tonight, police arrested two members of a notorious Brooklyn gang, Albert and Joey Jordan. They drove into a police car and took shots at two off-duty police officers in a Brooklyn restaurant. Police finally subdued the perpetrators and impounded their vehicle, which contained one hundred thousand dollars' worth of assorted drugs and several weapons including shotguns, submachine guns, automatics, and eight hand grenades. One thousand dollars in cash was also recovered. No motive was given for the seemingly unprovoked attack on New York's finest, but a spokesperson called the crime crack-related."

Jessica raised her eyebrows at me. "One thousand dollars?"

"New York's finest," I said. "Think the Jordan twins will do time?"

"Ten to life at least." She pointed to the small duffel bag I'd been toting since we left the Brighton restaurant.

I shrugged. "Who's going to miss a few weapons in that lot?"

"Or two hand grenades?"

"Even exterminators charge a fee for pest control," I said. "Besides, you never know when a hand grenade might come in handy."

Tomorrow at the office, I would enlist Jessica's help in moving the safe out of its regular position to get to our special, hidden, built-in floor vault where the firearms could be safely stored.

5

THE SMELL OF coffee woke me up Thursday morning. It was eleven o'clock by my wristwatch and I was on the couch in Jessica's den again. The coffee meant that either Jessica was already up or a very considerate burglar had been about. I pulled on my pants and got out of bed.

I peeked into the kitchen to see whether the kind-hearted burglar was still there. No burglar. No Jessica. Not even Mrs. Olsen with her can of Folger's. The kitchen was devoid of life except for the eager Mr. Coffee machine, which had finished brewing. A note was propped up against it.

> Red—I made you some of the hot, black, addictive, adrenalin-stimulating, life-threatening yet legal drug in liquid form that you crave. There's some white, powdered, concentrate of sugarcane in the cupboard and some cow milkfat in a container in the refrigerator. Enjoy!
>
> —j

I was probably grinning from ear to ear as I got the sugar from the cupboard and the cream from the fridge and made myself a super morning cup of coffee. I located a glass pitcher, a small hand juicer, and Jessica's supply of temple oranges. When I had squeezed about half a pitcher full of orange juice, I washed my coffee cup and put the pitcher on a small tray along with two tall glasses.

Both pitcher and glasses sported a festive border of painted red wildflowers and green grasses.

I started to carry the tray upstairs to search out Jessica when I noticed the basement door open and a light on down there. I carefully made my way to the innards of the Munroe house.

Over muted strains of Beethoven's *Egmont* overture, the slaps, kicks, and grunts sounded measured and controlled. Jessica was working out in earnest. I watched with admiration as Jessica went through one of the routines of her unique brand of street fighting.

She was even better at it now then she had been a few years back when she taught self-defense as an adjunct Instructor in Brooklyn College's Department of Physical Education and gave seminars in street fighting at the college's Women's Center. Jessica is the type of person who uses everything she learns. From an early age she attended demonstrations of various kinds of competitive fighting—boxing, wrestling, martial arts. During our college years, I was able to show her some of the things I had learned in Nam courtesy of Uncle Sam, and she taught me a thing or two of her own invention. Later she learned whatever the police academy had to offer. Now, on the occasions when she must use her fighting skills, she has an unlimited arsenal from which to draw—all without picking up a single weapon.

The type of practice Jessica was doing now was new to me. She was practicing kicks, side kicks, full-face kicks, back kicks, jump kicks, and some others I'd have to invent names for, against the large, eighty-pound heavy bag that functioned as her somewhat passive opponent. Her kicks were strong, she stretched her leg muscles to the limit. From her waist down, her body moved in wide, fast motions. Her legs were everywhere. The catch, I soon noticed, was that her upper body movement was hampered considerably. She had bound her wrists together behind her back with a wide elastic band.

The music stopped and so did Jessica, bringing both feet solidly to the ground and steadying herself for a moment against the heavy bag, which was still in motion from her last kick. She released her hands from their restraint, picked up a small hand towel, patted her face dry, and then tossed the towel around her neck as she turned off the portable record player. The room was set up as a sort of home gym. There were reinforced wooden beams against the bare stone walls and along the ceiling. The ceiling was pretty high for a basement, so I'd guess that the floor had been dug down a couple of feet at one time. There was an assortment of weightlifting equipment, a bench press, two speed bags, and the heavy bag.

Jessica walked toward me smiling. I suddenly remembered that I was still carrying the tray with the orange juice and found a chair to set it on. Jessica downed her tall juice in three gulps.

"What's the idea of tying your wrists?"

She smiled. "How'd it look?"

"Super."

"If you know you can't work with your hands," she explained, "your legs get much better and are more useful to you—like the way a blind person learns to sharpen other senses." She poured herself another tall one and started on it, a little slower than the first. "Most people would feel rather helpless with their hands tied behind their backs. If you try it, you'll see that there's plenty you can do with just feet."

"What if your feet are also tied?" I teased.

She put her almost-empty glass down with the air of one who has just accepted a challenge. "Come on," she said and picked up her elastic band again. Then she produced its mate from the low chest against the wall that doubled as a bench and proceeded to bind her ankles, then her wrists. She stood silent and passive, a prisoner of her own making. "Try to strangle me," she said.

"Seriously?"

"You won't make it."

"How are you going to stop me?"

I approached, and she seemed to stand more still, to be more helpless. I stood close to her, looking down, and felt the heat from her strenuous workout still emanating from her body. I circled my hands around her neck, but before I had a chance to squeeze, the top of her head had been thrust into my downturned face. My nose took the brunt of what I knew was nowhere near the full extent of her strength. She could easily have mashed my nose right into my brain. My arms and legs were free but quite useless as I sank into the floor.

"No fair," I wheezed. "You knew what was coming."

Jessica untied her bonds and came over to me with an ice bucket. She wrapped a few cubes in the hand towel and held the pack against my nose. I stretched my legs out in front of me and leaned against her shoulder. She didn't seem to mind. I know I sure didn't.

"But, suppose," I continued bravely, "that your legs and hands are tied and your head is immobilized. What would you do then?" I had her now.

She laughed and punched me in the shoulder, not too gently. "Don't press your luck, Reddy."

She went upstairs to shower in the bathroom off her bedroom while I showered in the downstairs bathroom. I thought this was a big waste of water and towels and told her so. Now that her arms and legs were free, I felt courageous. Nonetheless, we bathed and dressed in our separate quarters and made it to the junction by one o'clock. We hadn't had much breakfast, but that was okay. It was already time for lunch, and a late start wouldn't do our case much harm—especially as we had no idea where our investigation was going.

At the office we disposed of our usual mail and message routine in record time. There was little that couldn't wait a day for our attention.

"Munroe," I asked, "do you get the feeling we're running in circles?"

"Mmm," she agreed.

"There sure do seem to be some big pieces missing from the puzzle Althea Walters brought us. And we don't even know what color or shape they are."

"We're going to have to make some sort of a progress report shortly."

"We've made precious little progress," I countered. "Why not call it a lack-of-progress report?"

Jessica made a face. "Let's try and work through the logistics of this case. Brainstorm it. Maybe we'll come up with something intelligent for a change."

"Better than detecting without a plan. What do we have so far?"

"We have blackmail."

"For what? Money?"

"For now, let's assume the object is just what the videotape said—votes. Our client is a state legislator. She votes."

"According to Hartle, there were at least nine others like her, maybe more. Think they're all on the state legislature?"

"That would be something."

"I got a couple of descriptions. Not to speak ill of the dead, but I don't think the guy was smart enough to make them up." I consulted my notebook. "A very short, fat guy with a pointy, dark brown beard. Probably means a Vandyke. And a very tall, thin, blond-haired woman. He probably remembered these two just because they look different from the norm."

"Okay. That's one thing we can do, and Allie can help us with it. Get a lead on who those two characters might be. Also what they might be voting on. Then maybe we can turn up other politicians who have been illicitly filmed recently."

"Who would need to collect future votes like that?"

"Just about anyone, Red. A real estate mogul, certainly. Guys like Taylor need plenty of political favors, and politicians need the cash that guys like Taylor have access to." She paused a moment to reflect. "Except that, for a while there, Taylor was short on cash himself."

"But not on contacts. Those stay on long after the cash has run out."

"Could be this whole blackmail thing started as a way to finance one of his projects during lean times. Then he realized how he could use it in other schemes."

"We're getting into assumptions now, Jess."

"Right. Let's stick to facts. Matthew Andrew Taylor is a big fat cat—"

"Fat cat? Cool, man."

"—who lives in a big house in Brooklyn Heights. He throws great parties. He knows a lot of people. He contributes to just about every major local politician, Democrat and Republican. He was close to bankruptcy, and then some deals soured at the same time. He pulled through, rumor has it, by way of a business loan, but I have my own ideas about that. He is connected with our case because our client went to one of his parties and thinks it very likely that the horrid tape was made there. We don't know this for certain, however."

"But we do have Taylor connected to blackmail of at least ten stoned people videotaped while performing sexual scenarios in his house." I began rummaging in my desk drawers for a cigarette. I will occasionally toss one in there by itself when I don't feel like keeping an almost-empty package.

"Information obtained from a dead man."

I looked up. "Sure, but who's going to dispute it?" I pulled the drawer all the way out and found what I was looking for in the back. "Who killed them anyway? Big Jake and Tulip. It seems kind of ludicrous to be a donkey and a rabbit one day and smashed fourteen floors below your bedroom window the next." I lit up and took a long drag.

"Good question. I'd guess you'd need more than two people to pull off a stunt like that."

"More like three," I agreed, "at the least."

"It was neat. Efficient. No one heard anything until the two thuds."

"Sound like mob?"

"Could be."

"Don't all real estate people have mob connections?"

"Only in the movies. And, if you are referring to Sandy, he's only an—"

"Or is it that all mobsters have real estate connections?"

She threw up her hands.

"They own their own homes, perhaps?" I mused. "Anyway, maybe that's another line worth investigating. Does Taylor have any known mob connections? Who does he hang around with other than politicians?"

"And who bailed him out when he needed the dough?" A hard look suddenly came in her eyes. "Do you think it's time to give Boris some work?"

"Thinking about my business card?"

"Uh-huh. No sense borrowing trouble. Nobody's interested in us, yet."

" 'Course not," I smiled. "We don't know anything."

Jessica joined me in the smile. "Red, are we in the wrong business?"

"Nah," I said. "We'll get there. As you said, it's what we do. If it came easy, everybody would be a private cop."

"Have you looked at the yellow pages lately?" she said. "Just about everybody is."

There was nothing in the *Post* that we didn't already know, so I left it to Jessica to work out the crossword puzzle and went downstairs to pick up another container of coffee.

When I returned, the puzzle was half done and Jessica was drawing imaginative doodles all around the perimeter of the page as she talked on the phone. I busied myself with the electronic mail messages that had accumulated since the last time I'd checked. Some I discarded immediately. There will always be a few immature wise guys who think of their computer as a big electronic toy for grownups and are willing to spend their money proving it. There were a couple that required my attention—inquiries about computer crime and computer security systems.

Meanwhile, I figured out that Jessica was talking with our client, who was apparently upset. Reasonably so, I thought, since I couldn't see that we were getting anywhere at all.

The last letter was from a man who thinks he's still my boss just because I worked for his firm for several years. He still harbors the not so secret belief that I will someday give up this private eye foolishness. He dangles before my weary, cynical eyes such perks as pension plans, expense accounts, and two-martini lunches as one would dangle a carrot before a reluctant horse. I wrote him a letter saying no, politely, in five sentences.

"She got a note," Jessica said, replacing the phone with a small disgusted bang.

I swiveled around.

"Block letters. 'We have the tape in a safe place. If you try to expose us, who do you think will be exposed first?' Made her nervous. Most likely, they sent a note like that to everyone on their list."

"What a list to be on."

"It's not an especially long list. And the note's vague enough."

"I could tell she was upset."

"She's worried about her daughter."

"Her daughter's in Europe, having a ball."

"She hasn't heard from her in two weeks."

"Wow. Two whole weeks."

"She sent a letter to the hotel where—"

"She's nineteen, Jess."

"No response."

"A nineteen-year-old kid isn't supposed to write home," I offered. "It just causes fights."

"Allie panicked and called the hotel where Veronica is supposed to be staying this week. Venice, I think. They said her room had been reserved, not guaranteed. When she didn't check in on time, they gave it to someone else. Some American kids went off on overnighters, and Veronica went with them. They want to feel like real Europeans."

"Like real tourists, you mean."

"The rest of the group is there. Until tomorrow."

"She's with a tour group?"

"Apparently."

"Seems like being a mom isn't all it's cracked up to be."

Something in Jessica's eyes flickered and then was still. She penciled a word into her puzzle.

"Just joshing you, Munroe. Look, the kid went off on her own for a few days. Isn't that the logical explanation?"

"That's what I told Allie. She's still worried some

harm might come to Veronica because of this mess over here.''

''That ought to be the next how-to book to come out. *Parenting Without Guilt*—it'd make a fortune.''

''Meanwhile, Allie will work with us on our end. I arranged to meet her at the library tomorrow. We're going to look through some information on the current makeup of the state legislature and try to identify those other people who were filmed at Taylor's house.''

''That's a good idea.''

''Also,'' Jessica said, ''I tried to get a sense of the kinds of things she'd be likely to be voting on at the next session.'' I raised my brows. ''She's a member of the Energy Committee, but it doesn't do very much. What's important is when a bill comes up for a vote. Then, the entire legislature votes.''

''So we have to find out what bills are likely to be voted on when the legislature is in session.''

''Hmm.'' The alarm on Jessica's watch went off. She looked at it and registered surprise. Then she grabbed her purse and the key to the ladies' room and scrammed. Hot date for tonight. Myself, I had a free evening. Hell, I hadn't even been home in two days. I finished up at the computer and put it to bed.

Jessica returned from the ladies' room ready to leave in a flash, but not before I noticed a hint of red on her lips. I looked again.

''Jess! Lipstick?''

''Shut up.''

''Lipstick?''

''Watch it, Reddy.'' She turned on me. ''If you don't watch what you say, I'll put such a dent in you, Doris won't have to worry about birth-control precautions for a long time.''

''Doris is yesterday,'' I said. ''We're through.'' I grabbed my jacket and made for the door. Jessica rolled her eyes. We grinned at each other. "Give Sandy my best," I said. "Don't let him sell you any beachfront property in Arizona."

She kicked my butt on the way out.

6

I FINALLY MADE it home by my usual means of transportation. People who live in New York City and don't use the subway system are not true New Yorkers in my book. They might as well live in Cincinnatti. How anyone can walk through the streets, soaking up sights and sounds of Gotham, and totally ignore the netherland pulsating under the concrete beneath their feet is beyond me. Some might fear being accosted by drug pushers and their ilk in the unknown, dark regions, but there is nothing to fear. Drug pushers are afraid of working the subway platforms. There are precious few places to hide, and it is difficult to make a quick getaway. So dope entrepreneurs shun the stone and tile walls, the tall staircases, the fluorescent lights of the New York City subway system. Who wouldn't prefer fresh air? That's not to say that you can't find your share of kooks if you look hard enough.

I wasn't disappointed. As I emerged from the subway car at the Union Square station and prepared to make my way to the front of the platform and up the stairs to the street, I was approached by two girls in long flowing skirts and long flowing hair.

"Good evening," the older one said. "Would you like to study the Bible with us?"

The younger one slipped her arm in mine and whispered confidentially, "I found Jesus. He's the Jewish Messiah, you know."

I recalled noting recently that the Christian missionary

group known as Jews for Jesus had stepped up its proselytizing activities in the area. I've never understood the rationale behind the name of that particular group. To me, a Christian is someone who accepts Jesus. If that someone happens to be a Jew, calling that someone a Jew for Jesus doesn't make him any less a Christian. Next, I suppose, we'll see Moslems for Jesus. And, how about Buddhists for Jesus? Witches for Jesus?

Frankly, I was a bit insulted. Just the night before, Jessica and I had been doing some proselytizing of our own and I thought for sure the holy aura was still around me. Couldn't they tell?

Using the same confidential tone, I whispered back, "I'm not Jewish, ladies."

I was about to offer to show them proof of my gentile birth, when they turned abruptly and walked down the platform. Something in the way they squared their shoulders made me think they would be more careful in sizing up their next pigeon. Maybe he would have to show them proof of his religion. Lucky dog.

The night air was only slightly cooler than it had been during the day. From Union Square, I walked north on Park Avenue to 18th Street and east for a block and a half to my apartment—condo, actually, but I hate the yuppie sound of the word. Before entering my building, I reviewed the supper possibilities to be found in my kitchen. Mother Hubbard had nothing on me. I continued walking east to Third Avenue and the best little Hungarian delicatessen in town.

It's called Mario's Place, though the owner and chef is actually a Hungarian-born U.S. citizen named Laszlo. When he and his wife opened the restaurant a few years back, she convinced him that customers wouldn't be drawn to Laszlo's Place. Hence, the alias.

The food, however, is entirely authentic, and mostly great, though heavier than a lot of people like to eat nowadays. My personal favorite is cabbage leaves stuffed with a mixture of meat, rice, tomato sauce, and the occasional mushroom. Laszlo sure knows how to stuff a cabbage.

I made my way to the tables at the back of the restaurant, stopping at the deli counter on my way to greet Laszlo and give him my order. I noticed that a few of the tables were occupied, one of them by a young couple involved in a loud and heated disagreement. I selected a spot as far away from them as I could get, but, the dining area being rather small, it was impossible to avoid overhearing their animated exchange.

I waited patiently for my stuffed cabbage and tried hard to look as though eavesdropping was the furthest thing from my mind.

She was telling him, in a sweet but not at all uncertain voice, to please go away. He insisted on standing his ground until he wore her down and she changed her mind. About what, I wondered? Her dinner order? He was big, probably as big as I am and that's six-foot-two in stockinged feet. He had a couple of pounds on me, but his weight appeared to be mostly fat. Maybe he'd had some chest muscle at one time, but he'd let himself go over the years and his chest had migrated south of his belt. It's a bit of Nature's alchemy which I always felt was fitting punishment for those muscled beach boys in my native California who would eventually find something of interest besides pumping iron.

He was not what you could call handsome. Actually, I was surprised a woman could eat with him and keep her food down. His face was heavy and jowly, his features coarse bordering upon cruel. I didn't blame her for telling him to go, especially since I was here now, and, while I might never win any contest on my looks, no lady has yet thrown up her supper at the sight of me. In fact, if I tried hard, I could convince myself she'd seen me come in and that was what precipitated her cold attitude toward her companion.

It was a neat fantasy, especially since she was not only easy to look at but a real old-fashioned knockout. She was probably about four inches shorter than me—tall for a woman and that's how I like them. Her eyes were big and blue, and her hair was long, silky, and blond. Not a yellow blond, or a white blond, or a mousy blond, but all different kinds of blond blended together. You don't get that kind of color from a bottle. Still, you can't be too sure of anything nowadays, even hair color. This was something I could envision checking out more closely for myself. I am a detective after all.

Besides, if there is one thing I like more than a tall woman, it's a tall woman who doesn't think she has to starve herself down to anorexic dimensions in order to be attractive. This lady was a hit in that department, too. She had a full figure, top and bottom, with curves in all the right places, and a black crepe dress that outlined her proportions and lent assistance to my imagination.

Of course I couldn't tell much yet about her brains, other than that she was exercising excellent judgment by insisting that this rough bozo scram. Every time she raised her voice to reiterate her demand, it reinforced my conviction that she was the one for me. Unfortunately, her insistence also seemed to strengthen the conviction of her companion to stay and annoy her further. He started name-calling at her in a bellowing voice.

This he began innocently enough with derogatory names that one might use to describe any fellow human. Then he moved on to names for females, then names describing animals. I have to admit, he had it over me in name-calling. The blond knockout was by now quite red in the face and probably starting to cry. There were still a few diners in the room, but no one made a move. I suppose they, like me, were learning new words and afraid that if they did anything he might decide to stop the language lesson. Or, maybe they were just afraid of him. He was so mean and tough looking I couldn't imagine anyone willing even to enter an elevator with him. Sooner, an elevator shaft.

He eventually progressed to describe all different kinds of unusual familial relationships. I had reached for my notebook to take it all down for future reference, when the blushing face and large, blue eyes began pleading and somehow drew me from across the room into the heart of the fracas.

"The lady wants you to leave her alone," I said.

"Mind your own business, shithead."

"Look. We've already heard the full extent of your command of the English language. Why don't you just leave now and stop bothering the lady?"

"Go back to your table before I tear your stupid head off of your stupid shoulders."

I started to smile. I couldn't help it. "That's it?" I asked. "Stupid? You've run out of your supply of filthy words?" He started coming at me. At least it got him away from the table. "You know who's really stupid? You, you dumb bozo," I said. Then, in a stage whisper to the woman, who was sitting tensely at her table, I added, "I heard he's so dumb he can't win a game of tick-tack-toe with a three-move headstart."

She gave a little smile.

He said, "That's it, turdface. When I finish with you, the garbage men are going to carry you away in a paper bag."

"Turdface is better than stupid," I conceded, "but you're still a dumb bozo." Then, to the woman again, "I heard that when he was born, his parents made a large contribution to planned parenthood."

"Who told you that?" he snarled.

Obviously he didn't appreciate my sense of humor. A massive fist came roaring toward my face at about thirty miles per hour. I blocked with my left and caught him in the cheek with a right hook, then followed through with a solid left to the jaw plus another right-left combination. My dancing partner got weak in the knees, did a little half turn and slid to the floor like a screw into rubber. That's when Laszlo showed up at a run, through the swinging doors from the kitchen, with a meat cleaver in his hand.

I stood with my arms folded, near the fallen oak. Laszlo looked from me to the huge form on the floor, to me again. I elevated my eyebrows in the direction of the meat cleaver, which was still poised in midair. He looked at his raised hand as if he didn't know to whom it belonged.

"I thought you might need some help, Mr. Reddy."

I smiled. "Not a moment too soon, Laszlo."

He shrugged, grinning, and put the cleaver carefully into a deep pocket of his white apron. "I'm not as young as I used to be."

Laszlo did help after all. We carried the bum out the back door and dumped him into the garbage bin behind the restaurant. I cautioned Laszlo to wash his hands before handling my food, and he cautioned me against being a wise guy. "I still have the meat cleaver, you know."

Back inside, she was sitting at my table—all blue eyes, blond hair, black dress, and white, fine skin. I extended my hand. "Jason Reddy," I said.

"My name is Lisa Colford." She placed her hand in mine, and our souls touched. "Thank you so much, sir. I don't know what I would have done if you hadn't been such a gentleman."

"Skip it."

"I was so terribly embarrassed by his carrying on."

"Who is he?"

"I don't even know. I came in here to eat a nice, quiet dinner and all of a sudden there he was. I tried to get rid of him. But, well . . . may I?" I said yes, and she took a sip out of the water glass on her side of the table. I asked her to join me for dinner if she hadn't already eaten, and she accepted the invitation.

Laszlo himself brought our orders to us. Stuffed cabbage for me, and for the lady as well. It was clear that fate had thrown us together. We decided on apple pie for dessert, then spent a few minutes digging into our food and providing our stomachs with a taste of old-time Budapest.

Lisa said, "I heard New York City was a rough place, but that Neanderthal didn't want to take no for an answer."

"Forget about it," I said. "There are plenty of nice people in New York."

She flushed slightly and lowered her lids for a moment. "Like you, Jason."

"And you," I was quick to point out. "By the way, where are you from?"

She was a native of Houston, Texas, my fair-haired fantasy come true. She'd decided to set out for the Big Apple a couple of weeks back when she lost her job. I remembered a piece in the Times about the miserable economic situation in Houston. She'd always wanted to head east and take in that fabled crowded skyline. So she did.

"What sort of work do you do?" I asked.

"I'm in public relations."

"Well, I guess New York is the place for public relations jobs."

"It seems to be." She appeared uncomfortable for a moment. "I hope to find something soon. I'm starting to run low on funds."

"Where are you staying? With friends?"

"I'm at a small hotel—the Savoy—down the block a bit, across Third Avenue. Have you heard of it?"

I had. The Savoy was a moderately priced hotel that rented by the week or month. Of course what we call moderately priced in Manhattan probably bears no relation to moderately priced in Houston.

We finished up our respective dinners and continued to talk about this and that. I have to admit that although I have never been a believer in the love-at-first-sight phenomenon, I was totally intrigued—one might even say captivated.

We went for a walk and she was tall enough that we could hold hands without straining. Most of her job hunting had been either further uptown or further downtown in the financial district, so she hadn't had much of a chance to look around the neighborhood. I volunteered some historical information and small bits of gossip—common knowledge among us locals—about the businesses and private residences of the neighborhood.

"Gosh, Jason. You know so much about this area. Have you been living here all your life?"

"Just a few years. I'm from San Francisco originally."

We walked and talked for quite a while. She asked me what I did for a living and I told her.

"You don't look like a detective, Jason, Physically, you could be a boxer or a wrestler, maybe. But, on the other hand, you don't talk like a boxer or a wrestler. What made you decide on that line of work?"

"It's kind of a long, roundabout story."

She hooked her arm in mine. "I've got time."

"My partner and I met each other in college back in the seventies. I needed a change of scenery—sort of the way you feel now, I guess. That was after I'd come back to the world from working as cannon fodder for Uncle Sam in Nam. The GI Bill was available and I figured, by golly, I'm going to stick that white-whiskered geezer for every legitimate expense I can think of."

"You sound bitter."

"Frustrated idealist, I guess. Nam can do that to you. That's where I realized how impossible it is to fight for good against evil. You have to fight not only the enemy, but the thing you're a part of as well."

We walked a block in silence. Vietnam was over a long time ago, and I thought I had talked myself out on the subject. Obviously, I was wrong, Lisa Colford was an interested listener and I found myself opening up to her in a way that I hadn't done in a long time. "I was in the Special Forces. Green Berets and all that. Very patriotic. Glad as hell to be able to serve my country. I was part of a small unit that went on commando operations behind enemy lines. Our job was to disrupt the flow of supplies along the Ho Chi Minh Trail, supplies sent from the North Vietnamese to the Viet Cong.

"I soon found out that a lot of the guys I fought with were scum. Many of them enjoyed killing. Some of them enjoyed it so much they preferred to take their time about it. They had no ideals, where the war was concerned—at least, not by the time I met them."

Lisa's soft voice interrupted. I had almost forgotten she was there. "You don't really mean that all the soldiers were like that?"

"Why should they be otherwise? We were fighting and dying while the higher-ups looked around for ways to get rich. Did you know that some South Vietnamese officers sold American weapons to the enemy? Oh," I caught myself, "you're too young to remember. This must sound like an ancient history lesson to you."

"I'm not as young as I look," she said. "And, anyway, I'm really very interested."

"I don't see why. I'm just rambling on like a confused war veteran."

"If you were in the Green Berets, you must have started out to make the armed forces your career."

"Like I said, I was very patriotic. But the army killed that. I took my honorable discharge as soon as my term was up. Came east. Went to college."

"And that's when you decided to become a detective?"

I smiled. "Not quite. I don't think anybody actually plans that for a career. I happened to meet my present partner in college. Only she wasn't my partner yet, just a friend."

I thought Lisa's smile turned a little wooden for a moment.

I squeezed her hand. "Like I said, just a friend."

We walked another block—more slowly now than at first. She gazed at me. I gazed back.

"What did you do after college?" she asked.

"I put my degree to work. A bachelor's in computer science was not as common then as it is today. It got me a programming job with a large firm. Eventually I moved up to systems analyst with the same company. Then, I became the resident computer-security expert. After five years there, I thought I could make the job more interesting by becoming an independent consultant and working for several firms as a computer crime and security advisor."

"Was it? More interesting, I mean."

"Yes and no. I did enjoy being my own boss, and I suppose anything is better than corporate life. Still, at the end of the week I was hard-pressed to think of anything I had done of value. You know, it felt like I was just chasing the dollar."

"But you made out well, didn't you?"

"Oh, yes. A computer security specialist does quite well."

"You must have made more money doing that than being a detective."

I smiled. "I'm still living partly off of that money. And I do take on an occasional job when I have the time."

She shook her head. "If you were doing so well, how did you get it in your head to be a detective?"

"Remember I told you about this friend of mine from college? Her name is Jessica Munroe. Graduated summa cum laude with a degree in English literature and a minor in physical education. After six years on the New York Police force she came into a small inheritance and decided to go private. A couple of years back, I got a call from her about a job. She had a case that involved computer fraud and she called me in as a consultant. One thing led to another, and eventually she asked me to join her agency. It seemed like something meaningful, a job where I could make a difference."

She asked, "You must get some very interesting cases in your line of work. What are you working on now?"

"I couldn't begin to explain the case we're on now." I laughed. "I don't think I understand what's going on myself. But, if you're interested, I'll tell you about something we worked on this past winter." She said she was interested. I deliberately chose a case that Jessica and I had been able to solve without violence.I certainly didn't want to frighten Lisa off.

A large appliance store in downtown Brooklyn had been having some trouble. It seems a good portion of their inventory kept walking out on its own without benefit of sales slips. "They didn't quite know how to attack the problem because they didn't know its source—shoplifting or employee theft. Jessica and I worked undercover posing as store employees, for a couple of weeks. Did you know that employee pilferage is a much bigger problem than shoplifting?"

She shook her head.

"Well, that's what it turned out to be. It didn't surprise us much. What did surprise us was the ease with which we cracked the case." I cracked a smile. "One of the guys had the hots for Jessica and before you knew it he was showing off his five-thousand-dollar stereo, his three-hundred-dollar suits, his two-thousand-dollar color TV, his eighty-dollar custom-made monogrammed shirts. All on a salary of three hundred dollars a week. Jessica came right out and asked him how he was able to afford all those nice things on his measly salary. The yokel told her everything. He would throw a couple of small appliances—calculators, tape recorders, walkman's, watchman's, and the occasional VCR—out with the garbage and retrieve them from the trash bin late at night. We figured he averaged five hundred to a thousand dollars' worth of products weekly."

She shook her head. "I can't imagine anyone being that stupid."

"You'd be surprised at the things dishonest people will do to their employers."

We turned east on 18th Street. I said, "You must be dying of boredom. You're not going to believe this, but I never talk so much about myself."

She rested her head against my shoulder, and we slowed to a stroll. "I'm not at all bored, and I can sense that you don't open up very easily to people. I'm glad you feel you can with me."

I put my arm around her shoulders. It was happy there. We were standing in front of my building. "This is where I live," I said. "Would you like me to walk you to your hotel?" Was I smooth or what?

She looked slyly at me. "Do I look like I want to be walked to my hotel?"

I grinned. "You look like you want a glass of my best 1982 California Chablis."

"A good year," she agreed.

Moments later she was sitting on my couch, drinking wine, and listening to light pop music on an FM station. The night was young and I felt giddy. I kicked off my shoes and shrugged out of my sports coat. I tossed my necktie cavalierly across the room and opened the top three buttons of my shirt.

She hummed some bump-and-grind music.

"I'm not a sex object, you know," I said.

She opened another button on my shirt and poked playfully at some chest hair. "You could have fooled me."

We snuggled up to each other and tried a tentative kiss. It tasted like wine. I leaned back against the couch and sighed contentedly. "Now I know what I'm going to ask for when I reach those pearly gates," I sighed.

Lisa must have relaxed a little too much herself, because she suddenly started to choke on her wine. I helped by patting her back. Maybe I didn't help too much at that. I think I was patting a bit too low. Anyway, she got over it. But the mood was broken. I poured more wine.

"Hungry?" I asked.

"No, I'm not. Mario served a lovely dinner, didn't he?"

I thought it would be too much trouble to explain about Laszlo, so I just nodded. I had trouble saying anything more because one of her smooth, white hands was touching me in a private place. I reciprocated by touching some of her private places. Pretty soon we were all over each other's private places. I gathered her up in my arms—which was no mean feat. Her short, black, summer jacket and matching purse were still in her lap. I wondered at that, but not for long. A few moments later we were discovering those private places all over again in my big bed.

We fell asleep in each other's arms. Even in sleep, I knew I didn't want to let this one go.

7

THIS TIME I knew it was a dream. I used to dream about the war often, but hadn't for a long time. In this one I relived the months I spent as advisor to Captain Pham, although in the dream it took only a few minutes. Pham was one of the few South Vietnamese officers who knew what he was doing. An excellent officer, his men revered him; the Viet Cong despised him.

His problem was women. Here was this handsome, dashing guy and he just loved to fool around. It's not as if he didn't know that there was a price on his head and wanton sexual activity could be dangerous. It was his Achilles' heel. As cautious as he tried to be, there were always elements of those clandestine assignations that were difficult to control.

We were in this village near the border. She was maybe seventeen years old. A rare beauty with clear, Asian features, honeysuckle skin, fine, sturdy limbs, and unbelievably long, black, thick, shiny hair held together with a pair of brightly painted ivory hair ornaments. Pham was so darn proud that he had managed to get her to agree to join him in his hut, I bet he burst a button off his uniform that day. Of course, he had enticed her with the promise of a good dinner, probably the best she'd had in all her young life.

Middle of the night. The night noises seemed so real, the kind of real you only get in dreams. A scream, barely audible, from the direction of Captain Pham's hut, disturbed my sleep. I ran and ran, and unlike those running dreams where you never get anywhere, I suddenly found myself at the entrance to Pham's hut. The girl was standing over the prone form of Captain Pham, holding one of her hair ornaments. Blood all over. The captain's throat was cut, the hair ornament dripped blood. As I approached I got a closer look. It was a decorative "comb" bearing five metal spikes honed sharp as ice picks. As I ran toward the captain and the girl, moving through an ocean of jello, she was trying to cut him again and finish the job. But of course I reached him in time. Because that's what happened in real life.

We managed to save the captain's life, but he was never the same again after that experience. He had lost the better part of his legendary self-confidence. He just wasn't any good as a soldier anymore. Later, he told us that he fell asleep after the lovemaking, and the next thing he knew, he was getting his throat cut. That weak cry for help was all that kept him from a date with Saint Peter.

Of course, in my dream the story was not all that clear. Sometimes it was me being cut and sometimes it was Captain Pham. And, for that one awful second when I confronted the Vietnamese woman with the deadly hair ornament, the face she was wearing was Jill's.

I woke up in a sweat, my arms full of empty.

For a moment I didn't move at all. Through the slits of my almost-closed eyelids, I saw my Jill moving stealthily away from the bed. She picked something up from the floor. Her purse. Maybe it was an aftereffect of that dream, maybe it was a lingering suspicion I had been hiding all evening in a dark corner in the back of my brain, but I didn't wait to see what she wanted from her purse. I let my arm drop slowly to where I keep a spare .38 taped to the underside of the boxspring for easy access.

The room was dark, illuminated only by the faint glow

of the streetlight down the block as it filtered through my bedroom window. Jill was still naked. Her purse was now back on the floor and in her hand my dream was becoming reality. She held a small gun. In the dark it looked like it could have been a .25-caliber automatic. Maybe a Beretta. Its barrel caught the small bit of light in the room and reflected it, making it appear as if the gun had its own internal source of power.

She took aim.

I rolled out of bed and shot at her in one swift motion. My shot rang out seconds after hers. What happened next was all clouds and confusion and more gunshots and impossible to describe in sequence. In fact, for several minutes, I marveled at the capacity of a bad dream to feel so real.

The reality of it was that she was lying on my bedroom floor clutching her chest, her breasts and hands covered with pure red blood, and my pillow had a black hole in it where my head had been. I shook myself out of my inertia—or maybe the shaking was from shock—and moved quickly over to where her life was spilling into a red pool on my carpet.

I held her face for a moment and gently asked her, "Why, Jill?"

Her eyes glared at me. "For ten thousand dollars, you schmuck."

She expired then, before I had a chance to ask her any more stupid questions, or any smart ones either. Like who had hired her. Or, why. Or, how they had arrived at the ten-thousand-dollar figure for the value of my life.

I spent the next few hours with various employees of the New York Police Department. It wasn't too bad at first, until Slaker arrived and set a new tone by calling me a lady-killer, referring at once to my reputation with women and to the situation at hand. I pointed to the mass of human flesh on the floor that was just then acquiring an official white-chalk border and told him if there was a lady killer in the room it was there.

I think I mentioned that Sergeant Slaker doesn't like me. He likes me even less when I shoot someone. And even less than that when the evidence clearly indicates self-defense.

He examined my charred pillow. "You're a very lucky guy. She ought to have shot you, Reddy."

I gave him a look, which he returned in kind. "Thanks for the blessings, Slaker."

He reddened slightly. "You think you're so high and mighty, Reddy. You think you're above the law, that you can make up your own rules. Well," he comforted himself, "next time you might not be so lucky."

I didn't bother to point out to him that if I didn't live by some rules of my own devising, I wouldn't have been lucky at all. Somehow, I think that's what he was getting at.

I could tell that I would not be getting any more sleep that night. For one thing, tomorrow's sunlight was already streaming through the window. For another, my bedroom was no longer mine—it was evidence, and it was crawling with humanity. I decided to split.

"Don't forget to lock up when you leave, fellas," I said as I walked out the door. "You never know who might walk in off the street." They ignored me, which showed intelligence. Maybe the civil service examinations were getting harder.

I spent half an hour on the subway system. A bonus, since the trip can take anywhere up to an hour. I reached the junction at six-thirty, and it might as well have been the middle of the night for all the people that were about. The college community wouldn't start to mill around for at least an hour and a half. The stores wouldn't open for four hours, the banks for two and a half. The only people I saw were part of the early rush-hour crowd. They moved zombie-like past one newsstand or another, picked up their favorite papers, and descended into one or another of the subway entrances to make their way to Manhattan.

I grabbed a paper of my own, and the *New York Times* helped me through a breakfast snack at the coffee shop. I don't really know what I ate. To be perfectly candid, I don't know what I read either. The events of the night still weighed heavily on my mind.

When I got to the office, Jessica was at her desk, her legs stretched out uncharacteristically in front of her, feet up on the green blotter. She glared at me as I walked in.

Affecting an air of nonchalance that I did not feel, I sauntered over to my chair and pretended to relax. "Mornin', Jess. You're getting an early start too, I see."

"Jason Reddy, where have you been?" If looks could kill.

"Am I late for something? Did we have an early appointment?"

She pointed to the phone. "I've been trying to reach you. First, it was busy. Then, no answer. Later, I tried again and a man's voice came on. I said, 'Who is this?' He said, 'Who are you?' We danced around like that awhile until I finally had the brains to hang up on him. Then you show up here all bright-eyed and bushy-tailed like you don't have a care in the world."

I just stared at her. She put her feet down abruptly and busied herself at her desk. "Look," she said after a few moments, "we happen to be working on a case. And when we are working on a case, I like to be able to get hold of you if necessary. Even if you do have a healthy libido."

So that was it. She was ticked off because she tried to call me and, having trouble getting through, she assumed I was shacked up with a woman. Righteous indignation rushed through my body like oil through the Alaskan pipeline. Then it ran dry. I had indeed been with a woman.

"Uhm, Jess." She looked at me. "You know how you always tell me I have lousy taste in women?"

The story of my late-night adventure sounded clearer in the retelling than it had felt in the living, but that's to be expected. Of course, as clear as it was, the story also made me look pretty foolish. I finished with the cops' visit and the probable identity of the voice she heard on my telephone.

I wouldn't say that Jessica was ignoring me, but I didn't feel that she was giving my trial by hitwoman the attention it deserved. As she listened, she fidgeted. She doodled with colored pencils on a small notepad. She didn't even do any exercises that I could see. It was unnerving.

"Sorry I snapped at you," she said, finally.

"Hey." I was prepared to be magnanimous. "You didn't know what was coming down."

"In a way, I did. I'm a little tense and I've been taking it out on you."

"You okay, kid?"

She made a face. "I had a little experience of my own last night."

I felt my eyes open wide. "No kidding," I said. "Anybody hurt?"

She nodded and started from the beginning.

It must have started about 3 A.M. Jessica had awakened suddenly with the feeling that her house was trying to tell her something. Since she's been living in that house on Ocean Parkway most of her life, alone for the past couple of years, she is on intimate terms with its every squeak and whisper. It happened that, as she listened in the darkness, there was a creak followed by another one several seconds later. By then, she was wide-awake.

Assuming that someone was coming up the stairs, Jessica crept stealthily out of bed and pulled a very old trick. She punched up two pillows to look something like a sleeping form and covered it with the blanket. Luckily for her, it was a hot night and the air conditioner was on. This justified her using a blanket and also meant that her door was, naturally, closed.

"These guys were good, Red. The phone was dead. They had obviously cut the telephone line in addition to disabling my burglar alarm. I didn't hear a thing. My air conditioner is pretty quiet, but I still don't know how I managed to hear that creak."

I recalled my own good fortune. "Maybe you dreamed it."

"I realized that I had a minute at most before they would find me. There aren't that many rooms upstairs and the others are obviously empty."

"There's that one extra bedroom with no furniture in it."

"Then there's the one I converted into a study last year, and there's the bathroom. The spare bedroom and my room were the only ones with closed doors. I looked around for some clothes but nothing was handy, and it sounded to me like they were approaching fast."

"Since when did you start sleeping in the altogether?"

Jessica smiled grimly. "I was wearing a nightshirt, Red, but—oh, never mind." She went on.

She had taken her .38 out of the night-table drawer. She had no intention of using the gun unless it was absolutely necessary, but reasoned, quite accurately, that this was no ordinary burglary. Burglars don't cut off the phone in the middle of the night. They also don't generally like to work in groups, and the two creaks she heard on the stairs meant there were at least two intruders.

The door opened slowly, softly, and the first thing through was the silencer-equipped barrel of a 9mm. automatic. A few feet down the hall, someone was opening the door of the spare bedroom as well. The thick-barreled gun was attached to a guy with a thick-barreled body—all muscles, no neck, big ears, broad forehead, and clean shaven, including his head.

Jessica pressed flat against the wall next to the dresser, her gun hanging down at her side.

"I felt exposed and vulnerable, but he shot at the phony form in my bed three times before he noticed me."

"They're not making burglars the way they used to."

"I shot him twice and got him in the chest both times. He went down and I shut the door practically in his partner's face and locked it. By the time I turned back to the guy on the floor, he was already dead and a muffled voice was saying, 'The bitch shot Frankie and locked herself in her room.' "

"I hope you didn't get too upset about it. Granted, 'bitch' is antifeminist. But it's not as bad as, say, 'gal' or 'broad'—"

"I heard the other guy answer, 'He's probably dead. We'll burn her out. Go down and find something we can start a fire with.' "

"So there were at least two more of them."

Jessica nodded.

Not knowing how much time she had, but realizing that there was someone guarding her locked bedroom door, Jessica slipped into the closet. Her bedroom shares a wall with the adjacent spare bedroom, and the closets of the two rooms share a wall as well. A few years back, during what I referred to as a moment of paranoia, she had replaced the thick plaster wall between the two closets with a removable plywood panel. Now it provided her with an exit and very likely saved her life.

She made it into the other room with a minimum of noise. The door to the hall was ajar. A second no-neck, like the one she shot, was standing at her bedroom door, gun poised, his back to her. The third man had not yet returned.

Jessica shouted, "Drop your weapon!" and the guy swiveled quickly on the balls of his feet.

He fired two shots. He was fast. Luckily for Jessica, she was fast, too. His shots just missed her. She aimed at his chest and fired as he went into a crouch. Her bullet landed high of its mark—right in the middle of his forehead.

"You okay, Joey?" said a voice from downstairs. Joey didn't respond.

Suddenly there was the sound of footsteps heading not up the stairs, but toward the front of the house. The front door opened and closed.

Jessica catapulted down the stairs, prepared, underdressed as she was and angry as she was, to chase him all the way down Ocean Parkway. As she approached the door, she suddenly felt cold steel at the base of her spine. He emerged laughing from his hiding place at the side of the stairs. The hunter had triumphed.

"At that moment," Jessica said, "I actually did feel like a poor, little, captured animal. Seminaked and shivering." She wasn't looking at me now. "Almost like the way I had felt once a long time ago."

I waited for her to go on. I've long sensed that there was something terrifying in her past that she never spoke of. I had guessed that her interest in physical fitness was at least partially a response to—or, perhaps, therapy for—that something.

A minute passed. Two. She cleared her throat, and

when she resumed her voice was once more clear and strong.

The man behind her had said, "You killed my pals and now I'm going to make you pay."

He instructed her to drop her gun and turn around slowly. The voice was connected to a medium-build, swarthy-complexioned man whose hands shook. Well, they had a slight tremor, but what with holding a gun in them that tremor seemed a lot worse than it really was. He steadied the gun barrel between her breasts. His free hand slid down the side of her body, running over the curves of her waist and hip. It was clear that he was contemplating various methods of making her pay, as he'd called it. Jessica knew that her chances for survival had just improved if it meant he wouldn't kill her on the spot.

"I started to beg, to plead with him," Jessica said. "I whined. I made it look good."

"He must have been the tagalong, the schlepper," I said.

On TV and in the movies, the bad guys, even professional contract killers, regularly try to make out with their victims or else they run off their mouths to them, telling them everything the writers couldn't work into the story any other way. In real life, a pro never mixes business and pleasure. He just does the job and then gets back to his family in Scarsdale.

I saw that Jessica was having a little trouble with the words. "It must have been hard for you," I said to her. "You're strong. Strong people have a hard time with begging, even if it is a put-on."

She shook her head. "It's not just that, Jason. The whole situation brought me back to memories that I thought I had buried a long time ago. I was standing there pleading with this creep on the outside and tough as nails on the inside, and all the time there was this small, scared piece of me even further inside than that. It was begging, too, like a thirteen-year-old would beg." Her voice was thick with emotion.

I said, "Jess, there's a thirteen-year-old inside of all of us." She shook her head. Her eyes were shiny. "But that's not what you mean, is it?" She shook her head again. "Don't you think it's about time you told someone about it, instead of keeping the pain all bottled up inside?"

She shrugged and waved her hand. "It's nothing really," she said finally. "Happens every day in our fair city." I wheeled my chair over to hers so close that our knees were touching. She took my hand in hers and squeezed. "Just a nightmare," she said in a hoarse voice.

"Me and nightmares are old friends, Jess," I whispered back. "What happened when you were thirteen?"

"Sometimes, I lie awake at night and wonder how it could have really happened. Something woke me up in the middle of the night. I peeked out of my room and saw a very big, very vicious-looking man holding a gun to my father's head. My dad held some money out to him. My dad's hand was trembling. I had never seen him scared before.

"I could tell that the guy was barely in control. He looked crazy but he was probably just overdue for a fix. Still, the money wasn't enough for him. He hit my dad with the gun, over and over. My mom ran over to stop him, and he really went crazy. He shot her on the spot, I don't know how many times. When my dad tried to jump him, he shook him off easily, as if he were no more than a bothersome fly at a summer cookout. He shot my father, then ran out of the house.

"After I was certain he'd left, I called the cops and gave them our address. When I finally had the courage to approach my parents, I saw that my dad was still alive. He tried to talk, but it was very painful for him and the words came in a whisper that brought bright red bubbles of blood out of his mouth.

"He knew he was dying. I went over to him, trying not to look at what was left of Mom. He told me that he loved me, and those were his last words."

She let go of my hand, which was a good thing since by that time our palms were sweating. Her shoulders were shaking. She had a Kleenex and most of one hand covering her face, but I finally realized that she was crying.

This was new for me. Jessica never cries, and I didn't know what to do. Until that moment, my experience with crying females was limited to the sort of female that cries regularly. I knew just what to do with them—holding, hugging, patting, murmuring. This was different.

After some contemplation, I settled on a strategy. I'd do what would be appropriate if it were a male friend sitting there crying his heart out. After all, Jessica is just about the most macho person I know. I gave her a couple of firm, friendly pats on her shoulder and slid my chair back to its regular place. I checked my electronic mail and sent off some responses.

"So, anyway." She was in control again. "There I was, gun pointed at my chest, begging this guy to do whatever he wants with me but please, please not to kill me." She laughed, and her laughter sounded a little harsh, like a bitter joke.

She went on.

Jessica had realized that the guy was deriving immense pleasure from the sight of a half-nude woman crying and begging for her life. She played on that; she offered to fetch her valuable hidden jewelry for him; she insinuated that she would go to bed with him. He was a fool. His more intelligent cohorts were dead, and he was relying on his own limited wisdom to guide him. Besides, if he had only attributed a modicum of intelligence to his victim, he would have realized she'd know at once that he could not let her go with her life. She'd seen him and could testify against him.

But he liked being in the driver's seat. Meanwhile, he wasn't paying much attention to the gun. It was just hanging there in his hand.

Jessica, however, was paying close attention to such details—even as she continued to implore and cry pitifully. She pressed her palms together in front of her and steepled her fingers in the classic pose of supplication. At the right moment, she lashed fiercely out with her fingertips and smashed through his Adam's apple.

His eyes bulged. The gun dropped to the floor. He grabbed his throat, which was making little gurgling noises. Then Jessica's hand went smashing upward, mashing the base of his nose into his brain. Both blows are fatal.

A couple of uniforms on patrol from the 70th were the first on the scene. Two of the dead men were sufficiently well-known to be given names, Frankie Voss and Joey Santos. Later, she found out the third name—Iggy Pogue. Together, they had a list of priors that could stretch from here to Bensonhurst. They mostly contracted out to crime organizations and drug dealers, keeping people in line and eliminating competition.

"Do we know any of them?" Jessica asked.

"I think the name Voss sounds familiar. But I don't think any of those guys had a grudge against you. They were obviously working for someone, just like my little Jill."

"It's your own fault, you know."

"How's that?"

"A P.I. shouldn't have such regular and predictable eating habits." Jessica sighed and tossed her Kleenex in the wastebasket. "You know, Jason," she sighed. "I still find myself feeling guilty about my parents sometimes. For a long time I felt it was my fault. I should have awakened earlier. I should have helped them. They didn't have to die."

"You were thirteen. The only thing you would have done was get yourself killed."

"Guilt isn't always rational. My adult self denies it. But at the same time I resolved never to let myself feel helpless again."

"And it also influenced your decision to join the police force," I said. "I knew your parents were both dead, but I didn't know you saw them killed."

"I don't like to talk about it."

"That's an understatement."

"But when I found myself surrounded in my own home in the middle of the night by men aiming to kill me, it suddenly all came back in a rush, and I was determined not to be afraid and helpless this time."

"Even the toughest guys I knew in Nam were afraid. Courage comes in overcoming fear, not in being without it."

"Did you ever study Plutarch?" She recited from memory: " 'Courage stands halfway between cowardice and rashness, one of which is a lack, the other an excess, of courage.' "

"Plutarch's okay, but a little stuffy."

"Stuffy?"

"Yeah. You start quoting Plutarch at a party and pretty soon people will get the idea that you get off on feeling superior."

She grinned. "I do."

The phone rang just then. Jessica took the call and spoke a few words into the mouthpiece. She looked at me and mouthed a name, Slaker. I shook my head violently back and forth.

"No, Jonah, he's not here now. I really don't know

where or when he'll be back. . . . All right, I'll take a message.'' She made a face and stuck out her tongue at me as she wrote in her notebook.

''Well, Jason,'' she said after hanging up. ''Looks like they have a make on your dream girl.''

''You mean Jill Colford's not her real name?''

Jessica consulted her notebook. ''Linda Yarden. Twenty-five years old. Bronx born and raised. Used to work for the Rocco gang before going independent. Last few years, takes a job if the money's right. Suspected of being involved in some two dozen murders.''

''She said she was in public relations.''

''She was if that meant using her looks to gain access to her victims in their own homes.''

''Ouch.''

The better part of the morning had slipped by. We disposed of the mail in short order and then sat back and stared at each other. There was really nothing to do, and we were doing it.

''You eat yet today?'' Jessica asked.

''Not much.''

''I'm starved. How about an early lunch at Food for Thought?''

''Regular eating habits again?''

Over vegetarian chili and tacos, I prodded Jessica some more about her past. ''What'd you do after your parents died?''

''My mother's sister took me in—Aunt Rose—Professor Rose Baron.''

''I'd forgotten she was a professor.''

''Retired. Kingsborough Community College Department of English.''

''So that's who started you on literature.''

''My aunt was grand. We lived together in the house on Ocean Parkway until she died a couple of years ago. We got along great.''

"She never had children of her own, did she?"

"She was what they used to call a spinster."

"Uh-huh," I said, suddenly understanding a lot of things. "How did all the physical fitness stuff get started?"

Jessica smiled. "My aunt gave in to everything I asked for. I think she really enjoyed having a daughter to raise. She never married. She had her career, but—" Jessica sighed and shook her head. "Anyhow, I took Judo and Karate classes. I read books. I got weights, a chin-up bar, and all kinds of exercise equipment. My aunt fixed up that room in the basement for me. I would spend two hours a day there working out. Also, I took up running and cycling."

"They say a woman has half of a man's upper-body strength."

"It's more like sixty percent. By the time I was a senior in high school, I was the second-strongest student in the school. I guess you could say I was obsessed."

"What did your aunt think of all that?"

" 'A sound mind in a sound body' is what she kept telling me."

"How did she get it to sink in?"

"It was easy. She got me hooked on good books."

"Thank you, Aunt Rose."

"Why?"

"Otherwise, you'd probably be a professional wrestler today. I'd watch you on late-night TV. Maybe even place bets on you."

"You actually bet on wrestling?"

"Why not?" I switched direction. "Speaking of long shots, do you think New York's finest are finished yet with our respective digs?"

She shrugged. "Only one way to find out."

"Maybe we ought to wait a while." The less I crossed paths with underpaid automatons, the better.

8

FROM THE BROOKLYN Public Library's main branch at Grand Army Plaza, it was only a hop, skip, and a jump to the Park Slope office of the elected representative of Brooklyn's 51st Assembly District, Valerie Crockett. We drove.

Before that, we'd spent a couple of hours consulting with our client and with the *New York Red Book,* a publication that turned out to contain a storehouse of information about the state legislature, including bios and photographs. Even so, without benefit of names, it wasn't easy to locate two legislators out of one hundred fifty in the assembly and sixty-one in the senate.

By process of elimination, we concluded that Valerie Crockett of the 51st Assembly District was probably the tall, thin blonde. Mel Pierce of the 47th was pegged as the short, fat man with the Vandyke. Since the legislature had closed for the season a mere week ago, Allie was able to assist considerably in narrowing the field of possibilities.

We called from the library. Pierce was away and would not be back until Monday. Would we care to make an appointment? All of a sudden, Monday seemed a long way off, but we made the appointment anyway. Crockett wasn't in either, but the person who answered the phone gave us another number to call. We did, and she finally agreed to see us at her home on West 2nd Street near the park. Which was where we were headed now.

"Looks like we're the only ones working today."

Jessica shrugged. ''Friday in July.''

I put on my most engaging smile. ''If you work real hard today, maybe I'll take you out to a party tomorrow night. There's this rich guy in Brooklyn Heights that I hear throws a dynamite party.''

She smiled but looked serious. ''You still want to go? I thought you might be ready to back out by now.''

''Of the party?'' I asked. ''Or the detective business?''

We parked a block from Prospect Park, one of the city's most beautiful spots. The joggers were out—both singly and in herds. I noticed one in particular—a female by anyone's analysis—bouncing along one of the many little paths that wind through the park. The portable radio connected to her headset and clipped to the waistband of her shorts announced to all the world that she was oblivious to all onlookers. Her shorts, cut high at the hips, also announced that she wasn't wearing any panties. In fact, her entire outfit was designed more to reveal than to clothe.

Jessica regarded me seriously and looked as though she was working on a tough problem. She considered it for a few moments before speaking.

When she did speak, her voice was soft, almost tentative. ''Sometimes I wonder.''

I leaned closer to her. ''Yes, Mom. I really do want to be a detective.''

''You made a hell of a lot more moolah as a computer whatchamacallit.''

''Data-security analyst. And when was the last time you saw me strapped for cash?'' I moved closer and nuzzled her neck. She tilted her head to the side. A smile played on her lips as I murmured in her ear, ''I'm quite happy to go along as I have been, taking the odd job in the computer industry. Two a year are enough for me to keep current and maintain my contacts. Not to mention what I make as a detective, which isn't chicken feed. What about you?"

"We're not talking about me." Her neck pulled away, out of my reach. "Anyhow, what about me?"

"Are you planning to stay in the business? Does Sandy have any idea what he'd buy into with a P.I. for a wife?" Jessica fidgeted in her seat. She looked out the window. "Does he know that you have a .38 in your purse? Does he know that you know five thousand ways to kill a man?" She muttered something under her breath. "Did you tell him about last night?—What? I can't hear you."

"Bastard," she muttered. "Offspring of bastard. I shouldn't even have told you about last night."

"Wouldn't have made it not happen." I regarded her seriously. "Well?"

Her eyes flashed, but I didn't watch them. I watched her hands. She could flatten me. Hell, she could probably kill me. "Sandy thinks I'm going to quit the business after we're married." Her left index finger was making circles on her knee. "Maybe help him out. You know, credit checks. That sort of thing." She drummed her fingertips on the windowpane.

"Whatever gave him that idea?"

"Beats me," she sighed. "I never said a word about it."

"You probably couldn't get a word in edgewise."

She leaned back, took in a breath, let it out. "Sandy's a good guy."

"If you like well-dressed barracudas."

"He makes a good living. He's got a future. He could be a big shot in real estate one day."

"Sure," I agreed. "Like Matthew Andrew Taylor. Anyway," I added, "you're beginning to sound like your Aunt Rose."

"Oh, shut up."

I didn't shut, but redirected. "The problem with most

people with high-paying jobs—like Taylor, Foxworth, and corporate America—is that they try to optimize the cash they take in. Now me, I try to optimize my time and happiness, and so do you. The difference is, they have to maximize the hours they work and there's virtually no limit to that. We minimize in that area, and we're happy."

She stared at me. "That computer degree of yours really messed up your mind if you can look at life as a series of optimizations."

"And how do you see life?"

She shrugged. "I just try to do what's right."

"Oh." I grinned. "Like Robin Hood."

"Superman."

"Wonder Woman."

"Philip Marlowe."

"Now we're getting somewhere."

"Spenser."

That threw me. "The poet?"

She shook her head. "Fictional private eye. I just started reading the series. Why doesn't anyone write it like it really is for a P.I.?"

"Credit checks?" I asked.

"Oh, shut up."

Ms. Valerie Crockett answered the door in a bathrobe. She'd probably call it a hostess gown or a lounging robe but, in my opinion, a bathrobe is a bathrobe.

She received us in a large sitting room with high ceilings and shimmering parquet floors. We sat on separate sections of an overstuffed, sectional couch arrangement and found out that the good assemblyperson did not know about anything illicit going on at the house on Willow Place, that she knew about Taylor's parties but didn't remember ever going to one, that she may have attended one in the course of duty but couldn't remember as it was unimportant to her, and that she definitely knew nothing about anyone in the state assembly being blackmailed.

She was lying, of course.

In the half hour we were there, she chain-smoked a dozen cigarettes, offered us three drinks, which she downed herself, and jumped every time the word "videotape" was spoken.

Jessica and I spent what was left of the day in Prospect Park, feeding the animals in the zoo some kind of grain you buy for a quarter, while I fed myself hotdogs with the works. Although Jessica did join me at the hotdog stand, she ate everything but the frank and I think she really would have preferred the grains—she made sure to inform me with every bite that went into my mouth exactly what was wrong with it.

With the approach of evening, we went across the park to the Brooklyn Botanical Garden, where Beethoven—Jessica's favorite—was scheduled to be performed in the rose garden. There were folding chairs set out, but we selected a spot on the grass off to one side. Over the course of the evening our senses were stroked and massaged and pleasured and tantalized. We didn't talk about business. We didn't talk about marriage. We didn't talk about literature. We didn't do much talking at all.

It was pretty late by the time we got back to Ocean Parkway. The tinted window on the passenger side of the black Oldsmobile 98 parked on the service road in front of Jessica's house was open slightly. We could see the cigarette smoke puffing out of it into the night air. All the houses on the block were dark. We couldn't see who was sitting in the car, but whoever it was had made a mistake if they were trying to watch Jessica's house unobserved.

I was driving. I coasted slowly down the block. Normally, I wouldn't give a parked car a second glance, but this one was screaming for attention.

"Look at that," Jessica said. "You can even see the glow of the cigarette tip."

"Jerks," I agreed, although I couldn't see the glow of the cigarette tip. "Amateurs."

"Even without that cigarette, who the hell leaves a car parked late at night in New York with the window open?"

"Have a heart, Jess." Jessica is a perfectionist. She hates to see a job poorly done. Although, in this case, that might be just what eventually saved us. "They must have been waiting a long time. Got bored. Good help is hard to find."

"Bored, hell." She was on a roll. "You show me a smoker, and I'll show you someone who can't go twenty minutes without a fix." A self-righteous perfectionist. Admittedly, not an ideal combination in a partner.

"Well, let's see what we have here." I shifted in my seat as we rolled past the Olds. "Oh," I sneered, "it's just an unassuming parked car containing two large gentlemen, one in front and one in back." Probably couldn't both fit in the front. I looked at my partner inquiringly. "You don't suppose they're interested in *us*?"

The Olds started up before she had a chance to reply. Jessica's hand went out automatically to brace herself against the dashboard. I hit the accelerator and so did the Olds.

"I think we're in trouble," I noted astutely and kept the accelerator pressed to the floor as we speeded north on Ocean Parkway's service road, which runs parallel to the highway.

"They're following us."

With all due respect to Jessica, it did not take great powers of deductive reasoning to figure that out. It was close to midnight and we had the streets of Brooklyn all to ourselves. Ocean Parkway is not exactly the kind of area where you get down and party at all hours of the night.

"Well, what do you want to do?" I asked, as long as I hadn't a clue.

Jessica pointed to my left. The Olds was closing in, trying to pull up alongside us. "First of all, speed up, or there won't be anything we need to do." Something was sticking out of the rear window of the Olds in anticipation.

I don't question a direct order. I turned right and burnt rubber through a maze of side streets, leaving behind the image of something that looked like a silencer-equipped weapon pointing in our direction.

I didn't slow down. "Who are those guys?"

Jessica had the car phone working—this was only about the third time she's had occasion to use it—and was getting patched through to Boris. Now, that's thinking, I thought. Get Boris, the Russian Bear, out of bed in the middle of the night and, if the gorillas behind us don't get a clear shot, he can always finish the job for them.

The Olds was gaining again. I didn't pay much attention to Jessica's conversation with Boris. I could only hear her side of it anyway, and that was hardly more than grunts and nods and things I already knew. Anyway, I heard enough. At Beverly Road, I cut them off with a left turn across the main stream of traffic, and speeded along Beverly until we were back on Ocean Parkway, on the main highway this time. Only now we were going south. Toward Brighton.

"Okay, Red," Jessica nodded. "Boris is getting ready for us." The Olds maneuvered the turn and was still speeding along behind us. We were on a major highway now, and since there were other cars around us, we enjoyed a relatively peaceful, if speed-limit-breaking, drive.

"That's what I was afraid of," I said. "You wake him up?"

She grinned. "Don't worry. He's still pretty grateful for our assistance Wednesday night."

"How's his niece?"

"We didn't chat. He said if we can lure them onto the roof of his building, he'll prepare a nice reception."

"The roof?"

"Yes, we're to ring his sister's bell and she'll let us in. She's grateful too, by the way."

"And he won't be there to answer our ring, he'll be on the roof."

"Exactly."

"What else did he say?"

"Not to worry."

I looked at the rearview mirror. Not to vorrry. Oh, boy.

We drove down Ocean Parkway toward the ocean from which it took its name, left onto Brighton Beach Avenue underneath the elevated train tracks, then a right to our destination, frenetically escorted all the way. Boris's building, a twenty-floor complex of small and large apartments, was one of the older ones in Brighton Beach. We stopped short in front of it, ran in, and rang the bell to his sister's apartment. We were buzzed into the lobby and closed the door carefully behind us. We needn't have bothered. It was made of glass.

The elevator was waiting for us. A gun butt smashed with little finesse through the glass door behind us and a beefy hand reached through. Just as the elevator door closed, the toughs came barreling into the lobby. I grinned and waved. Too late, guys.

We rode the elevator to the top floor and walked up a narrow stairway to the roof. I was glad to see that Boris was already up there, waiting. It would take the gorillas a while to figure out where we went. We could use the time to set up an ambush. We didn't want to kill them. What we needed was information. If we could figure out who'd been trying to kill us, maybe we could make him stop.

Boris held out two shotguns. I didn't ask him where he'd obtained them and, to be truthful, at that moment I didn't much care. The greater the show of firepower, the more likely it was that our opponents would give themselves up and let us question them.

"You leave key in yourr carr?" Boris whispered.

"Yeah," I responded. "And the doors open. You sure it won't get stolen in this neighborhood?"

"Of courrse not," Boris grinned. "My sisterr drrive it arround corrner to parrk forr you. So police not take it."

"Very thoughtful of her." I put a hand out to touch his shoulder. "How's Nadia?"

"Oh," he responded grimly, "she get betterr. Little bit betterr everry day."

We barely had time to get settled when the roof door burst open with a powerful kick and the two thugs bounded out, pistols ready. Somehow, they didn't look much like amateurs anymore.

"Drop your weapons," I shouted.

They blasted a response, but our heavy artillery surprised them. Jessica fired her shotgun into the air over their heads. What surprised me was that none of the building's residents came rushing out onto the roof.

"It's all over," I insisted. "Drop your weapons."

Craziest thing. They saw the situation. But they kept at us, kept on shooting. At one point, I thought we'd be able to keep at least one of them alive by just wounding him with a handgun, but it didn't work out that way. Try and wing someone on a black roof under a pitch-dark sky. It just doesn't happen. Only the Lone Ranger and similar fictional heroes can perform feats like that. And—

maybe the guys on *Miami Vice,* but it'll be a while before I agree to go sockless.

Anyway, it turned out that we had to use the shotguns. And of course, once we did, there was nothing left to interrogate.

The activity on the street below suddenly seemed heavier than it had when we arrived. Windows were opened, friends called out to each other, nosy neighbors recognized that they had a job to do. Someone instructed someone else to call the police.

A quick search of the bodies turned up no information that we could use. The guys had names, as it turned out, along with pictures of their wives and kids and dogs. William Tucci. Marco Molloy. The names meant nothing to us. They were just some dumb guys making a buck the only way they knew. And now they were dead.

They were carrying over five thousand dollars in cash, but by the time the cops arrived, the money was gone. We decided to split among us what was probably a down payment on the lives of Reddy and Munroe.

The next day's news called it "a mob killing related to drugs." Why not?

9

OUR INVITATIONS WERE collected at the door by a big, burly guy wearing a suit with a bulge at the side and what had to be a custom-made shirt, since you can't get a size twenty-five-inch neck in Macy's. Another guy who looked just like him was stationed inside the door and cordially but firmly requested that we sign the guest register. There were already some forty people there. I couldn't make out everyone, but I did recognize some of the names on the register from our library work of the day before. There were several state and local politicos in attendance.

Jessica replaced the pen in its place above the register and whispered to me, "I wonder what happened to the last guy who neglected to sign the register."

"He's singing soprano," I whispered back. "For the Mouseketeers."

I was wearing my navy summer suit with a white starched shirt and a red-and-blue-striped tie. I felt like a Ken doll or maybe a sales rep from IBM. Any minute now, I would get an uncontrollable urge to marry Barbie.

I pinched Jessica on the behind. She stamped casually on my toe. I should have known better than to fool with Barbie without first buying her the five-piece wedding dress ensemble.

Jessica looked hot. Gone were the worn tennis shoes, the thick cotton slouch socks, the sweatshirt, the faded jeans. In their place was a form-fitting evening gown of soft, midnight blue, clasped toga-style at the top of her right shoulder. Her left shoulder was bare. She was braless and I could just make out the shape of her nipples under the soft silk. Her auburn curls were as unruly as ever, touched with a devil-may-care sparkle that matched the glint in her eyes.

The party was in full swing. A red-jacketed bartender was dispensing cheer—in a variety of glassware as well as tiny silver spoons and straws—from behind a mahogany-topped bar at the far side of the huge room. In physique and bulge under the armpit, he seemed to be related to the guys at the entrance of the house and to the two or three white-jacketed waiters who paraded tiny trays of hors d'oeuvres and half-full glasses among the milling guests.

Diagonally across from the bar, a Steinway's black and whites were being tickled and tinkled in a nonintrusive manner by a balding fellow with a round face and pink nose. He was accompanied by the full, warm sounds of a harp played by a rail-thin woman in a black satin dress that was too large for her frame. Her long, sinewy arms plucked the notes without error or feeling.

The oversized room was furnished with an ample collection of round cocktail tables and wooden bistro chairs, the occasional intimate cluster of sitting-room furniture, and a spacious expanse of smooth ballroom floor, perfect for the sort of entertaining that Matthew A. Taylor did to perfection. Along the side wall stood a closely guarded coatrack, as the wraps alone were worth a small fortune. Beside the coatrack, a richly carpeted staircase extended into the upper regions of the house, which was itself a lonely remnant from an earlier day of open Brooklyn grasslands and forests.

Jessica went off to do some detecting in that hotbed of information, the ladies' room, and I was free to watch the scenery and mingle. I wandered amid the muted strains of conversation and instrumentation and took in the various species of guest, bedecked in silk, satin, crepe, Italian wool, worsteds, and linen. Their skin was suntanned, their hair was moussed, their makeup immaculate, their perfume and cologne of the highest quality. Their necklaces and earrings and bracelets and rings and tiepins and cufflinks sparkled with the energy reflected from a huge, hanging, crystal chandelier. Nails were manicured to perfection. A Martian dropped down at this moment in this place would be hard put to figure out exactly what earthlings really look like in their natural state.

I picked a glass off a tray and set out to mingle. A serious redhead with large mauve-tinted octagonal eyeglasses was enchanting a small group of people with her appreciation of higher culture. The cocktail parties of the world are made up of two kinds of people. Some are great at talking and never lack for conversation, but are poor listeners. Some are great listeners, but mediocre conversationalists. Very few people excel at both. I'm a good listener. I can merge into a group of people, produce a few well placed uh-hums and oh-reallys, and move out again without uttering a syllable of any import.

The redhead was of the other type. She really could talk. She had a habit of interrupting people in midsentence, but no one seemed to mind. This was because she was so good at sounding intellectual and sophisticated that people simply assumed they deserved to be cut off by her. Anyway, that wasn't so bad. What was really exasperating was when she managed to begin an idea, get everyone to hang on to what she was about to say, and then do a quick turn and interrupt *herself*. The handful of people in her group—and it was very much her group—had a glazed, disoriented look in their eyes, even the ones that weren't high.

". . . problems in San Francisco," she was saying, "but I read an interview with Diane Feinstein, that she—" Her eyes stared off to the side for a moment. "Oh, that reminds me. There's a simply marvelous French film at the Bijou. Have you seen it? It's called . . ."

I don't speak French, but the title of the film sounded something like *The Duck That Peed on Me*. I don't think I'll rush out to see that one. Meanwhile, one man released himself from her spell and staggered shakily toward the bar.

". . . It had a simply marvelous message cloaked in the metaphor of . . ."

I never did like foreign films. They're boring. The people who watch them are boring. It's a condition that probably results from watching all those foreign films. Talk about a medium in need of redeeming social value.

I moved on.

A group of people, mostly men, were clustered around another woman. Her hair was alternately gold and platinum in streaks and had been frizzed out into a very avant-garde style. She was wearing a gold gown, of some kind of shimmering, shiny material, with silvery gold strands as straps holding up a low-cut bodice that did nothing to conceal her ample bosom. She was high, and fun to watch. As she talked, she waved a champagne glass in her hand, spilling a drop here and there on one or another of her eager companions. Once, she spilled some over the front of her dress—or at least where her dress should have been. I rushed to help her dry off, but there were already five guys ahead of me.

Somebody called her name. "Damn it, Ellyce," he demanded, striding over to her. "What are you doing here?"

"I was invited, Robert." She turned to the guy on her right and, as if in confirmation, kissed him wetly on the cheek.

Hanging onto Robert's arm was a woman whom a

more gracious soul than I might have dubbed a floozy. Introductions were made all around.

Ellyce volunteered to the floozy, "Lady, I don't know where you found him, but you ought to lose him again. I was married to the slob for seven years and I can tell you, he was perfect as a husband." She waved her glass for effect. "A perfect zero."

"Tell the truth, now, Ellyce," he countered. "Wasn't the movie *Romancing the Stone* the story of our love life?"

"You ought to know. You're dead from the neck up and the waist down."

Robert stage-whispered to his companion, "She's so cold, she wears all that makeup and perfume just so no one will take her for a lesbo."

"I only worry about that when I'm walking next to you," she replied. "Oh, and by the way. I looked into that sex-change operation you wanted. The doc said it would be minor surgery. He can do it in his office." She giggled and drained her glass. Her companions were not only unembarrassed, they appeared to be enjoying the entertainment.

Across the room, I saw Jessica emerge from the ladies' room. I started to make my way past the hundred or so people between me and her.

When I reached her, I grabbed her by the arm and steered her in the direction of the piano.

"Well," I asked, my left hand taking in most of the room in an expansive gesture, "what do these beauties really look like in the john, underneath their gorgeous gowns?"

"Red, you don't think—"

"Are the redheads really redheads?"

"—that we walk around naked—"

"Is there more makeup in there than in all of Bloomie's?"

"—in the ladies room. Do you?"

"Are they really in there plotting the overthrow of male domination?"

"I don't look over anyone's—"

"Anybody pee standing up?"

"—shoulder. I do my thing and leave." She rolled her eyes around and was quiet. That's a neat exercise she does. I'll have to try it sometime.

A few feet away from us, a guy was informing another guy about his approach to politics. ". . . Today, everything is marketing. You know, I wouldn't ever express an opinion unless my people do a study to find out what my constituents want. They can do a telephone survey with a representative sample in twenty-four hours. So, in twenty-four hours, I know how the voters feel and I can make a statement . . . What? . . . Phony? . . . Nah. Let me tell you something. In this business, there's only one thing that matters: you got to get the votes. . . .

"My people have it all figured out. You got your Blacks, you got your Italians, you got your elderly . . . Yeah. I tell the elderly how I support Social Security. The blacks want to hear about jobs—and sometimes I throw in a line about South Africa. To the Italians, naturally I talk about keeping down the crime rate and cutting the fat out of the budget. So I got my three basic speeches. That's marketing . . . What? . . .

"Hey, why not? My marketing guy tells me that Proctor and Gamble sells six different soaps. Get it? Six—from one company. They tell us to use Ivory for purity, Camay for women who want a creamy complexion, Safeguard to kill germs, Coast to feel fresh and wake up, Zest for deodorant, Lava for real he-men-do-it-yourselfers. If P & G can do it with soap, why can't we do it for political image? . . . I'm telling you, that marketing guy of mine is a genius. Now he's . . ."

"You learn a lot by mingling," I remarked.

"Hmmm. You learn that the kind of people you see at these parties are not the kind of people you want to be."

Later that night, we used the cover provided by a large group of people who were saying their early good-byes, finding their wraps, and being escorted to the door to sneak up the curved staircase.

Upstairs were five bedrooms, a study, and two baths, all elaborately furnished and decorated. None were blue like in the video. Between the bathrooms was a door that looked like it would open onto a linen closet. That would make it the only linen closet I'd ever seen that was fastened with a dead bolt. Good thing the goons at the door hadn't frisked anyone. I retrieved a burglar's pick from my waistband and handed it to Jessica.

When it comes to breaking and entering, Jessica's hands are golden. It's a craft she picked up during her six years on the force, from the cops and robbers alike. Being such a straight arrow, however, she doesn't often get a chance to use it. The lock was a Yale, which is decent enough for ordinary folk. We were through it in three minutes. A Yale is okay, but it's not a Medeco.

What a surprise. The room behind the door wasn't a linen closet. What it was, was another staircase, leading to the attic. Chivalrous as ever, I allowed Jessica to precede me up the cold, bare steps. They were remarkably creak-free and I considered we were lucky at that. As we ascended, I couldn't help but admire the muscles flexing on Jessica's buttocks just beneath the soft folds of her gown. Naturally, I didn't want to risk speaking, so I expressed my admiration with a few well-placed pats.

At the landing, Jessica stepped against the wall and motioned to me to continue in the lead this time. About the third step up, I jumped nearly three feet up in the air as I felt a light touch on my bottom, an invasion action that sent a tingly sensation through my body.

"That's it, treat me like a sex object," I muttered under my breath.

"Now you know what it's like."

"Yeah." I thought a moment. "It's pretty cool."

The attic was relatively large. I remembered noticing from the outside that the roof appeared to have been raised on one side from some modern-day renovation. There were just two rooms. One, with the typical slanted ceiling and exposed beams, was used for storage. The accumulation of junk was typical, although it didn't look like it could have come from any part of the house we had already seen. I suppose that's why it was in the attic. The other room was large, with an eight-foot flat ceiling, and it was blue.

Of course, we went in, but now that we had found the room that started the entire adventure, we weren't very sure what to do with it, or what we expected to find.

On the wall facing the big blue bed was a huge mirror. I said, "I'll bet your body against my body that's a two-way mirror."

"No bets, Red. Anyway," she grinned, "why would I give you fifty-to-one odds?"

"Fifty to one?"

"Sure. My body is at least fifty times better than yours."

"You know what? You're right," I leered.

The only remaining items of interest in the room were a chest of drawers on the wall beside the bed, and a large built-in bookcase at the side of the huge mirror. I poked my head into the adjoining bathroom while Jessica searched the chest of drawers. The bathroom was the kind of place I could envision spending the rest of my natural life in—maybe even the next life, should there be one. It was the Club Med of plumbing fixtures, with a Jacuzzi, a sunken tub surrounded by a marble ledge a foot wide all around, and—

I had barely taken a proper look around when Jessica called, "Look at this, Red."

The bottom drawer of the dresser was a cornucopia of sorts, depending on your inclinations. It held as rich an assortment as I'll ever want to see of chains, shackles, handcuffs, and masks.

"Well, that explains it," I said.

"What?"

"This room obviously belongs to some archeologist deep into the study of the artifacts of primitive people."

Jessica was at the bookcase. I went over to join her. She said quickly, "There doesn't seem to be anything here. Let's go."

"What are those?"

"Oh, just some video movies."

"The homemade kind?"

"I don't think these are the blackmail tapes, Jason."

I examined the titles more carefully. "Hey, these are classics."

"Classics?"

"Haven't you ever heard of *The Naked and the Bed? Gracie Under Pressure?*"

"Come on. We don't have all night."

"Of Mice and Real Men? War and a Piece?"

Jessica checked out the VCR and television that were set on the middle shelf. They were hooked up. "I hate to disappoint you, Red. But these are not exactly classics. They haven't even had time to ferment yet."

"Oh, they will. They will." I pointed to one tape. "Hey, Jess. This one really is a classic—*Little Women.* You remember that one?"

Jessica pulled the tape out a bit. There was a picture on the package. Four Pygmy women were wondering what to do with a guy with the largest male organ I have ever seen. I couldn't stop staring at it. I managed to steal a glance at Jessica. She couldn't stop staring at it either.

"I guess you're right, Jess. We ought to get going."

I replaced the tape, and just as I did, the bookcase and wall began to shake. The floor beneath us vibrated as the entire bookcase slid sideways right into the wall. We might have seen directly into the small room beyond had it not been for the two automatics held by the two goons who were blocking the way. One guy seemed to be about eight feet tall from my vantage point—with features that were all out of proportion to each other. The other was standard stock for his job. His midsection was round and narrow, his eyes were close set, he had but one thin eyebrow across his forehead, his nose had been broken more than once. Jessica and I stumbled backward and tumbled gracelessly onto the bed.

"Don't move a muscle," said Bigfoot. "It could get you dead."

Suddenly there were two more guys hovering over us. They had come in from the hallway. I recognized them as two of the guests at the party. In almost the same instant, I felt myself diving into a black void—which was merciful, as it followed a crash at the back of my head that hurt like hell.

I don't know how long I was out. Someone had taken my wristwatch—along with everything of mine that wasn't a wristwatch. I found myself spreadeagled on the bed in my birthday suit, which has seen some wear. Feeling not a little exposed, I gingerly tested my ability to move. No go. Each hand and foot had been shackled to a different corner of the bed frame. The bed was a large one and there was practically no give. Pain throbbed at the back of my head where I had been sapped.

I opened my eyelids very slightly, just enough to make slits of my eyes. I didn't like what I saw. The four guys were standing in a cluster between my bed and the mirror. I didn't like what they saw either. They were looking to my right, where Jessica sat tied to some kind of desk chair on wheels. She was also stark naked and her hands and feet were strapped securely to the chair. What made her look most vulnerable to me was not her nakedness, but that she was fixed in place against her will. I always thought it would take more than four men to subdue Jessica Munroe, but I guess the sap caught her unawares.

She wore her nudity like old armor, obviously comfortable with it—more comfortable than I was. Still, I didn't much care for the way the holding crew was staring at her. A smaller man might have been jealous.

In an attempt to direct their attention away from Jessica, I spoke up—or slurred up, it being my first attempt at speech since coming to. "That bookcase must open onto the room where you bozos do your filming, and there's probably a camera set up behind that mirror."

"You're not so dumb, Shamus," one of the guys said.

Oh boy, Shamus. That guy must be at least seventy years old to use a word like that. Actually, the geezer looked more like twenty-five. Maybe he learned his trade from an old-timer.

I tried again. The guy I addressed was skinny and had a skin condition. "Hey, Pigface." I figured he was probably tired of being called pizzaface. "Why don't you just undo these things so you and me can step outside and settle this, man to twit."

Pigface turned red and gripped his piece a little harder. Bigfoot put a hand on his shoulder just to make sure he didn't get out of control. That hand on a shoulder should be all the control anyone would need, but it was only partially effective. Pigface gave up on using his piece but lost it in the mouth department.

He spat at me and blurted out, "You—you just watch who you're talking to."

"Oh yeah?" I said. "Who's going to make me, nerd?"

He almost lost it altogether then, but Bigfoot managed to restrain him by whispering into his ear. I don't know what the big fellow said, but he's the kind of guy people tend to listen to. Pigface calmed himself down some, but he couldn't leave it alone. He had to get in the last word.

"Look who's talking like a big man," he sneered. "Just remember you're tied up and I'm not. I can walk out of here whenever I want. You can't."

His little speech would have been laughable, except that he was pointing his gun hand between my legs, after which he laughingly put his hand down at his side once again. I tried to remember to breathe.

"You probably can't get any broads interested in you. Now me," he continued, grinning, "when I walk down the street, girls crowd around, just dying to get their hands on me."

I couldn't help myself, I laughed out loud. "Yeah?" I responded. "Only if those girls are studying to be morticians."

Jessica was enjoying the show. She's never been one for much wisecracking herself, but she likes to listen. Maybe that's the real reason she keeps me around.

Now she said, "It's not nice the way you're talking to these gentlemen, Red. Some of them may have families—wives."

I picked it up. "Sure, Jessica. That fellow over there does." I indicated Broken Nose. "I know his wife. Just the other day, they called me down to fix the red light where she works."

Broken Nose looked a little nervous, but he didn't require the hand on the shoulder. He was no fun. Geezer seemed altogether too mellow, and Bigfoot was out. They were pros, and a pro never loses his cool. I went back to Pigface.

"And Mr. Pigface, there. I heard his wife is so ugly that she puts Preparation H on her lips."

That did it. Pigface apparently never felt the hand on his shoulder as he sprang toward me. He must have decided the pistol was too easy because he put it in its holster and drew a switchblade that looked pretty sharp and vicious. He slipped the blade inside my right nostril. It wasn't a perfect fit. I got a little nervous and tried hard to remember the last time I peed.

"One more sound out of you, smart aleck, and I'll slit open your nose just like in that movie *Chinatown*. You dig?"

I remember reading somewhere about discretion being the better part of valor. I kept my mouth shut. I don't know what he might have done if our charming and hospitable host had not happened to walk in just then.

Matthew Andrew Taylor seemed genuinely agitated. His face was pasty white. His hands, clenched at his sides, looked like fists, but they were wound too tightly to be of any use to him. When he opened his mouth to speak, the words came out with a slight stutter.

"All the guests have left." He turned to Bigfoot. "What are you going to do with them? I was just on the phone with Mr. M—"

Whatever he was about to say was cut short by Geezer's short, quick fist to the side of his face. It was a powerful punch that could have shaken some teeth loose. "No names, Taylor," Geezer growled. I wondered briefly why Taylor would take that kind of abuse from the help.

He seemed as nervous as a nudist climbing a barbed-wire fence. "I just meant to say you can't kill them here. This is my home." The tiny muscles at the side of his left eye began to contract involuntarily. He straightened up self-consciously, much like a drunk preparing to prove he's sober. "Enough is enough," he said in self-righteous anger. "Who does that bastard think he is? I don't care what he has on me. I let him use my house. I let him use my parties." Geezer squeezed Taylor's upper arm in a grip I wouldn't care to test, but he kept on. "This is kidnapping. I don't care what you do, but get them out of here. Who does that bastard think he is? I don't care . . ."

Geezer must have realized that Taylor was going off the deep end. For my part, I kind of liked the direction he was taking.

Geezer gripped Taylor's arm again. "You're coming with me, Taylor." To Broken Nose, he said, "Big R, you're in charge of the interrogation. Find out everything they know about the operation. Then dispose of them."

Big R, a.k.a. Broken Nose, took in Jessica and me with a single glance. When he spoke, his voice had faint traces of a Hispanic accent. "You think you won't talk, but hear this. Back in Colombia, I made tougher ones than you beg to talk to me. Just as you will beg."

Big R took the knife from Pigface. He sauntered over behind Jessica and used it to idly lift wisps of her hair. "Mr. Reddy," he said. "You will *certainly* tell me everything you know. You will tell me who hired you and everything that you have done and learned since you began working on the case. Some things I know already. It will be interesting to see how much more there is that you have been able to discover."

He gently lifted a lock of hair in his left hand. "The first lie I spot, I cut off your lovely partner's ears." As if to illustrate the sharpness of the knife blade, he slid it smoothly across the lock of hair he held in his hand. I don't think Jessica felt a thing.

"If you lie again, I will cut out her eyes." He released his fingers and let the strands of cut hair coast gently down to the floor. "While you are speaking, Miss Munroe will be with us in the next room. She will be able to see you, through the mirror, but she will not be able to hear anything. When you finish, it will be her turn." He turned to face Jessica. "Then she can get it all off her chest." A thick hand with hairy knuckles slid down her breast. She didn't flinch.

"Naturally, Miss Munroe, when you talk, Mr. Reddy's ears will then be in peril—and his eyes."

Big R brought a chair and parked it close to my head—as close as he could get, given the way I was stretched out over the bed. "Oh, by the way," he said as if it were an afterthought. "Your stories had better match." As he lowered himself onto the chair, his left forefinger caressed the blade in a manner reminiscent of foreplay.

Jessica was wheeled out of the room on her chair. Bigfoot pressed a panel and the bookcase slid right back into its original position.

What did two tough detectives do when faced with such a dilemma? What, one might wonder, did Brooklyn's own Dick and Jane Tracy do? What would Superman and Wonder Woman do?

We told all.

It wasn't much, but it seemed to satisfy. Consequently, we retained both sets of ears and a pair of slightly damaged egos.

Bigfoot went to get Jessica, while Big R was on the phone reporting to someone who seemed especially interested, not only in what we knew, but even more so in who we were working for—namely, Walters. Could it be Taylor on the phone? Bigfoot wheeled Jessica out through the sliding bookcase and gave the back of her chair a tap. A tap from him could register on the Richter scale. Her chair fairly flew across the large room and came to a crashing stop against the blue wall near my right hand.

"Hey, kid," I whispered. "Looks like we're heading for an ignoble end."

Her eyes smiled at me. "We're not dead yet, partner."

"If I don't turn my head away from you, a part of me

is going to be very much alive. Besides," I added, "my neck is starting to stiffen up."

"Such a little neck," she whispered.

A look from Bigfoot silenced us. I didn't want him to tap my bed.

I began to think maybe it had been a mistake to pick on Pigface. He took Big R aside and whispered to him, at the same time gesturing toward me and Jessica and in the direction of the mirror. Big R still held the knife. He was grinning.

"My associate has come up with a truly imaginative idea," he said. "You will like it, I am sure."

He went on to explain that we were definitely going to be wasted. So far, I didn't like it much. But, he said, out of the goodness of his heart, he would see to it that we got a few more hours of precious life before going to the great beyond. The only difficulty was the quality of that life. It could be pretty gruesome if we didn't follow instructions to the letter. If we did as we were told, well, we'd get a taste of heaven even before reaching those pearly gates.

These guys had decided to shoot a movie. A combination porno and snuff film with guess who in starring roles. If we cooperated, it would be just another homemade hard-core porno flick—except that our real deaths would serve as the culmination of a series of "little deaths." Oh, boy. And that was the good part.

Big R was really getting into it. "There are many ways one can die," he told us. "It can be slow and painful or it can be fast. And," he added with a smirk, "you will get to be in the movies." A real knee slapper.

Jessica had the right idea. "Don't hurt me," she whined pathetically. "I'll do anything you say." I didn't think she had that kind of crap in her.

Big R looked at me critically. He wasn't looking at my face. "First thing you will have to do, Miss Munroe—

may I call you Jessica?—is arouse Reddy, there." He shook his head sadly. "Such a shame. A beautiful woman naked in front of him and he can't even react like a man."

Oh, sure. I bet it was disco time in his pants. He sent my friend Pigface for the video camera. After all, why film behind a mirror, when your stars know the score? Jessica's feet had been shackled to her chair. Big R set about removing those shackles.

Jessica said softly, "Why not take the cuffs off my hands? I can't very well arouse Jason with my hands behind my back."

Big R stood up. "Why not? You got no imagination?"

Jessica began getting the feeling back in her legs, shaking them out, stretching the tight muscles.

"You'll think of something," he continued. "Anyway, we know you killed a couple of our guys, so I cannot take off those cuffs." He snapped the knife shut and returned it to Pigface, who put it in his pocket. He favored a gun now and so did Bigfoot, but they both held their weapons loosely, pointing at the floor, just as a precaution. What could we do, after all?

Pigface had his gun in a shoulder holster. His hands were occupied with the camera.

Jessica was still stretching her legs gingerly. It appeared that the feeling had not yet returned completely. The boys were becoming impatient, especially Pigface, who was the one holding the camera.

"Whatssamatta, honey, you got cold feet?" Pigface was enraptured with his own humor. He almost dropped the camera in a fit of the giggles.

Jessica started reluctantly to approach the bed. For the first time since we've known each other, I couldn't think of a sexual joke to save my life. Meanwhile, I must have blinked, because the next thing I knew Jessica had spun around on the ball of one foot and was kicking Big

R in the groin. His gun dropped to the floor with a soft thud. For that matter, so did he.

Pigface was still filming. Bigfoot started to move slowly across the room. He moved slowly but he had already proved to my satisfaction that he could get results. I hoped Jess would not underrate him. He was still not cognizant of the gun hanging down in his hand. After all, this broad was naked and her hands were tied behind her back. Who needed a gun?

He did.

She flew through the air and landed a kick, right in the middle of his belly. He didn't go down, but he felt it. While he was still doubled over, she turned and jumped again and applied a second kick to the side of his head. That was it. He was catapulted through the mirror and landed with his legs on our side of the wall and his head on the other, his back and head resting very still in an unnatural position.

Pigface finally dropped the camera and reached for his gun. Too late. Jessica ran full force into him with her head primed for a butt in his nose and her knee ready for a jab into his groin. There wasn't a damn thing Pigface could do about it. Upon impact, his gun dropped to the floor and, as Jessica whirled aside, he stood there a moment, blood flowing down his face, while he tried to decide what he should do with his hands. He couldn't grab for his nose and his groin at the same time. Decisions, decisions.

A moment more, and it didn't much matter. He slithered to the floor like a boneless, jellied mass. His face was bloody. His eyes were wide open with surprise, a look that would remain with him for a long time, perhaps an eternity. In the meantime, Big R had come to. He assumed a crouch and pointed his weapon at Jessica. He wasn't taking any chances.

I called out, "Jess, behind you!"

She pivoted and feinted to the left, then jumped to the right, flew through the air, and performed a sequence of moves I couldn't hope to describe. I'm not even certain I followed it all. When she landed, her knees were on his face and throat and he wasn't about to get angry about it. She had crushed his windpipe.

On a hunch, Jessica sat down with her back to Big R. With the help of my directions, she maneuvered her fingers behind her, feeling around in his pockets until she found a single key. It's not easy unlocking your partner's metal shackles with your hands cuffed behind your back, but she managed. After what we had been through in the last several hours, it was almost fun.

Once my own hands were free, I released Jessica's. She sat down on the bed and massaged her sore wrists and forearms while I undid the hardware on my feet. We found our clothes and guns and stuff in the dresser, folded neatly. Neatly, wow. I decided Bigfoot did it. Jessica thought it had Geezer's touch.

It was half past three. We had just notified the police department when the phone came to life again in my hand. I let it ring twice, then I aped Big R into the handset.

"Yeah."

" 'Lo, Big R. I'm sending you someone with a van to pick up the two packages. Did you get anything else before. . . ?"

I was surprised. It wasn't Taylor's voice. This one was used to talking in short, guttural spurts.

I kept at it. "Nothin'. They didn't talk any more after that. We wasted 'em."

Pause. "Who is this?"

Uh-oh. "What do you mean? It's Big R, boss."

"Yes? Who am I then?"

"You're the boss."

He snarled sharply, "What's my name?"

The jig was up. ''Shitface,'' I responded.

''I don't know how you did it, Reddy, but I assure you we will cross paths again.''

''The pleasure was all mine.''

The doorbell rang.

10

ONE . . . TWO . . .

I counted the rings and allowed the fog of my much-needed sleep to clear, while I waited for Jessica to pick up the telephone extension in her bedroom. I consulted my wristwatch—four and a half hours sleep—that ought to be enough to keep us until night. It was a nice feeling to wake up and find that I still wore my watch—and my pants, too.

It had been daylight by the time we drove wearily into Jessica's driveway, and after seven by the time we had completed a check of the house to our satisfaction. No bombs, no hidden terrorists.

Now, I was bunked out once again on Jessica's couch listening to her phone wake me up. I rolled stiffly out of my makeshift bed and padded heavily up the stairs to Jessica's room, planning to wake her up by hitting her on the head with the receiver. I don't like answering the phone in other people's homes, mainly because I never know what to say. "Munroe residence" or "Ms. Munroe's residence" would make me sound like some kind of overgrown houseboy, and just a "Hello" would have been likely to offend one or another of her suitors. That was before, of course. It sure as hell would bother Sandy, now. She answered on the fifth ring. I continued on up, anyway.

The local police had kept us at Taylor's house for several hours, going over and over the details of exactly how one small female, even a former cop, managed to create three corpses out of three living men while her buddy was tied to the bed and without using her hands.

The videotape Pigface had shot helped in that regard, but I still would rather have destroyed it. By the time I remembered about that tape, it was too late and, anyway, Jessica would never have agreed to it. She'd been a good, decent cop, which was pretty much the reason she wasn't a cop anymore.

The two cops who answered our call had themselves a field day with the videotape. I didn't think they had to replay it nearly as many times as they did. One was a rookie, a kid, maybe twenty years old. He was a big fellow, about six-foot-four, with rosy cheeks that couldn't possibly see a razor more than once every other day, and he was quite taken with Jessica. He asked her out a couple of times and followed her around the room like Mary's little lamb. It was all she could do to extract from his more experienced partner a receipt for the tape and a promise to lock it away in the evidence storage room.

Now, Jessica's bedroom door was open. She was sitting crosslegged on the bed, the telephone receiver perched on her shoulder. She was nodding and saying mm-hmm and rummaging in her night-table drawer for a paper and pencil. She's one of those people who can't talk on the phone without a paper and pencil. If she has nothing important to write down, she just doodles.

I suppose I should have knocked before I walked unannounced and unexpected into Jessica's bedroom, but I didn't. After what we had just been through together I didn't think that kind of decorum mattered anymore, but I was relieved just the same to see she was wearing a set of summer pajamas consisting of short pants and a blousy top.

I sat down on the bed, put my feet up, leaned my head

back against the pillow, and eavesdropped on her side of the conversation.

"No, I'm busy tonight. . . . That's right. . . . Sorry, I'm busy every night this week. . . . Yes, all next week too, and the week after that."

She rolled her eyes at me. I snuggled up against her and covered myself with the top sheet. It was too hot but felt good nonetheless.

"Look, Parker, you're a nice kid, but I'm old enough to be . . . Mm-hmmm . . . Listen, if I find out you're using that tape for anything but good police procedure . . . You liked my moves, huh? Well, those are nothing compared to what you're in for if you get out of line . . ." Suddenly, she sat up straight.

"When? . . . Where was he found? . . . How . . ."

I peered over her elbow to see what it was that she was scribbling ferociously. Under a doodle border of geometrically designed flowers, she wrote "M.A.T. Belt east Flt. 2 bull back head."

She shook her head in the negative. "No, Parker. We didn't know anything about it. We went straight home to get some sleep . . . He was right here with me the whole time." She hit herself in the head with the flat of her hand. "I didn't mean it the way it sounded . . . Oh, hell, forget it. I don't have to explain anything to you . . . Yes, we'll be down today to sign our statements. As soon as we can force ourselves to pull away from each other."

With a sour face, she rammed the receiver down onto its base. Jessica sighed. She leaned back and laid her head gently on the pillow close to mine. For a few moments, we huddled. It felt good, and it felt clean. For that matter, it was clean. Damn.

She grinned. "Maybe that will keep him away from me, anyhow."

"About Taylor?" I asked, not really needing to ask.

"He took two bullets in the back of his head. Some

poor weary traveler found the body when he pulled off the Belt Parkway for a rest, just east of the Flatbush Avenue exit.'' She turned to me. ''You know. Where the tall grasses grow?''

I nodded. It wasn't the first body to turn up there. ''I guess we can forget about pumping him for information.''

''Unless you happen to work for the IRS.''

''Yeah, they can get information out of *anyone*. We did learn something from him, you know.''

She looked up. ''When?''

''Before they took him away. He was yelling about a Mr. M-something, holding something over his head. That's probably who the boss of this operation is. Sure can't be Taylor anymore.''

''That's right. It sounded like Taylor was being blackmailed as well.''

''We may never know what the big boss had over him.''

''Probably he was the one who bailed Taylor out when he was short on dough.''

She waved a forefinger in the air. ''And he said that he let the guy have the use of his house—''

''For more blackmail setups.''

''—and the use of his parties—''

''For cover?''

''And because the people he wanted to blackmail would go to those parties anyhow.''

''He could help it along by making sure that enough invitations were left in the right places.''

I let my fingers trip idly up her arm. She shivered slightly and turned to stare in deep thought at the ceiling, her back pressed flat against the bed, her hands clasped behind her head.

I put my head down softly on her chest and listened to her heartbeat. ''Hey, you know what?'' I felt a hand moving softly over my hair and the side of my head. "You're alive," I said.

"You, too." She strained her neck forward and planted a kiss lightly on the back of my head. "How about that?"

Sometime later that afternoon, Jessica's car puttered happily down Flatbush Avenue. I was driving. We had already been to the precinct and signed our respective statements. By the time we left, Jessica had Parker convinced that her social calendar was filled through 1995.

"Persistent little twerp, isn't he?"

Jessica groaned.

"He does his job, though. He and his buddy sure put us through the routine." I stopped for a light at Glenwood and automatically checked the rearview mirror to make sure that all the clowns behind me did the same.

Jessica waved her hand. "That's crap. As long as the cops bother us about who we're working for and what we were doing at the party, it just means there's nothing real for them to sink their teeth into."

"They can't expect us to press charges against Taylor."

"Because he's dead. And they certainly can't hold us on that score, because when Taylor was shot—"

"Oh, did they pin down time of death?"

"They have it narrowed down, according to Parker. Anyhow, Red, we have the best alibi in the world. The cops were with us the whole time."

I stayed to the right, passed our office, and kept on going down Nostrand Avenue. "I'm still concerned about Allie. Until last night, we were the only targets. We got ourselves involved, asking a lot of questions, and maybe we stepped on somebody's toes. When Big R reported to whoever his boss was—I thought it was Taylor at the time—"

"So did I."

"—he was especially interested in who we were working for. And if you remember," I winced, "he got all the information he wanted out of us."

"And more." Jessica sounded as miserable as I felt at what had happened. "I've been thinking about that, too. I really don't see what they can do to her, Reddy. After all, she is an assemblyperson, she's in the public eye. They already have her compromised on tape, so all they have to do is get a message of some sort to her threatening to go public with the tape."

"They probably will, at that."

"And that just means we've got to work harder."

"And faster. Okay," I said, "let's chew on this. We've got blackmail. And we're assuming that there are at least a few New York State representatives on the list."

"Seems that way."

"Do you think they're being held for money?"

She shook her head. "If we can find out what the state legislature is going to be voting on in the next session, it may give us a clue."

I turned onto Avenue J. A blue Lincoln turned with us. "We can narrow it down. For starters, try the ones with a lot of lobbying activity." We reached East 20th Street and, even though it was Sunday, were slowed down by the late-afternoon shoppers.

"We'll have to get back to our client on that." Jessica twisted around to glance at the Lincoln through the rear window. "But maybe not right away."

I slowed down. "Company?"

"Some people don't know when to quit."

I coasted past the intersection at East 16th Street and double-parked in front of a small Jewish bookstore. We couldn't be absolutely certain that the Lincoln was following us or, if it was, whether its occupants meant us harm. Still, given the excitement of the past few days, it was best, in this case, to assume the worst.

The seven-block stretch along Avenue J between East 17th Street and Coney Island Avenue is a major shopping area for the neighborhood referred to sometimes as Midwood, sometimes as Vandeveer. Since my college days, this neighborhood has seen a continuing influx of observant Jews, as evidenced by an increase in the number of synagogues, large and small, and Jewish day schools. Along with this, the stores on Avenue J began to see less business on Saturday and more on Sunday, since Saturday is a major day of rest for Jewish people, when all business is suspended.

So Sunday became an important shopping day in this neighborhood, and on this particular Sunday afternoon, the stores were open, traffic was knotty, and cops were around to make sure that the flow didn't get snarled up any more than it had to. We didn't mind the cops at all. As long as they were around, we'd be around.

The blue Lincoln rolled past and we saw it make a turn on East 15th. It had tinted windows that were too dark to see into. Maybe we were just being paranoid. While Jessica waited in the car, I hurried into the bookstore and scanned the bumper sticker collection at the side of the counter. I already had an approximate idea of what I wanted. I was keeping an eye on the street through the dim, dusky glass of the storefront. The Lincoln, or its twin, passed by twice.

By the time I stuffed my purchases into a small paper bag, ten minutes had elapsed and a cop was in the process of presenting Jessica with a ticket for double-parking. That was okay. Our buddies in the Lincoln would keep their distance from anyone in uniform, even a traffic cop. They were probably circling the block waiting for us to make a move. I grinned at the officer, pocketed the ticket with appropriate good grace and, as soon as I saw that our tail was still with us, took off.

"Where are we going?"

"Women," I sighed. "Nag, nag."

Jessica punched me in the arm. She didn't use all her strength, she didn't need to. Good thing I had a spare. When I could move the arm again, I tugged playfully at her hair. "I have an idea," I offered.

"I could tell."

"Really?"

"You practically have smoke escaping from your ears, and a lightbulb went on over your head. It's still there." She picked up the paper bag from the seat and examined its contents. She waved a finger in my direction, pointing to somewhere a few inches in the air above my head. "Turn it off, will you? You want to make Con Ed rich?"

I grinned. "Aunt Rose used to tell you that?"

She pulled out my bumper stickers. "These seem innocuous enough."

"It would depend on how you used them."

"Why? Are they laced with cyanide or something?"

I grinned. "We're going to Williamsburg."

Her eyes opened wide. She read the messages on the bumper stickers again. "I hope you mean Williamsburg, Virginia."

I shook my head. "Brooklyn." I was still grinning. I had a plan, you see.

"Well"—she resignedly stuffed them back in their paper pouch—"how long have you had this death wish?"

I shook my head again. "A life wish," I said.

Williamsburg is an area at the northern edge of Brooklyn, anchoring the Williamsburg Bridge, which bridge could take you over the East River and into Manhattan's Lower East Side, if you wanted to go to the Lower East Side in the first place—which I didn't.

One of the largest ethnic groups represented there is a

group of ultra-Orthodox Jews known as Hasidim—specifically, Satmar Hasidim. This is a Hasidic sect that has its roots in Romania—a city called Satu-Mare, meaning Saint Mary. Today they number about a hundred thousand worldwide, approximately half of which reside in the Boro Park and Williamsburg sections of Brooklyn.

Jessica and I have done a bit of work for Satmar Hasidim in Williamsburg and elsewhere in the city and are thus somewhat familiar with their customs. What they are is what they aren't, and what they aren't is mainstream. They're different, all right.

I turned right on Ocean Parkway and headed for the expressway. I checked the rearview mirror. "They're still there."

Jessica was doing shoulder rolls. "Maybe they just want to talk." She began flexing and unflexing various muscle groups. She does this a couple of times a day. It helps keep her limber. "Anyhow, why are we running away?"

I decided to answer a question with a question. "Who's running away?"

She leaned across me to peer at the dashboard. "Oh." My hand was feeling better. I used it to muss up her curly hair. "You're right. Definitely not running." We were doing thirty-five. Traffic was somewhat heavy, which was not news.

The Satmar Hasidim try to dress pretty much the way their ancestors did several hundred years ago in Eastern Europe. The men have untrimmed beards and long, curly earlocks and wear ancient-looking black suits and distinctive black felt hats. Over their shirts, they wear a loose-fitting, four-cornered, woolen garment with fringes at the corners. They call it "zizith." What they don't wear are neckties, jeans, or bomber jackets. Also, they consider television to be an evil force akin to Baal worship. Who knows, they may be right about that.

They get married very young. Most are still in their teens when they say their "I do's." Or, the Yiddish equivalent, I suppose. They don't go to college. Hell, one guy—Jessica and I did a job for him—once told me that after fifth grade his education consisted solely of religious studies. No algebra, trig, physics, no social studies, no geography, no Shakespeare. There was a time when I would have drooled at his good fortune.

Then, being older and wiser, I naturally wondered—aloud—about the obvious. "How can a whole community scratch out a living without a college education?"

He smiled proudly and waved his hand expansively around us. We were standing in the middle of his privately owned, bustling electronics store—or, more accurately, electronics city. "What for I need college?" he asked. Beats me.

Most of the young men go into small businesses. Few, certainly, are as successful as he. Retailing is very popular. When a man completes his formal schooling, there is sometimes a father or father-in-law standing by to give him a boost in a new business. The women, for the most part, do not own their own businesses, although some will help their husbands out. Most married women take care of things concerning the home and the kids. Seven or eight kids in a family is not unusual, and I've heard cases of sixteen and more. Talk about women's work never being done.

"Remember the Horowitz case?" I asked.

"The diamond heist. Before your time."

We passed the exits for the Brooklyn and Manhattan Bridges. For a moment, I considered doing some fancy footwork—tire work?—and losing them in such a way as to send them on a wild goose chase into Manhattan. I soon decided against it. I wanted them to follow the wild goose—or geese, as it were—into Williamsburg.

"What do you mean, before my time? As I remember,

you were on the phone to me every night, complaining." We drove past the Brooklyn Navy Yard. "You were really pissed that they treated you like a woman."

"Well, that was before they got to know me."

"Before they found out you used to be a cop."

"That made a small difference." She was working on her legs and feet. It didn't look easy. When she finished, she took three deep breaths. "Anyway, it worked out all right in the end. Horowitz even sent more work our way. You know," she said, "I still get a card from him every September, before the Jewish New Year."

The work she was referring to was, for the most part, security and investigative work in the international center of the gem-quality diamond industry. This diamond center somehow manages to accommodate, on each working day, hundreds of firms and literally thousands of people in a single one-block stretch of Manhattan real estate, 47th Street between Fifth and Sixth Avenues. Quite a few of the people who work there are Satmar Hasidim.

Jessica and I agree that the Satmar are among the most charitable people we've ever met, supporting all sorts of organizations to help the poor. At the same time, they are also among the most dogmatic. Anyone who doesn't toe the official party line is considered to be somewhere between an idol worshipper and an ax murderer.

You almost never hear modern Hebrew, the official language of the State of Israel, spoken in Williamsburg. That's because the Satmar Hasidim are violently opposed to the existence of the State of Israel. Some have even been known to consort with Palestinian terrorists dedicated to the State's destruction. An official demonstration usually accompanies the visit of an Israeli dignitary to New York City. I don't pretend to understand this venomous hatred. I think the idea is that the existence of the State of Israel is instrumental in delaying the miraculous arrival of the Jewish Messiah. If there is to be such a State, the Messiah is the one who is going to set it up.

I guess it's a turf thing.

"Lunch," I said.

"Lunch?"

"Where we're going."

"It's four o'clock in the afternoon."

"Okay. Lupper." I turned off the highway and made my way through some of Williamsburg's side streets. I drove slowly. No point in causing our pursuers undue stress.

"Oh." She nodded to herself. "Horowitz's brother's deli."

I licked my lips. "Turkey sandwiches."

"What are you planning to do there with these?" She held up my bumper stickers for inspection. "If, indeed, your little pea brain is capable of planning on an empty stomach."

"Potato salad," I said. "Noodle pudding."

She stuck her tongue out at me.

"Pickled tongue," I said. "Corned beef. Pastrami."

Horowitz's Delicatessen is a small working-class kosher restaurant where you could get all those things and more, plus tea in a glass and pickles from a barrel. There was no reason in the world why we should not stop in on a Sunday afternoon for a late lunch or an early supper. We were on friendly terms with the owner and practically his whole family and practically his entire staff. We put in an order for turkey sandwiches and iced tea and took a table at the back. Jessica, for all her taunting, knew perfectly well what I had in mind.

A group of four men entered and we didn't have to wonder if they were our friends from the Lincoln. For one thing, they came in a few seconds after us—on our heels, you might say—and stared intently to keep us in view. For another thing, except for us, they were the only goyim, or gentiles, in the place. For a third thing, they were all of them over six feet tall, broad of shoulder, with serious, determined pusses. Oh, the fourth thing: they were definitely carrying. They found a table near ours. Cozy. They were so out of place in that joint, a 707 coasting through that front door would have fit in as well.

The waiter who brought our sandwiches was a guy of about fifty-five with a short, trimmed beard and a black skullcap. He wore a white, short-sleeved shirt, black slacks, and a white apron folded over and tied around his waist. He stepped over to our friends' table and politely inquired if they were ready to order. I found out that I was hungry and I guess Jessica did, too, because we both attacked our sandwiches with gusto.

One of the four ordered for all of them. "Shrimp salad," he said. "And make it snappy."

Jessica and I nearly choked. "Maybe that's how they planned to take us out," I wondered aloud once I could speak again. "Getting us to choke to death."

Our waiter didn't bat an eyelash. He explained patiently that, as this was a strictly kosher establishment, shellfish could not be obtained. After some dickering back and forth, they finally asked for steak and potatoes. He got them to settle for Hungarian goulash.

I could have saved them the trouble. I wasn't planning to give them a chance to eat much of it. Maybe I should have advised Horowitz to ask for payment in advance, but then I would have tipped my hand. I left my sandwich half-eaten and went to use the bathroom. I had to go down a flight of stairs to the basement to do so and I hoped, if someone was assigned to tail me, that he found his way all right. Should I leave a trail of bread crumbs, I wondered.

The first thing I did when I got to the men's room was enter one of the stalls and lock it modestly. Then I slipped out of my loafers, leaving them lined up neatly on the floor, and crawled underneath the partition to the next stall. Not a terribly noble move, admittedly.

I crouched on the toilet seat with my feet lifted off the ground, peered through the partially ajar stall door, and waited.

I didn't have to wait long, even without the bread crumbs. Two of the *big* crumbs from the Lincoln burst through the bathroom door and set about a procedure that made me feel they lacked certain social graces. Once they spotted the brown shoes in the locked stall, they immediately commenced affixing silencers to what I could only assume were a couple of very noisy automatics. Then they discharged their weapons fiercely into the empty stall. Like I said, no social graces.

My own .38 in hand, I burst out of my hiding place. I had them surprised and I had them covered. We went through all the required motions of conqueror and vanquished. Upon my command, they dropped their weapons and submitted to a frisk. I retrieved my shoes. Together we filed next door into a sort of boiler-utility room, where they obliged me by lying prone on the cement floor. I, in turn, did not shoot them.

I didn't actually want to shoot them. I wanted information. I wanted to find out who had sent them. Was it the Mr. M that Taylor was so afraid of? I wanted to know who was interested enough in our activities to send one operator after another to his, or sometimes her, death. I also wanted to rip their beaten and bruised bodies apart limb from limb and organ from tissue while they died the slow, tortured death of the unrighteous. But I didn't want to shoot them.

I provided each of them with a piece of paper and a writing implement and gave them the opportunity to write down the name and address of whoever had hired them for the job. I said I didn't want to shoot them. Somehow, I'm certain they believed me. Still, they did not pick up the pens, which were well within reach.

"You will both write down," I began calmly, "clearly and legibly, the name and address of your boss. The person who hired you. The person you will report to if you succeed in killing me. The person who will pay you." I was terribly calm.

"If the papers don't agree, I will shoot you both in some nonvital place. Like a knee. Or an elbow. Or a hand. Then you'll have another chance to get it right." See how nice I am?

I continued, "If you two don't agree the second time, I will shoot your other knee. Or your other hand. Or maybe one of each." I grinned at them and showed a lot of teeth.

Reddy's Law, you can learn something from anyone. And I had clearly learned a thing or two from good ol' Big R in Taylor's house.

"If it happens again, well . . ." I let it hang in the air, figuring that, with their backgrounds and chosen profession, they would be able to imagine scenarios far worse than any I could describe.

Well, that was the scene, and I thought I did it up pretty well. You know what? They balked. One guy was lying perfectly still, probably afraid to move. I could have sworn that the patch of pants between his legs looked darker than the rest. If Hemingway were writing today, he'd be a new kind of hero: *disgrace* under pressure.

His friend was made of sterner stuff. He called out in a loud voice, perhaps more for his partner's benefit than mine. "You're bluffing, Reddy. You're not going to kill us." The dark patch was spreading.

Who said anything about killing? I walked over to the loudmouth, stretched out his right arm on the floor, stepped on the elbow to steady it, placed the gun directly on his hand, and calmly put a bullet through the base of his index finger. Who said anything about killing? I repeated the procedure on his quaking partner. I used one of their own weapons, with a silencer. Their days as hit men were over.

I got the name I wanted—Frankie Falcone—and a Bay Ridge address, and two slips of paper contained exactly the same information, both written in shaky, immature, unformed scrawls. After all, they were using their left hands. I used their weapon one more time. Holding it by the butt, I knocked them both unconscious. Then, I wiped my prints off both guns and the knife I had recovered from one when I frisked them.

The boiler room had a heavy steel door that opened onto a narrow alley at the side of the restaurant. I propped it open and made my way casually past bags and bins of restaurant trash and the creatures that feed off of it to where the blue Lincoln was parked. From my pocket I retrieved my bumper stickers and surreptitiously affixed them to the rear of the car.

I hurried back to the alley and peered out from behind a huge commercial garbage bin. There were two bumper stickers. One had the flag of Israel alongside a proclamation, in blue Hebrew lettering on a white background, that said, "Israel must live." The other was a simply lettered Yiddish slogan proclaiming the superiority to Satmar of the Lubavitch Hasidic group.

Lubavitch is a Hasidic sect that originated in Russia and is centered today in the Crown Heights section of Brooklyn. To say that these two rival groups—which are, in truth, more similar to each other than they are to any other group in the population—dislike each other is a little bit like saying that the Turks had a minor disagreement with the Armenians.

I returned to my seat inside the way I had left, checking in on my two friends along the way. They were still out. One was snoring heavily. I hit them again. Jessica sat at our table, calmly sipping her second glass of iced tea.

"You'd better have the constitution of a camel," I said, tossing her one of the slips of paper I had coaxed out of our two friends downstairs. "We're going to be leaving here pretty quickly."

She read the name and address and slipped the note inside her jeans pocket. Then she raised her eyebrows.

"They won't bother us again," I explained. "They fell asleep." I finished my meal while Jessica paid the bill.

It looked like the two guys still on our tail had polished off their goulash platters and most of their lost companions' portions as well. They looked on quizzically as I ate, obviously wondering why I had returned alone. On my way out, I made certain to pass by them. After all, I didn't want to give the impression I'd be indecent enough to try to shake them. I flipped a piece of paper onto their table. The way they scrambled for it, you'd think it was a letter bomb. For that matter, it might as well have been. Their boss's name and address were scrawled on it.

Outside, Jessica turned to me. "Imagine," she said, pointing to the Lincoln, "driving into Williamsburg with those things plastered on your car."

"Tsk, tsk. Some people have no sense."

"Good thing the car's owners came out before too much damage was done."

I started the Cutlass and we watched the scene safely from inside our little urban tank.

The two toughs barreled through the restaurant door, anxious to keep us in view and get to their car quickly enough so as to hang onto us. I don't know why. We were in no hurry.

They almost missed the young Hasidic boy—about nine years old, dressed in white shirt, black slacks, black skullcap on close-cropped hair, with brown curly ear-locks framing a round, cute-as-a-button baby face—who was in the process of deflating the Lincoln's trusty tires while his friend stood watch. He was on his third tire and obviously enjoying the rush of righteousness brought on by his good deed.

The toughs were furious. One of them kicked the boy in the stomach and continued kicking him after he was down. The boy's friend screamed something in Yiddish, a scream for help.

Oh, yeah, I may have neglected to mention one of the quaint little customs in Satmar Williamsburg. If someone if being assaulted, he needs only to call out an SOS and every able-bodied man is honor-bound to stop whatever he is doing and come to his aid. The last few times a mugging was attempted in the neighborhood, several hundred Hasidim poured out of their stores, factories, and homes and pounded and pummeled the sorry mugger into the local hospital. You can bet muggers have learned to avoid that part of Brooklyn.

Not these guys, however. To add injury to injury, while that guy was kicking the boy who was down, his pal got hold of the kid who had screamed for help and began slapping him in the face.

Within thirty seconds, the street was filled to capacity with a sea of black-frocked, curly-earlocked, enraged Hasidim. After all, two strangers were brutalizing mere children. No one seemed to care that the strangers had big, ugly guns tucked under their arms. The strangers didn't stand a chance.

11

"FRANK FALCONE OWNS a discotheque in Bay Ridge." Jessica had spent the better part of the past hour on the phone with some of her friends from the force. "He's usually there, nights."

"Dancing?"

"Dealing."

"Oh." I tossed aside the book I had been reading. It was B. H. Liddell Hart's *Strategy,* and heaven only knows what a book on military strategy was doing on Jessica's bookshelves. "Why does Falcone want to bump us off?"

"He doesn't." She lowered herself onto the couch.

I grinned. "Scared him off, did we?"

"Falcone's disco does some regular business. Dancing, disc jockey, shows, and all that. It also fronts for a more lucrative dope operation. Mainly crack, cocaine, ludes and, of course, joints. Nice kids can take a date there and pick up some stuff at the same time. The cops have been onto him for a while, but . . ." She shrugged. "Anyhow, the profession he's in gives him access to certain—ah—contacts." She looked at me.

"Tough, mean contacts. So," I finished it up for her, "if you want to set up a hit on someone, he's the one to call. Is that it?"

"Right."

"So person or persons unknown want us out of the picture. They ring up this Falcone and order two hits to go?"

"Something like that."

"Then we really don't know any more than we did yesterday."

"That's one way of looking at it."

"You got another way?"

She sighed. "You could say we have one more lead."

"Oh," I said. "Whoopee."

"Besides Falcone, there seems to be one guy to watch out for. Serves as his assistant-bouncer-whatever. Name's Jock O'Toole. Apparently, he's famous."

"I should say so, Jess. Used to be a hockey player on a Canadian team. Vicious bastard. He didn't seem to care much for the sport—just played to break bones."

"If it was so much fun, why isn't he still a hockey player?"

"A few of the other players took care of him one night after the game, players from both teams, no less. He ended up in traction. When he got out of the hospital, he was still as mean as ever, but he wasn't much good for hockey anymore." I took in a breath. "So Jock 'The Ox' O'Toole ended up in Bay Ridge."

"And as mean as ever. Got any ideas?"

"Uh-huh." I tapped the book beside me. "I think Liddell Hart had good advice. Indirect approach, not head-on confrontation. After all, Falcone may be expecting us. Although," I added, "I don't think those bums we left at the restaurant are in any hurry to tell Falcone that we found out about him. I don't guess he takes too well to failure."

"That was a pretty dumb thing to do, tossing proof to the two guys at the table that you'd got what you wanted out of their buddies."

"Ah, but what a gesture."

"Listen, Cyrano, there's more to life than gestures."

"Like what, Roxanne?"

"Oh, shut up."

"Okay," I said. "Seriously, I think we should call Boris in."

"Already did," Jessica said, beginning a set of calisthenics. "He'll be there at eleven."

I raised my brows. "Without checking with your partner?"

She answered me with huffs and grunts.

Later, at the disco, our indirect approach consisted of playing a couple of nerds out to watch the swinging singles. It must have been a good part to play. There were others, at the bar and on the dance floor, doing the same.

The music wasn't too loud, not louder than an atomic explosion in an echo chamber. The place wasn't crowded; it was fairly spilling over with bored, lonely people trying faithfully to show what a grand time they were having. Hundreds of people were crushed together with a density rivaled only by the Japanese subway system, bravely looking neither right nor left, eyeing the floor, communing with some inner voice, or glancing at their partners if, indeed, they had any. Contact of arms, legs, or various other body parts was either studiously ignored, or flaunted in such a way so as to depersonalize or, even, dehumanize it.

"According to my sources," Jessica was saying, "Falcone keeps the coke and other junk in a safe in his office, which is way in the back. Anyone interested in buying, deals with Jock."

I looked around. I'd seen Jock O'Toole once in a televised hockey game. I spotted him immediately, but then so did Jessica, who'd never seen him before anywhere. It's not easy to miss someone who's six-foot-six and built like a cement mixer. He had the kind of face that recorded every fight he'd ever been in, and the kind of eyes that assured you the other guy looked worse.

During the next twenty minutes, we saw about a dozen people pass money to him and receive, in turn, a small envelope.

"This operation is practically out in the open."

"Hmm."

"Falcone must have paid off the right people."

Finally, Jock headed for the office. He'd either run out of little envelopes or it was time to unload some cash. When he returned, he went through the same routine as before, exchanging bills for envelopes, guarding against unruly customers, and generally doing what he was paid for. The next time he headed for a refill, I followed him casually, weaving my way through the crowded dance floor.

There was a desk in front of the office and a restroom some fifty feet away. About the only way I could keep going and not look conspicuous was to go to the restroom. A bathroom is not exactly a prize spot for investigative surveillance. Nonetheless, I valiantly observed, through the crack in the partially open door, Jock nodding to the armed guard at the desk and knocking on the office door.

I heard him say, "It's Jock." He was in there, all told, ten minutes, and then he went on another round while I rejoined Jessica and Boris at the bar.

Boris was sipping something amber over ice and making it last. I knew it didn't suit him. Anything less than a hundred proof he considers ladies' liquor. My theory is that they get used to that stuff in the Ukraine in order to escape the harsh realities of life. I was reminded of the story my uncle used to tell of the man who lost his job, wrecked his car, and found out his wife was divorcing him, all in the same day. The punch line has the guy shaking his head sadly and saying to himself, "Thank goodness I'm a drunk." I smiled to myself.

Jessica was in the midst of a sophisticated, intellectual

discussion with someone who was trying to pick her up. And why not—she was in her disco best: a full-cut dancing skirt, patterned hose, and a sequined unstructured top held up by matching shoulder straps. I listened in.

"Hey-baby-what's-happenin'-get-DOWN-you-look-real-hot-you-know-that?-Let's-dance-this-place-is-really-happenin'."

Jessica just shrugged his hand off her shoulder, smiled, and shook her head.

He gave a knowing wink. "Just took your medicine, huh? You'll be gettin' down in no time. Hey." He took on a confidential tone. "You got any to spare? Small stuff. You know."

"Medicine?" Jessica asked innocently. "Maybe."

She started rummaging in her purse. It was a prop, I knew. She never carries anything important in a purse when she's on a job. The dodo licked his lips and leaned obscenely against her looking over her shoulder into the bag. Then, she brightened and pulled out a box of cough drops. He became positively animated. Pensively, she counted what was in the box, withdrew two, and dropped them into his palm. He stared at them. She smiled sweetly.

"Something new?" he asked. She nodded. "Thanks. I'll try anything once." He popped them in his mouth. There was a strange expression on his face. He patted her shoulder. "See ya 'round, babe."

I leaned over and whispered in Jessica's ear. "Better watch it, Sister, or the Smith Brothers'll put you in the slammer for dealing without a license."

While the bartender was busy serving a customer at the other side of the bar, we powwowed. I told Jessica and Boris about the guard and the proximity of the office to the bathrooms.

"If Falcone is here, he's in there."

"My source says he's here every night."

Boris was still grinning over the cough drops routine. "Looks like ve come forr notting, Rreddy." Boris winked at me. "I didn't know vhat forr Chessica need us along."

Jessica smiled. "Okay." She stood up. "You boys want to watch?"

With that she sashayed her way through the sweaty, panting, plastered people with the painted smiles, in the direction of the office. Boris and I stared at each other for a second or two, then scrambled after her to my lookout point in the men's room. All right, we didn't exactly scramble. After all, we didn't want to attract any undue attention.

Jessica first stepped into the ladies' room, then emerged looking very upset. She glanced around and finally approached the guard at the desk. She lowered her eyes. "There's no, uhm, toilet paper in there."

The guard grinned vacuously. "Wait just a minute, lady."

He lifted his telephone receiver and turned to dial. He never completed the call. Jessica's trained right hand met the side of his neck in a vicious karate chop, no holding back. He was instantly unconscious. She propped him up in his chair against the desk, and perched herself on the desk, crossing her legs, and leaning on one elbow. She was partially blocking him. To all onlookers, a sexy lady was doing a little flirting.

It was several minutes before Jock came along. "You crazy, Sanchez?" He was furious. "Get the slut off your desk. Now."

Jock hurried over, grabbed Jessica by the shoulder, and pulled her off the desk. Then, he noticed that Sanchez wasn't participating much in the conversation. Jock's reaction time wasn't bad, just a few seconds too slow.

Jessica was already off the desk. She spun around and kicked him in the groin. Then, for good measure, she grabbed him by the hair and smashed his head against the wall. He had a hard head, but it was a hard wall.

Boris and I got there in time to see the finished product. Jessica was disarming the guard and I performed the same service for Jock. Jock slouched against the wall, his feet sprawled out in front of him. There was blood trickling down the side of his face. Boris whistled.

"Save your breath for the next task," I warned him. I pointed to the solid, wooden office door.

Boris sneered. "You call this doorr? In my countrry, vee yoos this kind vood forr firre." With that he heaved and we both hoed, and the door gave way in no time. Maybe Boris was right about the vood.

Falcone was in there. You could tell he was the brains of the operation because he was involved in real brain work. He was playing cards with someone. Boris went through the door first.

Just in case his visage wasn't enough to put fear into them, I came out with the obligatory "One move and you're dead" or something to that effect.

I covered the group while Jessica dragged Jock and Sanchez in to join the party. Then she covered them while I frisked them. Boris went out to his van to get some supplies. Falcone and his friend were both carrying. I noticed that the safe was open.

Boris returned carrying a knapsack and took out some thick duct tape. We used it to tie up Falcone, his friend, Jock, and Sanchez. Duct tape is much more effective than rope or twine. You can't work it loose. The only way to get it off is to cut it. While we were at it, we used the duct tape to gag three of them, but not Falcone. We wanted information out of him.

I had a vague feeling that there was something we'd forgotten. I don't get that feeling often, and when I do, it's not necessarily accurate. I went over to the safe. There was still a good deal of cocaine inside—also, a good deal of cash. Over ten thousand dollars, by my quick estimation.

"Father Ritter's organization is going to be very grateful for your contribution, Falcone," I said as I pocketed the funds. "And just think, you can get a tax credit."

Falcone made no comment. He was obviously too overwhelmed by my generosity on his behalf. Anyway, he was busy watching Boris taping him to his own chair, none too gently.

I'm always a little taken aback when I see how people react to Boris. To me, he's just a lovable teddy bear—a large, powerful, mean-looking, Ukrainian teddy bear. He hadn't yet done anything really violent, but Falcone and his pals were gawking at Boris in a way that told me they were at least a little afraid of him. They certainly didn't take their eyes off him, and Jessica and I were the ones holding the guns. It's enough to give a guy a complex.

I cleared my throat. Falcone's eyes flickered toward me, but he didn't let Boris out of his sight either. "Mr. Falcone," I began. "Frank." He frowned, opened his mouth, then shut it. I continued. "Hard as it is to believe, some nasty-looking characters have been trying to do away with Ms. Munroe"—I indicated Jessica—"and myself. They haven't been very good at it, but"—I raised my shoulders an inch and dropped them again—"it's a nuisance." I nodded at Boris and he started to fiddle with the knapsack. "So you see, Frank," I said, "nothing personal, but we'd like to find out who it is so we can"—Boris pulled something out of the knapsack—"reason with him." It was a tightly covered container made out of clear, solid glass. The kind used in laboratories. "We don't need much from you"—I smiled—"Frankie. Just tell us who put out the word about the hits and where we can find him. Oh, yeah, and why."

The container was marked "HCL" in capital block letters and contained some clear liquid. Falcone's eyes were bulging. I grinned. "Don't worry about my friend, there. When I told him we were going to a notorious doper's heaven, he remembered what someone had once told him about an acid trip." I laughed. "So he brought his own acid."

Boris was slowly working the cap off the container. I glanced over at Jessica; she just looked bored. Who says there's no fun in this business?

Boris held the now-open glass container aloft, over Falcone's head, then tilted it. "You say vat he vants to know," he said happily, "orr you vill look like monsterr." Like I said, a teddy bear. "You tink you so tough," sneered Boris, still holding the deadly liquid over Falcone's head. "You baby. In Siberria, I learrn how big boys play." Falcone snarled, but kept his eye on the container. Boris tilted it another degree. "I count to ten. You say fast.

"One." (Vahn.)

Falcone struggled against his bonds.

"Two."

He managed to jiggle the chair a bit—"Trree"—but Boris kept the container poised over his head. With each count, Boris tilted the container a little more precariously. "Fourr."

Falcone stopped struggling. Beads of perspiration had popped out on his square, ruddy forehead; one trickled down to the corner of his mouth. A thick, pink tongue darted out and tasted it.

"Fife."

"No." It came out a little hoarse.

"Vhat?"

"I—I'll—okay." He sighed. "Just put that damn thing down. You might make a mistake."

"Yes?" Boris appeared to consider that possibility.

"Mebbe." He switched hands, but kept the acid directly over Falcone's head. "I not make mistake," he said, "until I get tirred. You talk fast."

Falcone's overzealous eyebrows kept the perspiration out of his eyes, training it instead down the sides of his face. He was cowed and he knew it. Also, he was dead. He had no doubt but that Boris would dump the acid on him if he failed to produce reliable information. He didn't know how little we really knew, that he was our only lead, that we could not corroborate or test his information. From the look on his face, I didn't think he was going to take that chance. On the other hand, if he cooperated with us, word would undoubtedly get back to whomever had contracted his services. If Jessica and I were worth killing when we hardly knew anything, it stood to reason that he didn't have a prayer.

"Mihram," he whispered. "Kamal Mihram." The name meant nothing to me, but it did begin with an *M*. I tried to look like he was telling me something meaningful.

Jessica nodded. "Why?" she asked, sharply.

"Said youse were interfering in his business."

"Which one?" I tried.

He shrugged, very slightly. Either the tape constricted his movement that much or he was still mindful of the hydrochloric acid suspended above him. "I only know about the coke. I guess he's into other stuff, too."

"Interfering, how?"

"He said you iced some of his boys. I swear, that's all I know. Please get this animal away from me."

His voice seemed to go up an octave. He looked up at Boris to see if he was satisfied. I was still trying to figure out why I felt we had forgotten something. Boris nodded and was preparing to replace the container where it belonged, when he tripped and accidentally spilled most of it onto Falcone's lap.

"Oops."

The high-pitched shriek that filled the air brought to mind the sound of an alley cat getting the worst of a midnight fight. The only other sound was Boris laughing—a hearty, pleasant, Ukrainian laugh. The kind of laugh you'd like to share a drink with. As Falcone watched in horror, Boris brought the glass container to his mouth and drank down what was left of the clear, deadly liquid. He licked his lips.

"Wodka," he said. And grinned.

I grinned, too. But my shirt was sticking to me under my arms and the gun felt slippery in my hand.

All of a sudden, the back of my neck felt cold and the small hairs there stood up bristling and I knew exactly what it was that we forgot. The door to the office. We didn't have it covered. We couldn't lock it because we'd busted it on our way in. We didn't imagine that any of the customers would wander this far afield. Now the door was open and two brutes had their Uzis trained on us. Obviously, our big mistake was in believing that Jock O'Toole was Falcone's only protection. The newcomers looked around. They saw the disorder, the guns, the three guys tied up on the floor, Falcone tied to the chair, his pants wet.

"Drop the guns," they said to us, "and assume the position."

Jessica dropped her gun obligingly on the floor. I followed suit.

One of the new guys went around freeing Falcone and his pals, muttering under his breath about the job we had done with the duct tape. The other kept the machine gun trained on us. Just for fair measure, I kept my eyes trained on it, in turn.

I knew two things for certain—the name of the guy who had been trying so vigilantly to kill us, and that we were in big trouble.

12

We were in some sort of a storage room in the lower regions of the building which housed the discotheque. We heard it called "the dungeon," but there was really nothing sinister about it. It was just a drab, windowless, musty room, about twenty feet square, with crates of liquor piled up high against one wall. There was, against another wall, a huge, old-fashioned, blackened stove with six burners, a griddle, and two huge oven doors, a relic from the days when the resident establishment served more substantial fare than booze, pills, and white powder. On the wall facing the old stove was a solid steel door with no doorknob, leading me to conjecture that we might not be the first unwilling inhabitants to occupy this place.

As for us, we didn't look so hot. Jessica's hands and mine were bound with steel wire, which is even better for keeping a person out of mischief than duct tape. When used by a pro, steel wire can be secured so that it cannot be untied, worked loose, or cut through with anything other than wire cutting tools. Somehow, Falcone's pals didn't think to give us their cutting pliers. Spoilsports. Our feet were free because we'd had to walk down the stairs of our own volition; nobody wanted to carry us. We'd been relieved of our firearms and our pride—oh, and also of the cash I'd taken from Falcone's safe.

Boris was out on the floor, snoring heavily. The left side of his face, blown up to twice its size, was a mass of purple, blue, and red welts. His left eye was pasted shut and swollen so that even the slit was barely visible. He was out mainly because he'd been kicked down the stairs, but he'd been a little punchy even before that. The bruises on his face he got from Falcone by way of retaliation.

As soon as Falcone had been freed by his compadres, he'd grabbed one of the confiscated weapons and marched right over to Boris with eyes as hard as steel and twice as cold.

Falcone had raised the gun, holding it by the barrel, and obviously wanted to bring it down on the big guy's head. But Falcone was only about five-feet-six inches tall to Boris's five-feet-eleven and that wasn't going to work. So Falcone aimed for the gut instead and got enough momentum in the swing that Boris ended up sitting down in a chair that was behind him. Then he slammed Boris in the face with the gun. Repeatedly. Boris just took it. After all, the right side of his face, the side that could still see out of its eye, was staring straight into the one-eyed glare of an Uzi.

When Falcone finally got hold of himself, he said, "You two guys are going to die a very slow, painful death. You'll know you're dying, I'll make sure of that. But I won't kill you until you beg for it. And your broad, here"—he grabbed a scissors and deliberately snipped off one of her shoulder straps, exposing part of a breast—"she'll make my men very happy before she dies. She, too, will be begging for me to kill her."

Jessica rolled her eyes. "You bet," she muttered under her breath.

Falcone looked at her sharply but didn't respond. He motioned to the henchmen with the firearms. "Take this garbage down to the dungeon and lock 'em in. Let 'em sweat a little." He tossed a reel of steel wire. "Tie 'em up good. I gotta call Mihram to see if he wants them hisself.'' Falcone ran a pink tongue across his fleshy lips and glared at us from underneath bushy eyebrows. ''I sure hope not.'' He pounded his fist on the big desk. ''They're mine.''

Boris was starting to stir. He was lying facedown with his good side concealed from us, and what we could see of his face wasn't pretty. He shifted around uncomfortably. He was lying directly on his hands, which had been handcuffed together in front. While my hands and Jessica's had been tied tightly behind us, his big, burly body had not been able to cooperate too well by the time Falcone finished pistol-whipping him. So he was honored with the bracelets.

''Boris,'' Jessica whispered. ''You all right?''

Boris rolled onto his back and winced. His breath was heavy and came with difficulty. Aside from the ugly bruises, there wasn't much bleeding that I could see. ''Don't vorry,'' he said, heaving. ''In Siberria, I get vorrse beatings.'' He sneered and winced. ''Vhen arre they rreturrn forr us?''

''Falcone's on the horn with the big man. Mihram.'' Boris looked confused. I clarified. ''He's calling him up on the telephone. Before he decides what to do with us.''

''They're going to wait until this place closes down for the night,'' Jessica offered, ''before doing anything anyway.''

''Vhat they going to do?''

''Well,'' I said brightly, ''Falcone is going to kill us. Very slowly. But he's going to feed Jessica to his men first.''

Boris looked at Jessica. I don't think he could see well enough yet to notice that she was partially unclad. He tried a small smile. ''She vill eat them alive.''

''Funny,'' I grinned. ''That's what Sardine says.''

Jessica kicked me in the shin. ''Sandy.'' She was still wearing her heels and it hurt plenty.

I took a confidential tone. "Sandy says the two of them have a Plutonic relationship."

Jessica warily corrected me. "Platonic, you mean."

"Uh-uh," I countered. "Plut-onic." To Boris, I whispered, "They go at it like dogs."

Boris giggled, which I suppose made him feel better, but it brought out wet spots in his eyes. "It hurrts to laugh," he said. "You a bum, Chasun, you know dott?"

"I know."

"Yeah, you're a bum, Red."

"Vy you two arrgue all time?"

"Oh, we don't argue."

"Yeah," I said, "one of us resorts to physical violence." I stood my ground, feet spread apart, and challenged, "Go on. Kick them off, if that's what you want. I won't budge."

Jessica grinned and shook her head. "Too easy."

"Yeah," I agreed. "Big targets."

Boris was laughing so hard he was shaking. The swollen parts of his face were twisted into a grotesque grimace.

"Sorry, I forgot it hurts you to laugh."

He shook his head slowly from side to side. "You can't help it, you crrazy."

"That you are." Jessica came over and planted a tender kiss on my cheek. Which was fine, except that the proximity of her knee to my groin still worried me a little.

I walked backward to the wall and sat down against it. Jessica also sat, but she started doing leg lifts. Boris was shifting around again, and I got to thinking about his busted head and the hard, stone floor. I stretched my legs out and we managed to maneuver his head onto my lap.

Jessica finished a set of lifts and took a tour of the room. I followed her with my eyes. The crates of liquor, neatly stacked. The ancient stove topped with ancient grease. The floorboards. The ceilings and walls. The knobless door. She plopped down next to me. No, that's not right. Jessica never plops. She melted gracefully into a sitting position and leaned gently against me.

"Accommodations to your liking, ma'am?" Without waiting for an answer, I continued, "I wonder what Sandy would say if he could see you now."

Jessica snorted. She felt tense against my shoulder.

"Personally, I think he would say that he wants to take you away from all this."

"He's already said as much."

"Vy you vant to kip seeing such a dumb guy?"

"Hey, Boris. You're talking about the dumb guy she wants to marry."

Boris opened his one good eye wide. "Is umpossible," he said. "Umpossible. Dott's a big mistake. Vhy you vant to marry such a shtupid idiot?"

"She has to, Boris."

"Rreally?"

"She's old."

"Chessica? Old?"

I sighed. "Twenty-nine."

"Red, stop airing my dirty linen, etcetera."

"Dirty? Marriage isn't dirty, Jessica. Just think. Pretty soon—assuming we get out of this inhospitable dungeon with your pretty little face intact—you could be walking down the aisle in some staid, conservative church, wearing a flowing white satin gown. And then you could go home to a nice little white house in the suburbs, and wake up late, and have coffee with the other hausfraus, and amble into Sardine's—sorry, Sandy's—office at the respectable time of noon, do a few credit checks and traces just to keep your hand in, so you feel fulfilled. You'd leave a little early, of course, to get Sandy's dinner started, pick up his fine clothes from the cleaner's along the way. But, of course, it would all be worth it, because in due time you'd produce a little Sardine, and then another one, and then—why, you'd soon have a whole canful of Sardines!"

Jessica didn't say anything. I forced myself to look over at her. She looked miserable. I felt guilty as hell.

"Tventy-nine not so old, Chessica."

"Oh, what do you two know?" She practically spit the words out. She pointed her chin at Boris. "You'll get married one day soon—it doesn't matter when—to a wonderful woman who will have beautiful children by you and take care of them for you. You"—she indicated me—"have plenty of time, decades if you want, to decide to bring some genetically inferior offspring into the world. You guys don't understand what if feels like to have a biological clock working against you."

"Okay. You have this biological clock. You want to have a kid. But, does it have to be with"—I wrinkled my nose at her—"Sardine?"

She rolled her eyes heavenward. "Men!"

"Oh, that's a good response. You're really waxing articulate in your reproductive old age. Soon, maybe, you'll even burn your bra."

Suddenly, inexplicably, I started to laugh. It started innocently, and then built up to a hearty giggle. It had something to do with the fact that I suddenly realized that I was talking to a woman who very obviously had no bra to burn. Jessica smiled too.

Boris was sitting bolt upright. I don't think he ever sat up so quickly in his life, and it clearly hurt him to do it now. "Burrn," he said. And looked at the stove.

"We're all very articulate today," I said. "Must be the air in here."

"Dott's a gas stove. If is still hooked up to gas, ve can starrt a nice firre."

"Why would we want to do that? Aren't we in enough trouble already?"

"There must be a fire alarm system in a place like this, Red. It would bring help."

"Oh," I said. "I see. A Pyrrhic victory."

"Vhat's dott?"

"What he means is, the fire will kill us anyway." She shrugged. "Why am I translating for two educated males speaking the same language?"

"Falcone vill kill us, too. Anyvay, I know a vay. Trrust me." He added, with evident pride, "In Rrussia, I vas engineerr."

"Yeah, I know. All the other Russian cabdrivers used to be engineers, too."

Boris went to check out the stove. "Hum," he said. "Is to gas pipe connected. Dott's good." Using both hands, since they were cuffed together anyway, he opened one of the burners full blast. Nothing happened. Boris leaned over to sniff at the burner. "Dott's good." Gas was escaping. Apparently, the stove was hooked up and usable. Could be it was even still used occasionally for catering private parties. But it was old enough so that it didn't have a pilot light, or else the pilot was broken. We'd need to start it with a match. Only there were no matches around.

This didn't faze Boris in the slightest. In fact, he seemed perfectly pleased with the situation. "Rreddy, you open all the burrnerrs. Even oven. Chessica, ve need to find electrric virre."

I looked at him skeptically. He responded, "It vas us Russians who invented Molotov cocktail."

"Yeah, and then you drank it down." Oh, boy. "Trrost me," I muttered under my breath. I had to turn around and stand on tiptoe, and I still had a time of it trying to open the damn burners with my hands tied behind my back.

"I saw an outlet on that wall there," Jessica said, "at the other side of the door. Something was plugged into it, but I don't know what." They went over to investigate.

"Dott's good, too." Boris said. He reached out his hands and pulled.

I finished the last burner. The room was filling up with gas fast. "Boris, at this rate, Falcone won't have to worry about us. We'll die of asphyxiation."

Boris raised his eyebrows at Jessica. His good eyebrow, anyway. "Choking," she explained. He went back to pulling a cord out of the wall.

"What's that you got?"

"A wiolation," he said.

"What's a wiolation?" I asked Jessica.

Someone had drilled a small hole in the wall just above the electrical outlet. An electrical cord, probably an extension cord, went through the hole and its end was plugged into the outlet, so that all we could see on our side was the plug and a little bit of the cord before it disappeared through the hole in the wall. It's common practice among amateur electricians and do-it-yourselfers when a room with an extra electrical outlet adjoins one that doesn't have enough. In this case, the room we were in had no need for one at all; there were no appliances to hook up. It was a violation, all right. And a fire hazard. And Boris Radovich, one-time engineer, was going to start a fire.

Meanwhile, the air in the big room was becoming oppressive.

Boris had several yards of electrical extension cord in his hands. He tugged. It balked. Jessica and I stood behind him, wrapped a length of cord around our hands and we all strained in unison, just like a real tug o' war. The cord eventually gave way. Whatever the obstruction had been tore free, and the end we pulled through the small hole in the wall was all frayed, exposed wires. Boris peeled off more of the insulation and tied the exposed wire to one of the central grates on the stove top.

He went over to the liquor and swiped at a couple of cases. They fell to the floor with a crash. Cheap whiskey, cheap bottles. We helped him place some of the bottles inside the huge ovens and some alongside the old stove. Then, he took a bottle and tried to twist off the cap and seal. It was hard to get the twisting motion necessary with his hands restrained the way they were.

That didn't stop him. He raised the bottle with both his hands and brought it crashing down upon the stove top. He alternated pouring the whiskey onto the stove and into his mouth and I was getting nervous about the gas and all the noise we were making.

"Let's get on with it."

"Is finished."

Finished? "A room full of gas, and a wire attached to a stove top, and some broken bottles of liquor? And you call yourself an engineer?"

He put a finger to his lips. Even though he had to raise both hands to do so. There were noises at the door. Good thing. It was already pretty hard to breathe in there. The outlet was on the side of the door where the hinges were. The door opened inward. That was good. I think.

We all took up positions near the door, so that when it swung open the massive steel door would provide some protection from the havoc that we were getting ready to wreak.

Boris positioned the plug of the electrical cord over the outlet. When he inserted it, a spark would flare at the other end where the exposed wire was attached to the metal stove. We didn't need any matches. The spark would do.

We could hear muffled voices. Metal slid across metal as someone fiddled with a key.

"Tol' you there was a gas smell, Boss."

"What're those idiots tryin' to do, Boss?"

"I told youse to tie 'em up good. So help me, if they make trouble for me now, you guys are as good as—"

The door opened, the men ran by us into the room, and Boris made the connection. The next moments were a blur of white and orange and yellow and a noise as loud as the loudest silence. The metal door got hot almost immediately. Falcone had run for the stove and with him were Sanchez and the two guys with the Uzis. When I next saw them they were stretched out on the floor. Their clothes were catching fire. I marveled at the silence. A fire was raging that had already claimed four victims and would have killed us, too, if we hadn't been prepared for it, and it all happened in silence. I looked at Jessica. She was mouthing something to me, a message: "Let's get out of here."

I wondered why she didn't speak up. We went up the stairs in silence. Our feet made no sound on the old, bare, wooden steps. That wasn't right. Then, I realized that the blast of the fire started by that small spark must have temporarily deafened me, and perhaps Boris and Jessica as well.

"Ve get cutting plierrs I see in office," Boris whispered faintly.

Good, my hearing was starting to return. If we were going to get home, at least one of us would need two free hands in order to drive, so we headed for the office. The key to the handcuffs was probably already imprinted on someone's blackened flesh.

From behind the smashed door to the office, the unmistakable hulking form of Jock emerged holding a shotgun and meaning to use it. "I don't know what you bastards tried to do down there''—he took aim—''but you ain't never going to do it again.''

''Your boss is dead, Jock.'' It was Jessica. She was getting her voice back. Or, I was getting my hearing back. One of those.

''What happened to the boss?''

''Falcone's dead,'' I corroborated, softly. ''Why don't you just take the money and the coke from the safe and split? The fire department will be here shortly and the police soon after.'' As if on cue came the long, low wail of a distant fire truck.

Jock grinned. A broad, yellow-toothed grin. ''Oh, I'll take the stuff all right, but I'll leave you dead.'' His grin took us all in and settled finally on Jessica. He seemed for the first time to notice the soft curve of her exposed breast, made more alluring since the way her hands were pinned behind her thrust her chest out. I could swear he was drooling.

Jessica smiled and gave a small, self-deprecating shrug. ''Latest fashion,'' she said demurely.

Jock's grin widened but didn't get prettier. Jessica was closer to him now, smiling softly, leaning her breast against him. Then she was spinning and tripping him with such force that the shotgun slid down the smooth linoleum floor all the way to the rest rooms. It didn't take me long to get into the fracas. Jock had already managed to swing at Jessica hard enough to slam her against the wall. She wasn't out, but she was dazed.

Boris and I went at him like the Keystone cops. With my hands pinned behind me, and Boris's hands cuffed in front of him, and neither of us as good with our legs as Jessica, it must have been a comical sight. I wouldn't really know. I was too busy. I kept ramming into Jock, losing my balance, finding it, ramming him again. Once or twice, I got in a good kick in the general area of the groin. No Marquis of Queensberry rules for me. Maybe

Marquis de Sade rules. Boris used his cuffed fists as a club repeatedly—when he was in position—bringing them down on Jock's granite head, which was solid enough to be used as a hockey puck—and probably had been.

I wouldn't say I was getting tired. But I sure was relieved when Jessica recovered sufficiently to help us out a little. Well, actually, her little bit of help consisted of a series of killer kicks to the groin and head. If she didn't succeed in knocking his block off, at least he wouldn't be called Jock anymore. I swear, her feet should be registered as lethal weapons.

After a hectic few minutes we all stood back. Jock's bulldog head wobbled back and forth on his slumped shoulders as he slid to the floor.

Boris was coughing; I couldn't breathe too well. The siren sounded louder and was probably getting closer. I didn't really want to explain our restrained hands, Boris's brusies, Jessica's oddly styled dress, or the bodies. We hurried into Falcone's office, where Boris used the pliers to cut through the steel wire on my hands and Jessica's. The safe was locked. Too bad.

We split, like fugitives escaping from the fires of hell.

13

ALLIE WAS POISED and well dressed, all assemblyperson. She wore a lightweight navy blazer over a white linen dress, she carried a large purse of white leather with navy trim, and she had just taken a few short moments off from work to personally thank us for all we had tried to do for her. She sat chattily in our client's chair, smiling professionally, and occasionally illustrating a point with a nervous flutter of her hands. I liked her better when she was unsure of herself.

What exactly we had accomplished for her, other than nearly getting ourselves and Boris Radovich killed, I didn't know. But, as she seemed perfectly pleased, I smiled and nodded, generously accepting our client's generous praise for a job well done.

Jessica was pensive, biting her lower lip. From where I sat, it looked like she was doodling, but she shortly picked up the paper she'd been writing on and handed it quietly over to Walters. It was one of our invoices. Walters read it over quietly. It took her a long time. Her eyebrows went up, and for a couple of minutes it appeared as if she was going to say something. Then she pulled herself together. With her lips pressed into a tight, straight, horizontal line, she pulled a small checkbook from her purse and started writing.

I ambled casually past, glanced over her shoulder, and continued on my way to the window. On the street below, the college students were dressed in colorful summer wear and full of excitement over the start of classes for the condensed, intensive summer session. The shoppers and the local businesspeople bustled as they usually bustle, with the expectation that tomorrow they would be bustling anew. Of course, they were all blissfully ignorant of Mihram and his insidious activities. We didn't know much about him either, but what we did know was enough to make our blood curdle before it froze.

The invoice was for seventeen thousand dollars. So was the check. Not bad, for seven days' work. So Allie was writing out a five-figured check without so much as a wink or a groan. Now it was Jessica's turn to be surprised. One thing many people don't realize about private investigators—the honest kind anyway, which is what Jessica and I are—is that while seventeen grand may seem like too much for a mere week's work, and too little to get yourself almost killed for, it is most certainly not nearly enough for us to consider leaving a case unsolved. Even supposing that Mihram did not know that we were onto him, after what we went through last night and over these past few days, we'd have to be damn cold and selfish to drop the case for a paltry seventeen grand. Cold and selfish weren't whom Althea Walters had chosen to entrust with her reputation.

"Here you are, Jessica." Allie forced a smile. "I'll take back my tape now." Her tape? Getting proprietary, at the end? A little fonder of the thing now than when you dropped it in our laps, aren't you?

Jessica tried, "What difference does it make, Allie? They have the master."

"Oh, never mind about that," she waved a nervous hand at an insignificant problem. "It'll work itself out." I'm sure she said it to herself as much as to us.

That was my cue. "How's your daughter, Allie?"

She jumped four inches in the air, then covered it up by twisting around to look at me. I was still standing by the window. "What?" Her white-knuckled hands gripped the chrome armrests.

"Your daughter. You know. Veronica." I continued. "In Europe?"

A strangled noise escaped her parted lips, sounding like a cross between a hyena and a cat in heat. She was trying to fake a giggle. It wasn't working.

"You know te—eenagers," she said, still giggling awkwardly. She picked up her purse to go. Jessica was fiddling with the combination on the safe, and it was taking her longer than it had taken her to pick the lock on Taylor's phony linen closet. "Never mind, Jessica. I'll pick up the tape another time. Or you can just burn it."

"Have you heard from her yet?" I persisted. "Did she telephone? Write a letter?" Allie's eyes were becoming shiny and her nose pink. "Did she send a message with a friend?"

Allie crumpled back into her chair and sat there, weeping. Her trembling shoulders hunched forward, arms wrapped around her purse, face down into her chest. She was as close to the fetal position as one can get and still remain seated.

"Please." She looked up, first at me, then at Jessica. Her red, puffed eyes were begging. "Please. Stay out of this. Don't talk about it anymore. It's over."

"Why?"

"It's for the best. Just keep quiet about the whole matter. I'm sorry I ever brought you into it." She sighed and pulled a tissue out of the box on Jessica's desk. I made a mental note to declare tissue costs as an operating expense in our budget.

Jessica sat at her desk again and clasped her hands in front of her, all business. "Let me tell you what seventeen thousand dollars buys, Ms. Walters."

She then proceeded to report on our activities of the

previous week, including the attempts on our lives, in the impersonal tone she reserves for doing just that—reporting to a client. She reviewed in some detail the hours we spent Saturday night at Taylor's house, yesterday afternoon in the restaurant, and last night in Bay Ridge. She used her fingers to count off the people who'd been killed, until she ran out of fingers.

"A lot of people have died since we got involved in this case, Ms. Walters. I might even say, *because* we got involved in the case. True, some of them were crud, but they were also human beings. It seems that, since we began working for you one week ago, we have asked too many of the wrong questions, or, perhaps, the right ones. We obviously made someone very uncomfortable. Enough so that he's been trying to kill us since Thursday. Enough so—now that he knows on whose behalf we have been working—that he's increasing the pressure on you to pull us off the case, using the strongest weapon he could possibly hold over you. Allie. I can't promise you that Veronica is all right, but I can promise you one thing. If Mihram's boys have her, you won't see her again."

I winced. Allie's mouth popped open, and her hand flew up involuntarily to cover it. Jessica went on.

"As far as I'm concerned, this check is a piece of paper. Worth far less than that Kleenex you're holding because it's less useful. It can't keep us from finding out what's behind the blackmail of at least two other members of the Assembly. It can't make us forget the personal indignities we've suffered on your behalf over the last two days. It can't keep us from investigating Mihram's part in the attempts on our lives. And it can't keep us from searching for your daughter's trail and doing our best to return her safely to you." Jessica picked the worthless piece of paper up and, holding it with the thumb and forefinger of both hands, ripped it delicately and neatly in half. "You don't buy us, Allie. You just rent our bodies. We hold onto our souls, our thoughts, our wills. It's in the contract." She gave a friendly grin. "The fine print."

Allie took in her breath and let it out again. She reached deep into her large purse and came out with an eight-by-ten mailing envelope, which she handed to Jessica. I went over to have a look.

Inside the envelope was a sheet of plain white paper with a message of some sort and a passport in the name of Veronica Carol Walters containing a tiny photo of a blonde, long-haired beauty with a shy smile. Inside the passport was a four-inch length of blond hair. While Jessica read the note, I examined the envelope. There were no markings on it of any kind.

"I found it this morning, slipped under my door."

Jessica handed me the note. It was composed of letters and entire words cut from newspapers. Very traditional in the kidnap business.

"We have your daughter Veronica," Allie recited from memory. "Call off Reddy and Munroe. Next time, it will be an ear. After that, no next time. Your friend." She choked on the last word and finally spit it out with a sneer. Her eyes were hard. "Who is this Mihram you were talking about?"

"We don't have much more than a name at this point," Jessica responded. "Kamal Mihram. He lives in a beach-front manor in Queens, and he lives well. He probably has some legitimate business concerns or investments to justify his standard of living. He's certainly into a lot of dirty dealings."

Allie fidgeted. I could imagine her wringing out an imaginary handkerchief. "As soon as I got that package, I called Paris. That's where she was supposed to be. She wasn't there, I had to speak to the manager." Her eyes asked us to tell her it wasn't true. "My Veronica arrived in Paris with the group. She was there until yesterday. The manager informed me that I''—she gave a wry, humorless smile—''had sent a telegram asking her to come home at once. That I had arranged for a ticket to be picked up at the airport. It seems the wording of the telegram made her think I was ill. To think''—she twisted the imaginary handkerchief some more—''she gave up Paris for me.'' Her hands were suddenly still.

''He probably had some of his goons pick her up at the airport at this end,'' I said. ''She may be right here, in New York.''

''Do you think he's holding Veronica out there? In Queens?''

Jessica pursed her lips and shook her head in the negative. ''Not very likely, Allie. If he's as smart and as brutal as he appears, he probably keeps his personal life very separate from his business affairs.''

''So what you're saying is that you don't really know where to start looking for her.''

''I'm going to start by finding out what the cops have on him.'' She turned to me. ''Jason, you see what you can find out about his personal life.''

''Sure thing. Don't forget we have an appointment at three, Jess.''

She nodded. ''Allie, do you want to do something to help, or are you happy just criticizing?''

''Jessica, I didn't mean—''

Her voice softened. ''I'll bet you could trace Mihram's business interests for us. Find out what he's involved in. Especially if it's something that might come up in a future session of the assembly. Remember, the message on the blackmail tape said something about votes.''

''I don't know if I'll find out anything useful, but I'm glad to have something to do.''

''When do you think you'll have something?''

''Oh, I don't know.'' She considered. ''It depends.''

"On what?"

"On whether Mihram is trying to cover his tracks, for one thing. In that case, it would take a little longer."

"But it wouldn't be impossible?"

"Nothing is impossible, if you give it enough time. Every series of transactions leaves a paper trail. I have some contacts who can help me if I need it."

"Good. Use them. And let us know when you've about covered his operation."

We called on Mel Pierce at three o'clock in the office from which he represents the people of the 47th Assembly District. He was a short, ruddy man, round yet firm, with brown hair and blue eyes. A dapper dresser in a summer-weight Italian worsted, a soft silk shirt open at the collar, and matching suspenders. And a dark brown beard, neatly trimmed into a sort of Vandyke, which was not designed to hide the fact that he was a homosexual.

I suppose one might think I was jumping to a hasty conclusion, based on certain effeminate mannerisms of his. At least, that's what Jessica would think. She claims I'm homophobic, like many other of my ilk—male chauvinists, to be specific. I have enough ego to disagree with that judgment and have maintained to her on several separate occasions that sometimes you can just tell.

For all his dapper optimism and well-dressed enthusiasm, he was not a man one could by any stretch of the imagination call gay. That carefree adjective was belied by the assortment of deep and superficial frown lines on his forehead, around his eyes and down the sides of his face; the resolute set of his mouth; the worried jaw; the sharp, intelligent eyes.

I exchanged a glance with Jessica, leaving the brunt of the interview in her able hands. Maybe I am a little homophobic. At any rate, she gets along better with homosexuals than I do, both the male and female varieties.

"Mr. Pierce, thank you for seeing us. My partner and I happen to be working for a colleague of yours and we think it's likely that you may have found yourself in the same bind as our client."

Way to go, Jess.

Pierce just stared at her. His penetrating, calculating eyes willed, or dared, her to continue.

"Naturally, we can't divulge our client's name, but he"—I realized that Jessica chose the pronoun carefully—"is a colleague of yours in the state legislature. He was drugged and enticed into performing certain sexual exploits for the benefit of a hidden camera."

The expression on his face hadn't changed. I bet he fancies himself a poker pro, but I'd love to challenge him to a high-stakes game. Anyone who tries to feign disinterest in a story of drugs and sex and blackmail and political corruption is a fool.

"Our client wasn't about to take it lying down," which wasn't meant as a pun. Jessica is too straight for that. "He hired us to look into the matter. To find out who was behind it, what that party hoped to gain from it, and to retrieve the master tape or destroy it." She didn't bother to mention retrieving the client's kidnapped daughter.

There was a faint hint of a smile on Pierce's face. Either he wasn't as involved as we'd thought, or I should think twice about playing poker with him.

"Perhaps you've done some investigating on your own," Jessica continued. "Mightn't we all benefit from a pooling of resources?" Mightn't. Oh, boy. Only Jessica would try a word like that. Most people wouldn't know how to pronounce it.

Pierce let the smile beam. "Ms. Munroe, may I ask what made you think that I"—smile, smile—"was hooked into this ignoble scam? Just when and from whom did you get your information?''

''We heard it last week.'' Was it only last week? ''From an actor of dubious distinction named Vince Hartle, recently deceased.'' Straight from the ass's mouth, so to speak.

There was no look of recognition on Pierce's face.

''He also goes by the stage name of Big Jake Strong.''

Still no sign.

''He played in several of the incriminating tapes.''

''A support role,'' I put in. ''He played an ass.''

His eyes narrowed. So did his smile. ''That's all well and good, but I have to wonder what you are playing me for.'' His voice got stronger. ''You come in here quoting a dead man and expect me to jump right in and assist you in your investigation of another dead man.''

Jessica and I looked at each other. Then at Pierce, who was still talking.

''Yes, I know a little something about Matt Taylor's ring.'' Oh. ''There's been some scuttlebutt about it. But I've just found out that the man is dead. Happened over the weekend. That shouldn't have been too hard for a couple of crackerjack sleuths like you to discover. Hell, I was away all weekend and, even so, I obviously know more about it than you do. He was shot, by the way, and, for all intents and purposes, the blackmail caper is over.''

We sat silently, the three of us. A moment of silence for poor, dear, departed Matthew Andrew Taylor, whose timely death did nothing to stop the blackmail, no matter how convincing Mel Pierce could be to Mel Pierce.

''No, Mel.'' Jessica broke the silence. ''It's not over yet. No blackmail tapes were found in Taylor's house.'' I gave myself a little mental grin, noting that without the qualifier ''blackmail'' the statement would not be quite accurate. ''You see,'' she smiled, ''we do know a little something about it.'' Yeah. Enough to leave truly memorable body aches in all sorts of places.

Pierce leaned back in his chair. He eyed us cautiously, apparently measuring our capacity to damage him or, perhaps, to help him. ''Mel,'' Jessica countered, ''we can get past the did-you-or-didn't-you block. Let's just say that you didn't. From what you just told us, you heard certain rumors. You're a concerned citizen,'' she allowed. ''If you weren't, you would not have gone into politics in the first place. So, you don't like to see your colleagues hurt. Besides,'' she added, ''any stigma attached to a number of legislators could hurt the entire body.'' He was listening intently. ''So, say you decided to do a little investigating on your own.''

''Forget the rumors.'' He shook his head and smiled sadly. ''Let's just say, ahh, a close friend of mine in the assembly told me what happened. He swore me to secrecy so, naturally, I was reluctant to open up to you.'' He spread his hands wide in a gesture of openness. It was sincere. I was starting to like the guy. ''There are no rumors. I haven't heard a whisper from anyone else about it.''

''What happened to this friend of yours?''

Pierce's story—or his friend's—was achingly familiar. We compared Allie Walters's episode to his, leaving out names in both cases, of course. His friend had been to a party at Taylor's house in Brooklyn Heights and lost time somewhere between his second drink and 5 A.M. when he awakened in his car. Some time later he received the tape in the mail. He had a starring, if unattractive, role romping indecently in bed with a couple dressed up as a donkey and a rabbit.

''Ironic, isn't it? Having all that fun and then not even remembering a bit of it.''

''Was there a blackmail demand?''

''Not really. Not specifically. That was the strange

part. It was pretty vague. The idea was clear that sometime in the future my friend would be approached and told how to vote on a certain issue. Seems some people just like to have a politician in their pocket."

"Is your friend going to stay in politics?"

"Well, the activities on that tape are not what you'd call politically popular, Jessica. May I call you Jessica?"

"Of course."

"Is that what people call you? Or, is it Jessie?"

Jessica made a face. "Jessica will do just fine."

"Well, Jessica, this friend of mine was always ambitious. Always cultivating important contacts. Hell, that's what he was doing at Taylor's party in the first place. He never expected to stay in the assembly forever. But," he concluded wistfully, "he figured to be moving up—not out of the game altogether."

"Did your friend go to anyone else with his problem? Besides you, that is."

I smiled a little. I couldn't help it. Pierce examined his hands. "If you're asking did he hire a private investigator, no. He didn't think of it." He examined his hands some more. "He was used to playing his personal life close to the vest."

He looked up. "I, ahh, we did some heavy thinking about it, though. And a bit of light research into the assembly's activities. Until today, that is. When I returned to the city and found out that Taylor was dead, well . . . I just assumed that . . ."

He looked to the ceiling in a classical pose of supplication. Looking for divine intervention, perhaps? If so, he was connecting with the divinity of fluorescent lighting. Jessica and I are definitely not divine, although sometimes a girlfriend will tell me that I am, but I felt it was about time we held up our end of this give-and-take.

"I think maybe we ought to fill you in on what's going on at our end," I said, "because we know definitely that the blackmail scam is still on track. That's something you'll probably want to get back to your friend about." He rolled his eyes. I've got to ask Jessica if that's an acquired skill or if you're born with it, like good bone structure. At any rate, I was liking him better all the time. "You see, Mel—Is that what people call you, Mel?"

"Sure."

"Not Melvin?"

"Mel's fine," he said drily.

"Melrose?"

He looked at Jessica. "Some wise guy, your partner."

"Melville?"

"Mister Pierce to you." He grinned. "And may I say that with a name like Jason, I wouldn't think you'd go around casting stones."

"Okay, okay." I grinned back. "Anyway. Jessica and I happen to know that no blackmail tapes were recovered from Taylor's house, because we were there when the cops went through the place. And, Pierce, weren't you afraid that someone would find the tape and contact you? The cops? Whoever?"

Pierce looked uncomfortable, but if he noticed the pronoun he didn't say anything about it. "Haven't you ever heard of wishful thinking, Reddy?"

"Sorry, I was out of line."

He waved a hand. "That's okay. I already know you're a wiseass. Fact is, I'm starting to be kind of glad you two stopped in today and set me straight. One thing politics teaches you—whatever the reality is, whether you like it or not, it's there. You gotta work with it." Words of wisdom. I hope he hires a speech writer come election time.

"Anyway," I continued, "they say that all roads lead to Rome, and all our leads are leading to a guy by the name of Kamal Mihram."

"Is he connected? I never heard of him."

"We don't know much about him yet. Except that he lives in Queens and deals in controlled substances and favors the direct approach."

"Meaning what?"

"Meaning since we started on this case, he's been sending out hits on us, Jessica and me, like tennis balls out of one of those machines they use for practicing serves."

Pierce frowned and looked at Jessica for confirmation. She nodded. "Compared to that kind of action," he said, "a little blackmail sounds almost tame."

"Like standard operating procedure?"

He shook his head. "Not at all standard. In fact, that's what seemed funny about this whole thing to start with."

"What do you mean, Mel?" Jessica asked.

"Well, whatever happened to plain old-fashioned lobbying? Contrary to what the media will have you believe, corruption is not our usual way of doing business."

"Do you think this has something to do with the mob?"

He considered a moment. "It seems like it could. But, I don't know. I have some contacts who are connected—" He paused for a second, but only a second. "So does my friend. And you'd think they would have sent feelers out first before trying such a heavy-handed stunt. But if this were a massive operation—Do you know how many legislators are involved?"

Jessica shrugged. "Perhaps ten or a dozen or so."

"I don't know. It could be that some of the families are behind it, but it really seems too heavy-handed, even for them. And I never heard of this Mihram guy."

"Should you have?" I said sharply.

He gave a wry smile. "Maybe a blackmail ring can still shock me, Reddy, but I never said I was a virgin. I got some contacts. You have to, in my business."

"Getting back on track," Jessica said, getting back on track, "you said that you and your, umm, friend did some heavy thinking. Do you mind sharing it with us?"

Pierce didn't answer right away. He put his feet up on the desk and leaned back comfortably in his chair, clasping his hands around his paunchy middle. He stared at the ceiling for a moment and then closed his eyes. "First of all, I think we can dispense with the crap about my friend," he said softly. A smile flickered on his face. "It was getting awkward anyway.

"When I realized that I had been filmed in a very compromising situation for the sake of my vote in the legislature, I asked some vague and hypothetical questions of those contacts I mentioned, the ones that are connected to the mob. I came up empty. I really believed that they weren't behind it, that it was someone operating independently of any of the New York families. But, I didn't know if I was singled out for this attention or if other politicians were involved as well. Frankly, I thought my closet was being raided." He looked at me for a moment, then closed his eyes again.

"That's understandable," I said.

He smiled. Jessica rested her hand lightly on my knee. It felt good. It was a gesture of approval, but I thought it would burn a hole through my slacks.

"Then I thought—votes! Whoever is doing this, is after my vote. Whoever it is went to an awful lot of trouble for my vote. Whatever it is, it must be important, it must be big bucks, it must be more votes than just mine that they're after." He crossed his feet on the desk and uncrossed them again. "So, I decided to check into what I might be voting on in the next session, which begins in January."

"Why didn't we think of that?" I asked Jessica.

"Nobody's perfect," Pierce said. He held up the middle three fingers of his left hand. "I decided that of all the bills that are or might go through the assembly in the next session—that's when we do our most important work, when we vote on bills—there are three that might be profitable enough to warrant such a heavy, ahh, initial investment." He counted off on his fingers. "One. A major highway is scheduled to be built somewhere in the vicinity of New York City. So long-distance haulers can bypass the traffic on Manhattan Island, should they so desire. I don't know yet what route the highway is supposed to take." He shrugged. "Maybe that's still being worked out in committee.

"Two. A casino gambling bill will be proposed in the next session. Similar to one that was defeated in the last session, but by a shaky margin. It'll probably go through."

"Statewide?"

"Naw. It's gotta be in a specific region. Like New Jersey has Atlantic City. They're considering four areas, far as I know. Coney Island, Long Beach, the Catskills, and Far Rockaway. A lot of developers and some little guys have been buying up land in those areas. Right now, it's still cheap. After the bill goes through, forget it." He considered. "I know some guys who are investing heavily in Long Beach.

"Three. Somebody's gonna be awarded a juicy contract—something about converting garbage into high-yield energy. A lot of companies are fighting for the privilege—some of them so new, the paint on the door is still wet." He made a face. "So we're gonna vote on a bond issue to raise the cash. It'll take plenty of cash, believe me."

He held up a fourth finger and waved it in the air. "Or, I could be dead wrong about these three. There could be something else that hasn't even been put together yet.

"You know, through it all, I keep thinking of the saying, the one about your sins coming home to roost.

There's one sin I've committed, there is, and it's got my soul in a grip so firm I can't ever get loose. Just one sin."

"What's that?" I asked.

Looking me straight in the eye, he responded, "I got into politics."

Then he laughed.

14

"IS ALLIE STILL going to meet us at noon?"

"That's what she said." Jessica stopped eating to look at her wristwatch. It was 12:25. We had agreed to meet at the restaurant to share what we had each learned since yesterday. She shrugged.

"Think she backed out again?"

"You still haven't told me what made you decide that Mel Pierce is a homosexual."

"Just a feeling I got, Jess."

She nodded and went back to her food, some kind of vegetable masquerading as meatballs.

"Hey, Jess. Did you ever think that maybe humans weren't intended to eat grasses and other vegetables? Look at that, for example. We're always trying to make vegetables look like something else so people will want to eat them. Vegetarian burgers, meatballs, chopped liver, chili, franks. Did you ever think that maybe all of that's telling us something?"

She gave me a blank stare.

"I mean, you never see meat made up to look like celery."

She returned her attention to her plate.

"Or sprouts." I pierced my steak with a fork and slit through it with the knife. Brown and red juices trickled onto its leafy bed. "I wonder if Allie came up with anything interesting on Mihram."

"So do I, Red."

I signaled the waitress for some coffee. Jessica was

working on a lime Perrier. "I finally finished the bathroom."

"What?"

"You know, the book you gave me about the ladies' restroom."

"You're crazy."

"Isn't that what it was called?"

"It's called *The Women's Room,* as you very well know. Not *The Bathroom.*"

"Oh. I got mixed up. Probably because it belongs in the bathroom."

"Well, I'm sorry you didn't like the book. Every one of my women friends found something in this book to identify with, some personal experience to refer to and say: 'Yes! That happened to me, just that way.' "

"I'll read it through again."

She grinned. "I don't think it'll do you a bit of good."

"I'm hopeless."

"You're okay."

"She should have married that guy in the book."

"Maybe." She munched a little, musing. "You have to understand her point of view–"

"You have to understand his point of view, too."

"He wanted children, she didn't."

"Of course, he wanted children—he didn't have any. She did. She was being selfish."

"She executed her free will, made a choice."

"She ended up a lonely old cat lady on a lonely beach."

She thought about this. "Remember 'Match, hot'?"

"Huh?"

"At one point during her suburban housewife years, she described the feeling of responsibility that a mother has toward a small child as 'Hot! Match hot!' Meaning that no matter what else you are doing, you must always be on the alert for any trouble the tot may get into. For instance, if you see the little one playing with matches you have to be ready to stop whatever you are doing and warn 'Match hot!' It's a heavy responsibility from which there is no relief."

"Still," I said stubbornly, "He had a right to have children, one child. A baby would have been a joint effort—" I grinned. "I mean even after it was born. They could have done anything they desired, together. Even with a baby."

Just as Jessica was about to respond Allie slipped quickly and quietly into her seat. I hadn't noticed her arrival. It was 1:20.

"Sorry I'm late," she said breathlessly.

Her face looked drawn, the skin around her eyes, which jittered nervously back and forth as she spoke, was puffy and darkened. Her brown hair hung flat and lifeless, held in place by two oversized bobby pins. Her simple cotton shift, yellow-flowered on white, contrasted sharply with her mood—a heavy air of unexpressed depression and anxiety.

"How are you holding up?" Jessica asked.

"Oh, fine," Allie said, not sounding fine. She ordered a bowl of lentil soup and when it arrived she crumbled four huge whole-grain crackers into it. Jessica and I were on our dessert.

"Any word about Veronica?"

"Huh? Yes, I'm fine. I just told you I was fine, didn't I?" Allie lifted her teaspoon from the table, examined it, put it back down. Then she picked up her soupspoon and stirred her soup idly as she sat staring into it.

"Allie, cut it out. You don't have to put on an act for us and you're not doing a very good job of it, anyway." I watched the cracked crackers swim around and around. The sinking feeling in my stomach completely eliminated any appetite I'd had for my dessert.

"I did all right at the office. Nobody realized that anything was wrong. Or, nobody cared."

"We're not nobody," I continued. "We're friends." The cracker pieces moved slower, like so many abandoned life rafts. "Or we'd like to be."

"Friends, sure," she said. And stirred some more.

I waited. Jessica sipped her Perrier.

"I had friends once," she said, ruminating.

"Once?"

"Then I got married, and Arthur was my friend. Then Veronica came along, and I was too busy to keep up social contacts. Somewhere along the way I think I lost the ability to keep a friend, or be a friend."

"You mean you have no one to go to now?" Jessica asked. "Just to talk?"

She ignored her. "Arthur and Veronica were enough for me." The American dream. "Then, when I started working again, friends were people you networked with because you might need them one day. You know, something to be cultivated. Then I lost Arthur, and . . ." She stared into her lentil soup in the manner of a drunkard about to start crying into his beer. "So don't tell me about friendship. I don't have any real friends, I never needed any before. Besides, I'm paying you and you're working for me, and that's the only reason you're even here right now."

"Also, the food's good," I said, wide-eyed. She smiled. I reached across the corner of the table and took her hand. It was warm and moist. She seemed about to pull away, but then she didn't. I squeezed her hand gently. She squeezed back.

All of a sudden, she didn't seem so hard anymore. Her features softened and her eyes looked wet. I pressed my advantage. "You're right, Allie," I said. "You're paying us to do a job and we're doing it. But I like you," I said simply, "for free. And if I had to make a guess, I'd say

Jessica feels the same way. So," I took a breath, "maybe you can lower your guard a little and let us in? We can use a friend, too, you know."

She shook her head. A strand of hair grazed the top of her soup and she pulled her hand away to wipe it clean. Then, surreptitiously, almost shyly, she replaced it in mine. "I don't have anything to give to a friendship right now. And I was never really the type who could take without giving something in return."

"Allie, you're in a tough spot, but I am confident that both you and your daughter will come out of this all right. Jessica and I will do everything in our power to see to that, but it won't just end there. We've been through too much together. We're with you for the long haul."

Jessica took hold of Allie's other hand. "That goes for me too, Allie," she said. I noticed that each clasped the other's hand tightly.

Allie pulled away and mopped up her moist face with a table napkin. She wasn't wearing any makeup. "Goodness," she said eyeing her plate. "This looks awful." Jessica signaled the waitress and I ordered an omelet with a side order of Greek salad.

"Got to have those veggies," I said.

Allie ate a little, if listlessly. "You guys have a special rate for friends?" she asked.

I put down my coffee cup and looked over at her. "Sure. We charge friends more." Jessica was stacking our dishes for the waitress.

"More!" in mock shock. "Why more?"

"Naturally, we assume our friends would be grateful for the opportunity to help our little business succeed."

Allie rested her chin on her palms, her elbows on the table. She looked better. Somewhat better. "I miss her," she said simply. "I started to miss her as soon as she got on the plane with the rest of her group. When she was young, I used to resent being tied to her and her diapers and the kitchen and the laundry room. I used to feel somehow it was her fault—maybe in collusion with Arthur—that I was imprisoned in a world of my own making. I used to fantasize about the future, the so-called empty nest stage—when I would be free and on my own. Well, let me tell you something." She crossed her arms, resting them on the table, and hugged her elbows. "That's a fiction. There's an invisible umbilical cord that never gets cut. Call it apron strings. Call it what you like. You're happy with them, you're sad with them. You worry about them. When you have a kid, you really sign up for the long haul." She smiled. "When she's sixty and I'm eighty-four, I'll probably still worry about her." She bit her lip and glanced at me. "How's that for optimism?" she whispered.

"Admirable," I said and signaled Jessica that we could get back to business now.

"I don't know about you," Jessica began, "but I didn't turn up anything on Mihram before the early eighties. Either he kept his nose very clean and his profile very low, or else he just wasn't here." Jessica spread her notes out on the table. The waitress had removed the dishes except for the coffee cups, which she refilled with fresh brewed decaf and Jessica's second glass of lime Perrier.

"He wasn't here." Allie dug a stenographer's notebook out from her large white purse. "He arrived in New York City in 1980, from Lebanon. Whether he's a native Lebanese or not and where he's from originally, I could not determine."

"I think most Lebanese started out being from somewhere else," Jessica said.

"Sounds like the U.S. of A."

"Not quite." Allie made a face. "But, anyway, I would guess he'd feel more comfortable in New York than, say, Nebraska."

"That agrees with my information," I offered. "He bought his house, the manor in Queens that he lives in now, in 1983. I don't know where he lived before that."

"In Brooklyn," Jessica said. "Atlantic Avenue. That area. There's a small Moslem-Arab community there. Depressed economically."

"I know it," I said. "I pass the neighborhood stores sometimes."

"Some of his real estate holdings are in that area, although they're not at all profitable. I don't know why he holds onto them."

"Oh, they're profitable," Jessica corrected her. "There's just no paper trail." She used her fingers to count off. "Drug fronts. Prostitution. Numbers." She looked at her fingers with disgust. "He used to keep a small army of soldiers and hire out the muscle, but it seems he got out of that business and now"—she looked at me wryly—"he hires his own muscle elsewhere as he needs it."

"Who does he get his thugs from now, pray tell?"

"I can tell you who he used up till a couple of days ago. Now, I don't know."

"He does keep a full-time armed guard on his house," I said, "in six-hour shifts, so there's got to be at least three or four guys."

"*Six*-hour shifts?"

"He wants them alert. Rumor is he keeps a lot of cash around. Maybe he doesn't trust banks or, more likely, he just needs plenty of cash at hand for his business."

Jessica shrugged. "Since we're talking personnel, he has two guys that have been with him from the beginning. In the early days, he used to hire them out or send them on jobs, but recently they've been with him at all times. Bodyguards, I suppose."

I nodded. "I know. He's rarely seen without them."

"Hassan Nesar. Five-foot-five, but don't let his size

fool you. He's an expert with a knife. Throwing, stabbing, slashing."

Allie turned a little white. I didn't blame her. I don't much care for knives either.

"Norton Jackson. Six-foot-three. A tough ex-con. Spent ten years in the slammer for manslaughter. Mihram picked him up on practically his first morning out."

"Should we try to get some pictures of them?"

I reached into my shirt pocket and pulled out a photocopy of a newspaper article, a wedding announcement to be exact. The headline read, "Real estate tycoon to wed Long Island beauty." Obviously not the *New York Times*. Together with the accompanying photographs, it seemed almost like a retelling of the story of Beauty and the Beast. There were separate photographs of Mihram and a pretty girl with an open face and a hopeful smile. The article was dated February 12, 1985. The girl, Betsy Ashton, was twenty years old and a former Miss Long Island.

"He's still a bachelor," I clarified. "Forty-one years old, five-foot-nine inches or so. Vicious temper from all accounts. Weakness for blondes." Allie winced. I could have kicked myself. The two women examined the photograph. It showed a swarthy, slender man, with shaggy eyebrows and a thick, bushy mustache, who looked every one of his forty-one years. "He won't win any beauty contests," I said.

"You're not one to judge," Jessica said with a grin. She's right. When they were giving out handsome, I must have been taking a nap.

"He likes to keep five or six women at a time," I said. "One at the house, sort of steady, and the others spread out around town. Not always the same women."

"Ahh," Jessica said. "A soul brother."

I showed her my fist. "I ought to belt you one."

"This is a wedding announcement," Allie pointed out. "Why do you say he's a bachelor?"

"I can fill that one in," Jessica said. "A guy I used to work with said he heard that this Mihram once had an American girlfriend who ditched him for somebody else. As a matter of fact, I think it was this same girl, he said she had been in a beauty contest. Anyhow, soon after, the girl went off to California—alone. Her lover staggered into the hospital one day with his face dripping blood. It had been slashed and needed hundreds of stitches. One of his ears was missing. Word was, the girl received the ear in the mail shortly before she left town."

I pointed to the headline. "Is this his cover? Real estate?"

"It's more than just a cover," Allie responded. "It's a legitimate business concern. Strong and growing." She flipped a few pages in her notebook. "He picked up some lucrative parcels over the years in Staten Island, Brooklyn, and Hoboken. One in Manhattan. Some very wise investment decisions, except for that Atlantic Avenue area which is a loss on the books. He turned a few over at a large profit. Built on others and is reaping nice rewards. He has his own management company to oversee construction, maintenance, etcetera.

"He's still investing." She consulted her notes again. "Now it's upstate New York, in the Catskill Mountains region. Some of the land is very cheap up there. For good reason—it's a low-activity area." Jessica and I exchanged looks. "He's done some heavy buying near Swan Lake and Liberty and elsewhere. I've got the listings here. He's already purchased five old hotels that folded, and the grounds around them."

"Part of the so-called Borscht Belt."

Allie went on. "He's concentrated at least twenty million dollars into Catskill properties. Highly speculative." She turned to me. "He also has that piece of real estate in Queens, but that's for his personal use."

I nodded. "Mihram's house is a twenty-room mansion on a quarter-acre plot in Belle Harbor, Queens. Right on the beach. The beach is a public one—it belongs to the city—but it's far enough away from subways, parks, and the boardwalk so that it's practically private property. There's even an entrance to the house from the beach."

"Alarmed?" Jessica asked.

"Natch. To the hilt. But no dogs, he hates dogs. Just the armed guards and, of course, his own two personal bodyguards, when he's at home."

"What about the safe?"

"Burglarproof, fireproof, what-have-you-proof. And huge. It's a vault."

"One thing I couldn't trace," Allie said, "is where his funds came from originally. I think there would have been some record if he arrived in this country with a large sum of cash. Certainly, if he wired it over. If it's important, I can keep searching."

"Don't bother," said Jessica. "You'd probably just find that he supposedly raised the capital from among his friends. More than likely he made it the old-fashioned way—by cheating the less fortunate slobs of society out of whatever pennies they managed to get ahold of. Those Atlantic Avenue businesses again."

"Sounds like he's his own mob," I said.

"That's true," Jessica said. "He's not connected with any of the New York families. In fact, the story goes, when another group tried to muscle in on his territory—a small Brooklyn gang, headed by one-time Black Panther Franklin Davis—the move was suddenly aborted. Police found Davis and his four top guns in a deserted third-floor loft on Fourth Avenue. Their throats were cut. Very messy."

"Mihram walked?"

"Certainly. No evidence."

Allie appeared preoccupied. I tapped her on the shoulder. When she came out of her reverie, she asked, "What's the chance that my Veronica is in that house on the beach?"

"Uh-uh," I said. "I don't think so." I already knew where we'd have to go next.

She sighed. "How are we supposed to know what to do now?"

I tapped her notebook. Jessica said, "If they're holding your daughter in New York, the probability is that she is in the Catskills right now."

"Jessica's right. A deserted hotel provides a perfect spot for someone to hide out with a kidnap victim, or for any other reason."

She looked confused. "Is that what he's buying all that land for? Hideouts? It seems to me like overkill."

"No, I think the land is intended for another purpose," Jessica said. "Remember a bill you voted on last session, Allie? The casino gambling bill."

Allie nodded. "It was defeated. We'll probably be voting on it again next year."

"How did you vote?"

"I was opposed, of course, Jessica. That's what my people pay me for."

"If the bill passes," I asked, "where will the casinos be built?"

"Well, when the bill comes before the legislature we're going to be considering several—" Her eyes opened wide. "One of the areas being considered, not too seriously, is the Catskill Mountain area. But you knew that already. How?"

While Jessica explained to Allie about our visit with one of her esteemed colleagues, I paid the tab, which included some food packed up to go. Healthy fast food: a contradiction in terms. Thick sandwiches, oversized bran muffins filled with blueberries and walnuts, some drinks, paper plates, plastic cups, and utensils. We needed the provisions for our quest, which would take us through the mountains of New York's Catskill region, looking for the fair-haired daughter of our fair assemblywoman.

Match hot.

15

THE LONG DRIVE up to the Catskills was uneventful, marked by uninteresting if pleasant chitchat and prolonged silences. Jessica and I could not engage in our favorite current topic of conversation, namely, marriage and babies, specifically, marriage to Sanford Foxworth, Jr., and having his babies. We refrained from that sort of talk because Allie had hitched herself along with us, if not for the duration then at least for the ride, and any mention of children was liable to put the droop back in her eyes and an anxious silence on her parted lips. Allie returned to the subject of New York Catskill real estate.

"This area has been really depressed, in a financial sense, for perhaps fifteen years. Plenty of hotels and resorts have been forced to close down in financial ruin. Buyers are not exactly swarming in with offers, although there have been a handful of individuals interested in summer homes—a few developers, and some hopeful speculators. Mihram had no trouble picking up those five parcels. He could easily obtain five or a dozen more."

"Looks like the Borscht Belt boom has fizzed out."

"What happened?" Jessica asked.

"I'm not really sure. Maybe people are simply vacationing elsewhere. Also, more planning and effort goes into vacations nowadays. People have more discretionary income than they used to and, rather than simply taking a Greyhound to the country, they go on cruises, to the Islands, Acapulco, the West Coast, or else to a more fashionable country spot like the Poconos. The Catskill facilities are old-fashioned and run-down. As the money left the area, a lot of places weren't maintained very well."

"So, if casino gambling is approved for this area, there's suddenly going to be a lot of activity here again."

"That's true, Jason. And Mihram stands to profit outrageously."

Jessica nodded in agreement. "A lot of the people who owned run-down properties near Atlantic City's boardwalk became instantly wealthy."

"Speaking of boardwalk and other means of access," I asked no one in particular, "how does Mihram expect all those gamblers to flock to casinos out here? It's a long trip from the city, and some of the smaller roads you encounter once you get off the highway are real killers. They can be narrow, slippery in a rain, unlit. And don't forget the huge, crippling snowstorms they sometimes get up here."

"You know," Jessica said, "he might just be planning to sell once the bill goes through. That in itself will net him a tidy profit."

"That's true," added Allie, "but from what you've told me about Mihram, he seems more like the type to go after the profits that can be made off of a going gambling concern. Anyway, if the bill passes, whoever gets involved in construction and development is going to have to consider the access problem. Maybe," she mused, "a heliport. Yes. That might just do it."

Over halfhearted protests, we dropped Allie off at a motel just outside of Monticello, with promises to call just as soon as we had any information about Veronica. It occurred to us belatedly, getting back in the Cutlass, that whereas we had gladly left the oppressive heat of the city behind, neither one of us had thought to bring a jacket or sweater, necessary protection against the cool mountain night. It was just late afternoon, and the air was still summer warm. Jessica was driving. I snuggled closer, anticipating the need for warmth. I didn't have a jacket, after all.

We had drawn up a list of Mihram's Catskill holdings. Our first stop was in Swan Lake, some 120 miles out of New York City, at a darkened empty resort once called The Fisherman. What we expected were cabins shaped like fishing boats, decor held together by a motif of coarse and fine fishing nets, rods and reels, bait and tackle, and plenty of large and small mounted trophies representing the luck of the fisherman and the skill of the taxidermist. Instead we found a large, staid old main house on a small grassy hill set off from the surrounding acreage, white stucco and shingle surrounded by a comfortable expanse of wide porch made for rocking, quiet conversation, and appreciating the scenic woodland beyond. Here and there, tattered strips of canvas rippled from a metal frame that had once formed the spine of an elaborate awning.

The area around the house was covered with several varieties of grasses grown long and wild. Off to the side was a cluster of crabapple trees. A quick rustling of leaves caught my eye, and I could just make out the elated thrust of a small squirrel's furry tail, its bearer making good its escape with the small green prize of an early crabapple.

In the distant background, a bevy of large, unrestrained blueberry bushes, grown wild with neglect and heavy with fruit, beckoned invitingly to the busy squirrel and its woodland comrades. My mouth watered.

Although we would have preferred to leave the car somewhere out of sight from the hotel, the road that took us there was a narrow country road, barely wide enough to allow one to pass oncoming traffic let alone maneuver around parked vehicles. We drove up on the embankment and parked the car under the shade of the crab-apple trees.

The place looked quite deserted. There were no other structures in sight, and we approached the large house stealthily, circling round about and to the side. Our .38s were tucked into our waistbands; we held our flashlights loosely at our sides. The windows and doors appeared to have been boarded up a long time ago. We looked in vain for signs of fresh footprints, for places where the grass might have been trampled, for signs of recent vandalism.

In the back, beside the old water main, we found an opening at the ground level where a wooden barrier had been ripped away to expose a portion of a glassless window. The damage did not look recent: the torn ragged edge of the wood was as weatherworn as the clean-cut surface all around. We were barely breathing. Jessica lifted herself through the opening. I followed.

It took us about an hour to search the house from bottom to top, but when we finished we were certain that it had not been inhabited recently, even as a temporary stopover. Veronica Walters wasn't there.

She wasn't in Liberty either, where the place in question had been known in its heyday as the Liberty Manor Resort and was located near the old Grossinger's Hotel and Resort, famous for its spacious grounds, country hospitality, and down-home Jewish cooking. We passed Grossinger's on the way. It, too, was dark and quiet. I remembered hearing somewhere that it was to be renovated into condominium apartments.

The buildings and grounds were enclosed within a fence of chain link eight feet high. This is it, we thought. But it wasn't. The fence had been erected some years previously, probably when the place folded, in an effort to keep local vandals from further reducing its resale value. We climbed the fence easily.

In addition to a large main house, which was similar in

structure to the one we'd visited in Swan Lake, there were about a dozen one- and two-room cabins arranged in a semicircle around the main house, a pool house, and several clapboard cabanas, which were still standing, along with a large single-room structure that we guessed had been some sort of meeting room. Needless to say, it took us considerably longer to complete a thorough search of the manor and its appendages. By the time we were satisfied that we were through, we could see twilight in the shadowing skies and felt it in the chill of the air on our bare arms.

The town of South Fallsburg was the next stop. We each had a sandwich in the car. I downed a cup of coffee hurriedly purchased at a small diner that was closing for the day. Things sure close down early in the country.

"The folks in the diner said that there's a little motel just two miles out of town"—I looked around—"if you can call this a town."

"The next place is around here somewhere."

"It's getting kind of late, Jess."

"There's still some light yet. Night falls fairly late this time of year."

"And cold. But the main thing is, the way this town is closing down—and we're on Main Street, no less—if we don't at least register soon, the motel will probably put on its no-vacancy sign."

"You're not tired, Red, are you?"

"Who said anything about tired?" I said huskily. Then, "A little," I admitted.

"It's all that coffee you drink. You're fairly intelligent. You should be able to understand that the jolt of caffeine that you get produces an equal and opposite reaction, a letdown effect—"

"Let's go, Jess." I sighed. "Drive."

I swear, she was holding back a smile.

There was no fence surrounding the Lakehouse Inn.

In the hazy onrush of nightfall, we could make out no human footprints in the grassy path, no telltale light within, no broken windows. We did, however, pick up on the brown Chevy parked just in front of the gaping, abandoned swimming pool.

My throat tightened. For the thousandth time I cursed my favorite sweater for staying put at home without me. It was getting dark quickly.

The name "Inn" did not do justice to a sprawling country mansion of no less than three stories, which had probably at one time—even before it was converted into a hotel—boasted a hundred rooms, a grand spiral staircase, many servants, and a fine country gentleman and lady to run it. The ubiquitous wooden boards covered the windows. Here, too, the overgrown native flora was in a state of active encroachment. On the east side of the building, which had once been mostly windows, one of a row of ugly plywood sheets had been carefully removed. Unlike the Chevy, it would hardly be noticed from the road.

The window opened into a huge formal dining room, large enough to hold a couple of hundred hungry vacationers. We trod silently across dusty parquet floors. We didn't hit any loose floorboards, thanks either to our good fortune or to the construction of a manor that had been extremely well maintained. The dusty, musky air was practically overpowering. I tried not to breathe too deeply.

As our eyes adjusted to the darkness, we could see heavy, satin drapes framing what would have been a wall of continuous windows overlooking a panoramic mountainous view. Some large, round tables and some small, square ones lay overturned in a corner. The few wooden chairs in sight, scattered here and there, had seen better days. A frayed tapestry clung to one wall. On another, a set of swinging doors appeared to lead to the kitchen.

One of the two large double doors opposite us was slightly ajar, just a crack really, enough to allow for a pencil-thin line of artificial light. We headed for it. No creaks, please. No creaks.

The room we were looking into as we peered through the crack in the door had once been the main lobby of the establishment. It was huge. The front entrance opened onto a room with elegantly ornate wall and ceiling decorations, now dingy and withered; lush oriental-patterned carpeting, now faded, frayed, and worn; and, very probably, a tasteful arrangement of overstuffed, inviting, and elegant furnishings, now missing. At present, the only pieces of furniture in the room were a card table, on which stood a small, battery-powered lamp providing light for the room; a pair of large sofas, unusable with stuffing escaping from the ripped upholstery, springs exposed, broken legs and spine; and a single army cot.

The jean-clad girl on the cot sat in repose, legs stretched out in front of her, hands in her lap, face cast downward in thought. Her blond hair hung forward listlessly. We could see where a chunk had been snipped off. Three sleeping bags angled at each other on the floor next to the cot.

A scan of the room revealed three weapons: two in the shoulder holsters of the two guys—one blond and bearded, the other a cleanshaven redhead—playing cards at the small table, and a sawed-off shotgun resting on the floor in the right hand of the third guy, sprawled out in front of a slick magazine. He looked a little like Charles Manson. As we watched, he turned the magazine sideways and some spittle ran down his moldy beard. He was, clearly, the cerebral one of the group.

Across the lobby, along the west side of the building, were the remains of the guest-services area. The long marble counter still remained, along with the matrix of cubbyholes behind it. The fourth wall had two doors. One bore the legend *Cowboys*, the other, *Cowgirls*.

Approaching the situation via the door we were peeking through was out of the question. The heavy couch blocking the doorway was piled high with junk, and any noise on our part would put them on their guard immediately. We didn't want to do that. The element of surprise was still on our side and we wanted to keep it there.

As if reading my mind, Jessica backed carefully away from the door. We slipped out again through the same unboarded window and searched for another way in.

Around back, the water supply had been turned on. I wondered whether the ancient plumbing in the building could still support a supply of pressurized water coursing through it. Two bathroom windows, clearly the respective domains of the Cowboys and the Cowgirls, were small, set high, and impossible to see through—one more so than the other because it was boarded up solidly. The plywood on the other window hung on a single, rusty nail and came off easily.

I made a trip to the car for our trusty supply of duct tape and a glass cutter. Applying a strip of tape to the windowpane, wrapping the ends of the strip around my left hand and holding tight, I reached up and applied the glass cutter with my right. A jagged rectangle almost the full size of the window itself adhered obligingly to the tape. I removed the glass carefully and Jessica laid it on the ground just as carefully. The quieter we could be, the greater the impact of the surprise when we showed up inside.

I held my breath as Jessica lifted her butt gingerly over the sharp, jagged cut edge and let herself down into the dark bathroom. For good measure, she wore the roll of duct tape around her slim wrist, like a bracelet. You never know when you'll need a roll of good, strong tape.

I'm a little bit broader than Jessica. And I'm not referring to my political/social orientation. The glass cut me on my right upper arm, although after the initial shock I hardly noticed it until much later.

"Surprise!" The door to one of the cubicles slammed open.

He was holding the sawed-off shotgun in one hand and arranging his fly with the other. I wondered briefly why he needed to take a shotgun along with him when he went to the bathroom. I didn't know what he'd had in mind, but if asked I could make a few pointed suggestions.

The door to the lobby, Cowboys, from the looks of things, was open a bit so that a weak beam of light filtered through. His matted facial hair parted to reveal a yellow-toothed grin. I could have done without the light.

Charles Manson's lookalike frisked us more expertly than I would have thought him capable. But then, I wouldn't have thought him capable of fixing his fly either. He wrenched the roll of tape off of Jessica's arm and tossed it on the floor in disgust. Then, he discovered our unconcealed weapons and flashlights and dropped them on the floor along with the tape. One of the flashlights rolled toward the door. He looked for more items, apparently believing that Jessica had hidden something dangerous in her bosom or in her panties. It took him a long time. When he decided he was finished, he was still grinning at us. Trickles of warm, slippery blood slid down my arm.

The small, battery-powered lamp served to keep the large room shrouded, but it was at least more dim than dark. You couldn't really hope to read except right near it. The cardplayers at the table were probably barely able to make out the faces on the playing cards that dropped from their hands as we were marched in from the john. Veronica looked up but didn't say anything.

Manson's shotgun poked us in the back and directed us toward the card table so that the others could get a good look at us. The redhead jumped up and drew his weapon, followed quickly by his fellow kidnapping card shark.

"Do you know who you got there, Meat?" he asked Charlie Manson. I didn't think I wanted to know why he was called Meat. "It's the detective lady and Dick Tracy. They're worth plenty to us dead." I wondered briefly why Jessica always got top billing.

"Yeah?" Manson-Meat grinned and steadied the shotgun expertly at our backs. Maybe he never stopped grinning. "Guess it was lucky I was in the john, huh, Duke?" The redhead was Duke and obviously in charge. Probably, that's the reason he'd been awarded a royal title.

Jessica said to Veronica, "You all right, hon?" Hon? From me, that would be considered sexist.

"You dummy, you're *always* in the john."

"I'm okay," she answered, looking at me. The right side of my shirt was soaked with blood. "You're not very *good* detectives, are you?"

"Don't call me dummy." Still grinning. "I'm not dumb."

BlondBeard was silent.

Then all proverbial hell broke loose.

The card table was introduced to Jessica's foot and tumbled over in appreciation. The lamp hit the floor, breaking its plastic casing and sending the batteries rolling. This, I'm guessing. As soon as the lamp hit the floor, everything went black. There is no dark quite so dark as a night in the countryside in an unlit house with boards covering its windows.

Meat was still behind me. I just didn't know how close. I dropped to the floor and rolled quickly in his direction. Two revolutions and I rammed against his ankles without stopping, tripping him and freeing the shotgun from his grasp. The weapon bounded away, discharging a lonely blue blast a couple of yards off. No one cried out.

Just then, BlondBeard made the mistake of firing at Jessica's moving form. He did this in an attempt to save his pal Duke the Red. Undaunted by the darkness, Jessica had already disarmed him and delivered a blow to his groin and a butt to his head. At the shot, she left Duke to come out of his daze on his own and zoomed in on the flash from BlondBeard's gun, which had given away his position. I heard a crack followed immediately by a snap, the kind of sound sequence that I was sure meant a fatal kick to the chin. Jessica can be fun to spar with but when it's for real, calling her a lethal weapon is not an overstatement.

You might say that the odds were even now. I heard Jessica tussling with Duke. I heard Meat slowly picking himself up. I took a chance.

"Veronica are you still—" Suddenly, I lost air. Big, beefy hands encircled me from behind and squeezed my chest. The winner of the Most Foulest Breath contest was breathing his prize-winning rot on my neck. Meat was full of surprises. For one thing, I didn't expect him to be so darn strong. I made sure I had enough leverage and swung my head backward quickly, smashing the soft cartilage in his nose. If I was lucky, pieces of it would pierce his brain, such as it was. "—on the cot?" I wheezed.

Small voice. "Yes."

"Good. Stay put. You don't want to be mistaken for a bad guy."

Jessica and Duke were still charging at each other. He tried not to let her get far enough away to start using her legs, but he wasn't always successful. I asked her later how she could be sure it wasn't *me* she was destroying. Or, didn't she care?

"Aftershave," she replied.

"What?"

"Don't you know that a woman's sense of smell is superior to that of a man? I kept sniffing for the scent of your aftershave. Whenever I got a whiff of where it was, I simply stayed away from there."

"Is there any area where women are *not* superior to men?" I whined.

She grinned and shook her head.

I didn't need a superior sense of smell to know when Mulchmouth was near me. Talk about gross. I could swear he'd eaten a compost heap for dinner. I kicked and punched and grabbed hair and kept smashing his face into the floor, nose first. After several minutes or hours of this, I noted a slackness in his head and neck that made it seem unconnected to his shoulders. He was deeply out, maybe he wasn't dead. I listened for breathing. Nothing. No maybe about it, then, the state he was in, it didn't really matter. If he lived, he'd have the kind of face that would scare little children.

Something round and cold rolled against my leg. I hoped for a gun, but it was the next best thing—our flashlight. Okay, I could use that.

I shone the beam around the room and spotted Jessica standing over Duke, who sat propped against the side of the marble-topped desk in the guest registration area. Dazed, he was opening and closing his eyes without seeing anything. The light seemed to hurt his eyes.

I found our weapons. Jessica rubbed her hands together and said, "Let's go." She took hold of Veronica's hand and made for the dining room.

I helped her move the couch. "Don't you think we ought to be more certain of him?" I indicated Duke with my chin. He was beginning to look around. His eyeballs were out of sync.

Jessica shrugged. She walked over to the bathroom

and retrieved the roll of duct tape from the tiled floor. With it we rendered the redheaded Duke immobile. He, at least, would survive, but we made damn sure he'd have trouble getting to a phone for a while. We would call the state troopers ourselves in due time. Right now, our immediate plans would work better if Mihram did not know that he'd lost the ace up his sleeve.

Once outside, Jessica beckoned me to follow her in the direction of the pool. The brown Chevy was still there. She reached in through the window, put the car in neutral, and we gave it a pretty good shove backward into the bottom of the dry, gaping pool.

"Be kind of hard to drive that out of there," I ventured.

She grinned. "Impossible."

The three of us piled into Jessica's Cutlass—Veronica in the back—and Jessica maneuvered smoothly out onto the road.

"What a gesture!"

Jessica just grinned and said nothing.

"I don't believe you did that."

She still said nothing.

"You're usually so straight, how'd you ever think of doing a twisted thing like that?"

Jessica spoke: "Shut up," she said.

I leaned back and gladly bloodied up Jessica's front seat.

"How's your arm?" It was Veronica.

"Okay," I turned to look at her. "It's the shirt that really worries me."

She showed that she knew how to smile. "Are you another bunch of bad guys like those idiots who picked me up at the airport or did Mommy really send you to rescue me? They also said they were working for my mother."

I feigned indignation. "What? You can't tell a cavalry when you see one?"

"Yes, Veronica," Jessica said, "Allie really sent us to get you. And we're going to bring you to her right now."

I continued, "A knight in shining armor?" I pointed at Jessica. "See my white horse?"

She laughed happily. "Are you two really friends? You don't seem to agree on anything."

"Sure, we—"

"Are you lovers?"

"Well, it depends on what you mean by—"

"Did you ever sleep together?"

"Uh. We had a date once."

"Couldn't get to first base, huh?"

I laughed. "That's about the size of it." I glanced furtively at Jessica and stage-whispered, "You see," another glance, "Jessica doesn't go for hunks like me. She only likes—" Jessica's back stiffened. Veronica was all ears. "—nerds."

"Nerds?"

"You know. Like real estate agents."

"Oh. I thought you meant like computer whiz kids and stuff."

I looked at her suspiciously. What did she really know? Jessica's shoulders shook. Perceptibly. Probably shake us off the road.

Veronica was looking from one of us to the other. "Boy, you two would be dynamite in bed."

I smiled. "We're dynamite anywhere, hon."

"Hon." She leaned back in disgust. "Chee. I just *knew* you'd turn out to be a male chauvinist pig."

Chee.

The Walters reunion was just as somber and pompous and proper and sophisticated as I'd expected. Which is to say, not at all. All the way back to Brooklyn mother and daughter, together in the back seat, hugged and cried and hugged and laughed and kissed and held hands and touched shoulders and hugged. It was just as sickening as it sounds.

Jessica kept her eyes on the road. I leaned back and closed my eyes. Later, I would spell her so that she could get some rest, too. We still had a lot of night ahead of us. My left hand, the good one, found its way onto Jessica's right thigh, where it rested. She let it rest there. Once, on a long, open stretch of highway, she even patted it.

16

I SCOOPED UP a handful of sand and sifted it through my fingers. The damage to my upper arm was not that bad after all, for all the blood. It required only one butterfly bandage: everything else was already starting to heal. I had cleaned up at Jessica's house after we deposited the Walters women to the comfort and security of their own abode. We promised to call Allie the next day. Which was, by then, the current day. My shirt was still slightly damp where I had done my best to wash out the blood. It felt nice and cool in the warm night air.

Belle Harbor, Queens, rests on a long, narrow strip of land between Jamaica Bay and the Atlantic Ocean. The beach adjoining Mihram's modest house is part of an eight or so mile coastline stretching over the Rockaways.

The night air was fairly warm here at the shore, but the sand running through our fingers was somewhat cool to the touch. We were alone on the beach, Jessica and I. We'd expected nothing less. It was, after all, three o'clock in the morning and the only characters you'd be likely to find on the beach at that hour are either legitimately insane or the kind of lunatics who'd attempt a B and E on a gangster's well-guarded, fully-alarmed, and otherwise secure dwelling. We were waiting for Boris, who said he knew where to get some chloroform, which we were going to need to handle Mihram's formidable entourage. And we were trying not to fall asleep. The chloroform wasn't the only reason we needed Boris. He was our acknowledged engineering expert. Self-acknowledged, to be sure. Every Russian immigrant I know claims to have been an engineer back in the old country.

"You sure Boris knows burglar alarms?" I asked.

"All I know is that when I laid the situation out for him he simply said he'd bring equipment and meet us out here. Then he hung up the phone."

"Uh-uh," I said. "What he said was 'I brring ikvipmont, Chessica,' " I qvipped.

A strong rush of fish odor charged in from the sea, the kind of smell that always made me think of San Francisco although that was a different ocean entirely. "Isn't it funny how a smell is all it takes to transport you to an old memory?"

"Mmm," she said. We were lying side by side, hands clasped underneath our heads, looking at the moon hanging over the deep waters. Aside from the moon, the beach was lighted only by a distant streetlight. The darkness of the sky met the darkness of the sea at the purple-black, invisible horizon. "What are you thinking about?"

"Oh, just memories of my youth in the big city. The other big city."

"San Francisco?"

"Yeah."

"The crazy city, you mean."

"That, too."

"What are you remembering?"

"Nothing. Lots of things. My"—stage sigh—"naive youth."

"You were never naive."

"You didn't know me before Nam. I mean, I actually enlisted, Jess."

"That's not naive. It's nuts." She flipped over onto her stomach and brushed the sand out of her hair. "You're not so jaded as you'd like to think, Red. You're still just a romantic idealist at heart."

"How do you know what's in my heart?"

I got a friendly punch in the shoulder. "I'm your best friend, remember?" I rubbed my shoulder—my left, luckily—to get the blood circulating again.

"Okay. I remember, I remember."

"Anyhow, if you had really lost all you're naiveté, you'd still be in the computer industry now, making the big bucks. You would never have accepted my offer. Actually," she added, "I wish Sandy were a bit more like you."

"Jessica," I said suddenly, "what do you really see in Sandy?"

She considered my question seriously for a moment before answering. A long moment. "Well," she said finally, "part of me is very attracted to part of him."

"You mean there are some things about him that you like, that are attractive to you."

"That's right."

"And, that's it?"

"Isn't that enough?"

"Oh, it's enough of a reason to have dinner with him, sure. Enough to have a few laughs, spend some time together, sure. But, enough for marriage? If a client came to you with a case, would you give a part of you to a part of it? Hell, haven't you ever heard of love? It's a fine institution, Jess."

"Oh, yes. It's a fine institution. But it seems to be reserved for other people. I'm twenty-nine years old and I've never been in love."

"Never?"

"Surprised?"

"Well, yes."

"Haven't you ever noticed that I'm somewhat freaky?" She produced a wry grin. "I'm different from any other woman I've ever known. Most of the men, too."

"Oh, come on, Jess. Everyone's unique in some way. No two people are alike, you know."

"Don't humor me," she said icily. "I know who I am. And I was raised with too much honesty to be anyone else. In fact," she added, "I like myself. I never wanted to change. But now," she said softly, "someone likes me well enough to want to marry me. And all it would take on my part is a little role playing. Is that too much to ask for the family that I might never get another chance at?"

"Buying into a lifetime of hypocrisy? Yeah, it seems like too much to ask. I can understand that you're determined not to remain childless like your Aunt Rose—"

"What do you—"

"—but, Jessica, you couldn't do it long. And still remain Jessica Munroe."

Jessica smiled. "So that's why women have to change their names when they get married."

"I'll tell you what," I said. "I'll make a deal with you."

She hunched forward on her elbows. "I'm all ears."

"No you're not." I was looking down her shirt. "The deal is this. You tell Sandy no. And you keep on looking for that lucky man who will love you because of what and who you are. Who will love you passionately, will never want to spend a moment away from you, will take on your problems as his own just as he shares his with you."

"Do you have any part in this deal?"

"I was coming to that." I cleared my throat. "If you still, uhm, haven't found him by the time you're—uhm, say—thirty-five, then we'll just go ahead and make a baby together."

"We?"

"As in you and me."

"Isn't this just a little arrogant of you?"

I took a breath. "Yes."

She grinned.

I pulled my right hand out from behind my head and offered a handshake to seal the deal. She looked at my outstretched hand suspiciously. "What if you're married when I'm thirty-five?"

"A deal," I stated, "is a deal. Besides," I shrugged, "I don't think I'm the marrying kind."

She patted my hand down, securing it down at my side in the process. "I'll have to get back to you on that one, partner."

Boris, his poor, bruised face looking worse even though it was surely on its way to getting better, decided to approach the house from the beach. The house, actually a two-story custom-built mansion, was much larger than most of the other homes in the predominantly upper-middle-class area. In fact, most of those homes were not much larger than Mihram's servant quarters—a more modest structure situated at the end of his driveway, behind a carport. There was also a separate garage large enough, by my estimation, to shelter four cars snugly.

Although Boris's ego was definitely about as large as his exuberant frame, it proved, in this case at least, just as substantive. He was through that burglar alarm in minutes. We all put on gloves. Not a sound was heard, no one came crashing out of the house with a shotgun, not even a curtain rustled. Now, all we needed to worry about was that a silent alarm had been tripped that was connected to the local police department. But something told me that our friend Mihram's ties with police anywhere were kept on a less-than-intimate plane.

Boris had the chloroform in an unlabeled brown glass container, stored that way to keep it from decomposing.

It had been diluted to approximately a one percent solution: enough to put someone out, but not so much that they would become sick or suffer permanent liver damage—all in all, a very sensible and practical tool for what we had to do. He also had an empty, hard plastic spray bottle—the kind used by hairdressers to spray a lacquer mist over blue-gray hair teased within an inch of its fragile life and then nudged into place one strand at a time. Boris filled the spray bottle from the brown bottle.

The first floor was empty except for the armed guard watching a videotape on the television in the den. The television was turned on low so that he would still be able to hear important sounds like those made by vicious criminals breaking into his turf. Fortunately, we were turned on low, too.

Jessica managed to sneak up behind him. Whatever was on the screen obviously had his attention. Come to think of it, it almost caught Jessica's attention as well. But she overcame the urge. Just as the guard started to look around uncomfortably, she hit him from behind, applying the side of her hand to the back of his neck. Before he could recover, Boris sprayed him full in the face, directing the spray to the nose and mouth area. The guard's eyes stopped blinking very suddenly. Boris nodded and made an okay sign with his thumb and forefinger, indicating that everything was going fine. I taped the gentleman's wrists and ankles together. We weren't taking any chances.

Two men fitting the descriptions of Nesar and Jackson were sleeping in separate bedrooms on the upstairs level. We gave them the same treatment as the guard downstairs, only we didn't have to hit them first. All we wanted was some uninterrupted time alone with Mihram—or with his safe, whichever proved easier to crack. We felt sure that our client's master tape would be in that safe. But I must say that the strength of our conviction was based mainly on the fact that if the tape wasn't in there, we knew of no place else to look.

We spotted the master bedroom and kept it under surveillance while we assured ourselves that the other rooms were unoccupied. The master bedroom was most definitely occupied. It might have been hard to identify and sort out the mass of tangled flesh in what had to be the largest bed I have ever seen anywhere, including the movies, were it not for the definite and obvious differences among the occupants. Mihram, himself of swarthy skin tones, was nicely offset by the coloring of a blond-haired, white-skinned lovely and that of an ebony-colored Black American with a close-cropped Afro. On the dresser were some dusty coke paraphernalia.

While Boris set about spraying his chloroform mixture on the Bobbsey twins, Jessica and I worked quickly to tape up Mihram before he had a chance to awaken fully. We applied the duct tape to his wrists, binding them in front, then we taped his ankles, after crossing them for him. He sure was a hairy bastard—back, stomach, legs, everything. He was covered all over with a thick mat of black wool. Whatever he was paying those women, it wasn't enough. Jessica found a dirty—and I mean dirty—sock on the floor and stuffed it in his mouth. He was coming around. Talk about heavy sleepers.

Boris had made sure that the two girls would be out for several hours, but I taped their wrists and ankles, too. That was one job I did all by myself. I refused to let Jessica help me at all. I'm such a gentleman.

You couldn't miss it. Next to a long walk-in closet, a set of carved wooden doors, polished to a brilliant shine, fronted what appeared to be a large built-in cabinet. Jessica poked gently at one of the doors. It swung open on silent hinges revealing another door, a more formidable one, constructed of a heavy gray metal with two combination locks inset at one side. It was the kind of safe—more of a vault, really—that you might find in a jewelry store. Jessica gave each of the locks in turn a slow twist, in the hope that the safe, being in such a well-guarded house, had been set for easy opening. It hadn't. Jessica crossed over to the bedroom door and locked it. The air-conditioning provided us with a convenient sound screen.

It's hard to sneer with a sock in your mouth, but Mihram was making a pretty good go of it. Mihram was fully awake by now. I went over to him, nudged his trussed-up legs to make room at the edge of the bed, and sat down facing him. I removed the sock,

"Hi, honey," I said, patting his hairy chest. "What say you tell us how to get into that big beautiful safe of yours?" I searched his eyes for the fear I hoped I would find there. What I found instead was a pair of blazing black fireballs.

He fired a shot of spittle in my direction. "I heard your client's little girl is missing." It landed on his stomach. "What a shame."

I grinned.

He went on. "If you're as smart as you think you are, you'll get out of here right now."

Boris returned from where he had been checking out the adjacent private master bathroom. I heard water running.

"Perhaps," Mihram offered with a smirk, "I'll even help you look for her."

I was still grinning. "You don't have that ace up your sleeve anymore, Mihram. Veronica Walters is home safe with her mother."

Jessica put in, "He doesn't even have a sleeve anymore."

"Chessica, Chessica," Boris said. "You not rreally looking at naked man?"

"I'm looking," came the retort, "but I don't see anything."

Boris looked around the bedroom, spotted the nineteen-inch color television sitting on its stand, and nodded approvingly.

"He looks to be durrty, no, Rreddy?"

Jessica and I just stared. We had no idea what he was up to.

"Come," he motioned me to the open bathroom door. "You carry him to pool in bathtub. He vill talk and get clean at same time."

"Sort of like getting clean and coming clean?" I asked. I still didn't understand, but I'm nothing if not obliging.

The water flowing in just covered Mihram's legs, which stretched out nicely with room to spare. The bathtub was something else. It was a sunken bathtub, more of a small swimming pool, really, big enough for several people to bathe comfortably. Two or three, certainly. There was gold-veined marble, gold-plated plumbing fixtures, and a gold-covered handrail. Marble steps led down into the tub. Boris waited as more water rushed in. Then he shut the flow of water off.

Mihram still wasn't talking. But then, taking a bath wasn't exactly on par with burning bamboo shoots under one's fingernails, hanging upside down by one's big toes, or being buried neck-deep in the hot, dry desert sand and abandoned. I think Boris knew this and was about to make it more interesting.

Three pairs of eyes watched, one with more than passing interest, as Boris returned from the bedroom carrying the television. Zenith, color, nineteen-inch. One of those tabletop models that some cynical marketing genius once called portable, and the name stuck.

Balancing it on one hand, Boris took the cord and plugged it into an outlet over the sink. It went on immediately. A *Kung Fu* rerun was playing. "You everr vatch TV in the tub, Rreddy?"

"Sure," I said.

"Mebbe is betterr inside tub?" he asked innocently. "Is closerr."

"I don't think so," I said. "The surgeon general warns about bathing and watching. It's kind of like drinking and driving. Smoking and sleeping."

"Nah." He waved one hand in derision and the television tottered precariously over Mihram's lap. "You vatch too much mofies. You think a little TV in the vaterr has so much electric? Pooh." He turned to Mihram, "I vas engineer in Rrussia," he said proudly.

"I don't know about inside the water," I offered, "but you're welcome to come over to my place anytime and hold my TV for me while I take a bath."

"Uh." He shifted the weight around a little in his arms. On the screen, young Grasshopper's mentor was delivering a lesson in moral self-defense in his characteristically slow, stilted speech. I recalled that all the violence on the show had been in slow motion. "I don't think so. Is verry heffy." He sighed. He had been holding the television directly over the middle of the tub and his grip had become somewhat shaky. He twisted his head around the big box and peered at the screen.

"Is nice?" He asked it pleasantly enough, but his fearsome visage belied any thoughts of good humor. "Vood you like mebbe a differrent station?"

Mihram was becoming distinctly uncomfortable. He maintained his silence, but he kept looking toward the door as if salvation would soon be forthcoming. If I knew anything at all about Kamal Mihram, however, it was that salvation in any form would be a long time coming. Anyway, Jessica was in the bedroom, waiting to try out the combination on the safe as soon as he revealed it, keeping an ear at the bedroom door and an eye on the windows. We remembered too well the trap we had set up for ourselves in Bay Ridge.

Mihram spit to show his disdain for us. His disdain didn't reach all the way to his eyes, and his spittle dripped into his own water. But when he spoke, it came out tough. After all, one didn't run a successful illegal operation without a coating tough as steel wool. "You're not going to kill me. Not you, Reddy. Or," he indicated his human television stand, "your big friend here. That's one thing amateur punks like you don't do very well—is killing in cold blood." He said it like it was a character flaw. "If you really wanted to kill me, you would have done it right away. I have nothing to fear from you." He finished his little speech with a tone of conviction. I think he almost convinced himself.

Can't have that. I said, "You jerk. Don't you realize I could snuff you in a minute? It wouldn't bother me in the least. In fact, I'd enjoy it immensely. In the past week, your boys have taken more shots at me and my partner and, yes, my friend here, than I can count without taking off my shoes and socks. But—" I wondered whether I have any unconscious facial expressions that give away when I am lying. Like a tic. Or, some people avert their eyes when they are about to tell a lie. I directed mine straight into his. Or, on the other hand, some people purposely look directly into their victim's eyes. I blinked. "—my partner is weak. She is a woman after all." Forgive me, Jessica. "She does not like killing. Ms. Munroe wants only to get into your safe and retrieve our client's tape. As far as I'm concerned, however, we'd be better off killing you where you lie and burning your whole house down, and to hell with you and your tapes."

I shrugged. "Of course, my friend here"—Boris was indeed showing the strain—"may not be able to serve your entertainment needs for the same length of time as you can keep quiet about the safe and—" Boris let one corner slip. It almost touched the water. Mihram's taped-up knees jerked together to the side, exposing the holes in his tough facade. "—if it's an accident, well . . ." I shrugged once again.

Boris sighed. "You talk too much, Rreddy. I tirred. Is heffy." He slumped forward treacherously.

The rest, as they say, was easy.

Mihram yielded the combinations to the safe and ended up back in his bed, dripping wet. The safe yielded a virtual treasury: cash, jewelry of all types and sizes, ten baggies full of some white powdered stuff that we assumed was not sugar, and papers—deeds, documents, business records. Oh, and a nice little cache of videotapes. The tapes were labeled, each with a different name. I recognized the names of some state representatives. Among them, Althea Walters, Mel Pierce, and Valerie Crockett.

The television was back on its stand. The sock was back in place keeping company with Mihram's teeth. Mihram's bed partners were still out. Good thing. If there's anything less appealing than an overly hirsute man, it's a soggy, overly hirsute man.

Jessica took charge of the tapes. Boris still had the chloroform, which he proceeded to apply to Mihram's furious countenance. I stuffed the cash into the roomy pockets of Boris's lightweight safari jacket. I left the safe open and untied one of the bags of coke, letting it spill open onto the dresser next to the snort apparatus.

Some of the deeds were for properties in the Catskills and were made out to various corporate names. There were a lot more than the five we already knew about. We considered ourselves lucky to have found Veronica at all that night.

A large manila envelope contained some floor plans, architect renderings, and operating plans that clearly spelled out Mihram's confidence in his future casino gambling empire in upstate New York. It was one area, according to our client, which was not being considered as seriously in drawing up the casino gambling bill and still wouldn't be, now that we had recovered the blackmail tapes. Still, someone ought to stop Mihram in his tracks. I took the envelope with me, leaving the records of various current operations intact in the open safe.

Before departing, we checked the duct tape on the two sleeping beauties, on the sleeping ugly, on the two ineffectual bodyguards, and on the still-armed guard in the den. The videotape had finished playing.

"How long are they going to be out?" I whispered to Boris.

"Don't vorrry," he said. "Mebbe lasts couple hourrs. They vake up soon." Boris took his chloroform and the spray bottle with him into his van—and the cash I had parked in his pockets.

"Don't spend it all in one place," I warned.

He smiled. "I hold forr you till I see you." He waved a big hand at us through the open window as he pulled away.

We took Rockaway Boulevard to the Marine Parkway Bridge. I was driving.

"You just passed Riis Park."

"Okay. I just passed Riis Park."

"There are telephones at the park."

"Oh." I U-turned and pulled up alongside a bank of Ma Bell's Finest. "You make the call."

"Me? You know I can't do that kind of thing."

"A woman's voice is better. Besides," I added, "who was it tossed a car into a swimming pool tonight?" I had the number of the local police precinct in the pocket of my jeans. From what I heard of her side of the conversation, she did very well.

"Hello." Her voice sounded older, kind of naggy and nosey. "I want to report a burglary . . . No, not my house. On my block. That nice man, Mr. Miriam." She gave the cops Mihram's address. ". . . I think they are there now, you better hurry . . . I don't know, but I heard a shot. Maybe two shots . . . Maybe three shots . . . Oh, yeh, I don't know about those burglars, maybe they're crazy men . . . Why? Because, you see, these two naked ladies ran out of the house and they just dragged them back in . . . That's right, naked. Very attractive, too . . . Now, it's none of my business what those gorgeous ladies were doing in poor Mr. Miriam's house, let me tell you. I'm not one to pry, but—" She replaced the receiver gently in the middle of her own sentence. That way the police would think they had been cut off before they had a chance to ask for her name.

"What's the idea of the naked ladies bit?" I asked once we were on our way again.

"You're the one who's always complaining about how long it takes the cops to respond to a call."

"Yeah. Twenty minutes when they're in a hurry. Oh." I grinned appreciatively. "That's good. How many cops do you think will respond to a call involving a couple of beautiful, allegedly naked women?"

"How many would you say are on duty this time of night?" she asked rhetorically.

"Unfortunately, I don't know if our friend Mihram is going to spend much time in prison," I commented. "But he's sure going to have a hard time explaining the cocaine that's out in the open."

"Oh, yes. That was a good idea," she said. "Otherwise, it would be called an illegal search."

"Yeah. Like this, they were legitimately on the premises, called in to investigate a burglary."

"And what do they find? The occupants of the house tied up and just coming out of a chloroform stupor. It certainly seems like burglary to me."

"It was," I patted the papers on the seat between us.

"Quite frankly, though, I really don't think that the cocaine alone is enough to keep him out of commission very long. He must have some decent lawyers to be able to stay out of prison like he has. He can be out on bail and fighting this rap in the courts for years."

"Hmm," she agreed. "And in the meantime, he's still after us, vindictive now. Also, Allie and Veronica may not be safe."

"And he can just go find himself some more legislators to blackmail."

"Or buy."

I nodded. "That's why I took these documents. I want to get them into the hands of the right people. The kind of people who tend not to worry about illegal search and seizure when they go after someone who is messing with their turf."

17

NEW YORK HAS five major crime families: the Genovese group, the Luccese group, the Columbo group, the Bonnano group, and the Gambino group. It's not something the Chamber of Commerce puts in its promotional literature. Each family has its own counselor—often called by the name *consigliore*—but Howard Garvin is an attorney on friendly terms with all of them. He has been known to lobby for them at the state level and to serve in the capacity of mediator in the occasional interfamily dispute. Mel Pierce set up the appointment for us. I suppose Garvin was one of the contacts Pierce had tried to impress us with. One thing did impress us—he agreed to see us the same day.

It was hard to believe that less than twenty-four hours had passed since we set out to search for our client's fair-haired daughter in the wilds of Upstate New York. Working on four hours sleep and several cups of strong coffee is not new to me, but it's not something I want to do every day. Just as we were cleaning up after a late breakfast—the only way we could have had an early breakfast was by not going to sleep at all—Boris stopped by to unload the cash. He didn't want to have it on his conscience if anything happened. Boris kept a ten-thousand-dollar share, Jessica took charge of another ten. I matched her ten grand with my own. We decided to split what was left between two individuals whose charitable institutions deal regularly with the ravages caused by Mihram's operation in under-the-counter drugs: Father

Ritter and Mother Hale. That came to $27,500. Each. Boris agreed to deliver the money, in cash. After all, we didn't want to get onto some kind of charity-suckers mailing list just because of one windfall—and an illegal one, at that. Jessica and I made a few phone calls, setting up what was left of Tuesday. Our appointment with Garvin was at two o'clock.

Howard Garvin's law firm was just your average multi-partner organization with a large staff and offices inhabiting the entire tenth floor of a major Park Avenue office building.

I recognized his face immediately. Why not? It had been on the six o'clock news often enough. Every year, he would take on one or two charity cases. Inevitably, these cases were sensational enough to keep his sympathetic, alert face and quotable comments plastered throughout the news media for weeks.

Howard Garvin had the long, lean face of a thoroughbred. His chin jutted out slightly as if his unconscious mind were always trying to get the edge on the competition. His light-gray vested suit, well tailored and supremely fashionable, went as well with the hair around his temples as the handkerchief in his breast pocket went with the muted colors of his perfectly knotted tie. Like everything else in the office, the air-conditioning was superb. Not overdone, but enough to take care of sweaty brows and prevent unsightly crescent-shaped stains under the arms. One didn't have to work with mobsters to be a successful New York lawyer but, at least in the case of Howard Garvin, it sure didn't hurt.

"As you can see, I'm a very busy man," he began. We saw nothing of the sort. His gleaming mahogany desktop was totally bare. "But our mutual friend, Mr. Pierce, is very persuasive. He led me to believe you may hold information that could be of interest to some of my clients. I've learned to be skeptical about such offers, but . . ." He raised his shoulders half an inch and let them fall again, spreading his hands wide. The first ball of an ill-defined game had clearly been tossed. "Well, Mr. Reddy?"

I had the manila envelope, but Jessica had the ball. I deferred to my senior partner.

"That's true," Jessica confirmed. "We uncovered some information which could be useful, if not vital, to certain of your clients."

"Which clients would those be, Ms. Munroe?" There was absolutely no expression on his face.

"Oh," Jessica matched his indifference with her own, "any of your clients who might be interested in legalizing gambling in New York."

His eyebrows went up a degree. "Now there's an interesting subject. But"—his chin jutted out a little more—"I couldn't say which of my clients might be interested in such information as you may have to offer. This is, after all, a large concern." He smiled crisply. "How much do you want for your information?"

"Please." Jessica's hand was raised in front of her, palm turned out, as if he were about to force a check on her. He wasn't. "We're not asking for any money. During our latest investigation, we uncovered information about an individual who is attempting to set up his own gambling empire in the area and we simply knew immediately that it would be a terrible travesty were we not to bring it to the attention of the proper parties." Garvin's mouth twitched slightly. "Of course, there is one additional complication."

"What's that?" Twitch.

"This man—not a very nice man—is involved in many illegal enterprises and has been trying very hard to kill us, myself and my partner, Mr. Reddy."

I nodded.

Garvin pressed his lips together and shook his head sadly. "Why would he want to do that?" he asked.

"For one thing," I offered, placing the envelope on the desk within easy reach, "he really wants these back."

Garvin emptied the contents of the envelope onto his desktop and looked the documents over carefully, with evident interest.

"Perhaps," Jessica continued, "if you find that some of your clients are indeed interested in the information, they might simply apply a little gentle persuasion to this man, Kamal Mihram—in a most friendly way, of course—and ask him to refrain from annoying us any further."

Garvin packed the papers back in the envelope. "I'm sorry, Ms. Munroe. Mr. Reddy. These documents are not as important or interesting as you had hoped. I don't really see how I can help you." He slipped the envelope carefully into a drawer of his desk. "Have you tried going to the police on this?"

Jessica shook her head. "There's no evidence linking Mihram with the attempts on our lives so, naturally, we saw no reason to involve the police."

He nodded. "Well, I can't make any promises for my clients. Of course, you understand that none of them is involved in the type of shady operations that this Mihram"—he grimaced with distaste—"apparently relishes."

That was as much as we could get out of him, and it was plenty. He'd kept the envelope, after all, and we could be sure it would not remain in his desk drawer very long.

Meanwhile, I couldn't remain on my feet very long. I wanted to go home and get some real sleep. I had trouble remembering the last time I was in my own apartment.

We'd already been to Pierce's office earlier in the day

to deliver to him the master tape of the production in which he had a starring role. Then, after meeting with Allie in our office, providing her with a full report, and leaving the master tape with her name on it and the copy from our safe in her grateful hands, we were left with eight very hot videotapes to take care of.

"Drive right down Park," I instructed. "I want to go home and get some sleep."

"Disposing of the tapes is going to be a bit of a problem."

"That's right," I agreed. "Don't forget the turnoff."

"If we deliver the tape to each of them," she sighed, "that will involve a lot of time and no fee. And, what am I supposed to do while you sleep?"

"Why no fee?"

"Because they are not our clients, no fee was agreed upon in advance, no contract entered into. Besides, private investigators have an awful reputation and they might be afraid that we had kept a copy and taken over the blackmail business."

"On the other hand, if we simply send each of them a letter stating that the tape was found and destroyed, they might very well think the same thing."

"Yes, that's right."

"And, I don't care what you do with the next few hours, I'm hitting the sack. Anyway, you have a"—I made a face—"dinner date with Fish Face."

"And his family," she said miserably. "At six o'clock."

I checked my watch. It was almost four. "Don't you have to fix yourself up? Put on a new dress to meet the family?"

"Shut up."

"Spend some time with the makeup mirror?"

"Anyhow," she said, pointedly ignoring my pointed jibes, "destroying the tapes without telling them so would be cruel. There you have eight legislators, sitting on trembling heinies, waiting for the sky to fall.''

''Heinies?''

''Perhaps we should call them all together in a meeting and give each of them back his or her tape, assuring them that their problems are over?''

''I don't think so, Jess. None of them will appreciate being publicly associated with a video blackmail scam, even if it's in a small, exclusive group.''

''Looks like we're back to personal delivery.''

''Without a fee,'' I concurred.

''Who knows what future business might come our way out of this,'' she said thoughtfully, pulling up in front of the building where I occasionally lived and slept. ''We could leave a card.''

I yawned. ''That's what got us into this mess in the first place.''

18

MY EYES HAD hardly closed when I suddenly found them wide open again. I looked at the clock: 10:40. P.M.? A.M.? The room was dark, even though I'd left a window open for air. It must be six hours sleep—unless I'd somehow slept through an entire day—felt like six minutes. I felt lousy.

Then I realized what had prodded me awake. There were noises coming from the living room or the kitchen.

Mihram.

This is it, I thought. Garvin left the envelope in his desk drawer. Or he didn't leave it in his drawer, but he took his time getting it to the mob. Or the mob took its time getting to Mihram. Whatever the case, time seemed to be running out. I looked at the clock: 10:45. Can't stay in bed. Wearily, I reached for the gun near my bed, and wished I weren't so fond of sleeping in the altogether.

The noises I heard sounded like they belonged to more than one person. They were talking. I tiptoed stealthily down the hall and stopped short. That was the television. Why had Mihram's men put on the television? Perhaps, to cover the sounds of a struggle? I looked in cautiously, keeping myself in shadow.

It was hard to see anything. The living room was dark except for the blue-white glow of the television screen. The volume was rather low, too low to conceal gunshots or screams for help. There was a lone figure sitting on my couch, watching the tube, a glass in her hand. Immediately I knew something was wrong. She was watching a tribute to the shining years of Hollywood.

Jessica noticed me standing in the doorway. "Sorry," she said. "I didn't mean to wake you." She took a sip from her glass. My glass.

"That's okay." I suddenly realized that I was brandishing a gun, and that was the only thing I was brandishing.

When I returned, I wore a pair of pajama bottoms. Somehow, I felt that getting properly dressed would be like renouncing any chance I might have for getting back to sleep that night. I made myself comfortable on the couch and took a sip from Jessica's glass. Water. What an imagination! She obviously wanted to drown her sorrows. I poured myself something stronger and brought her a refill.

"Do you want to talk, or are you just going to allow yourself to be consumed in glass after glass of New York tap water?" Someone once told me I have a way with words.

"You have a way with words."

"Where was this family dinner, anyway?"

"At Sandy's folks' place, In Hempstead. His parents were there, and his sister and her husband, and the brat."

"You shouldn't call Sandy names. I don't."

"His nephew. Sandy was there, too."

"You look like you fit in just fine." She was wearing a yellow silk suit with a white silk shell. Very Island.

"Certainly. Until we started chatting."

"Oh." I mimicked, " 'So, what do you do?' "

She smiled. "That's what started it. But it came out a little different. The father said, 'I hear you work in an office.' "

Oh, boy.

"I said, 'I spend some of my time in my office. I'm a private detective, in business for myself.' "

"Oh, that made it better."

"No. The brother-in-law giggled like a ninny and the sister's eyes glazed over and she went to see what the brat was doing."

"I suppose the sister isn't the working type."

"She works at being a pain in the ass. You know, she's *so* busy with the brat and the big house that she couldn't possibly *imagine* having time for a *career*. And, anyhow, brother-in-law supports the family *so* well, and she's *so* very thankful that she doesn't *need* to work."

"Don't you feel sorry for her? She just never got her consciousness raised."

"It would take a derrick."

"How about Mom?"

"Mom sits home all day and worries about Sandy and sister and gets sloshed."

"You can't possibly know that. You're not officially part of the family, yet."

"Oh, yes I can. She was half-sloshed when I got there."

"Oh, well. That's different."

We watched the closing credits in silence. Ed McMahon came on and tried selling life insurance to people over fifty. I felt overqualified.

"Then the father came back with, 'So, what does a private detective do?' Just as I opened my mouth to answer, dear Sandy blurts out, 'Oh, you know, Pop, credit checks and things like that.' At which the father nods his head because he suddenly understands and, just to show us how smart he is, he says, 'Like the girls at the insurance company.' "

Now that called for sympathy. I put my arm around her shoulders and said, "Think it's easy being an in-law?

One day you'll be a mother-in-law, and then you'll find out how hard it is."

"You're a big help."

The eleven o'clock news had started. A male and female team, both handsome and perfectly coifed, both between thirty-one and forty-two, both looking as if they couldn't understand the news let alone cover it and trying hard to show nice smiles without making the mistake of smiling at inappropriate news items. I think that was their hardest job. Jessica reached over and turned up the volume.

"What is it really, Jess? You've taken that kind of flak before."

. . . A nine-year-old boy was rescued by neighbors from a burning building that took his baby sister's life. The neighbors did not know she was in there . . . The mayor called a press conference to discuss the latest of his friends and political allies to step down amid charges of corruption. It was sparsely attended . . . In South Fallsburg, in an old abandoned hotel, three men were found dead—

We sat up. Three?

—one of them from a gunshot wound to the head. Cause of death of the other two has not yet been officially determined at this time . . . The water level is dangerously low, due to the drought. The city has begun using processed Hudson River water.

"Well, I'll be." I looked at Jessica. She looked at her glass and put it down.

"Mihram," she said.

"Hard to get good help nowadays."

"Especially if you go about killing them off."

"Afterwards," Jessica said.

"Huh?"

"That was the worst part. You know. After the family dinner on Long Island."

"Oh. Afterwards."

"We were having tea in the parlor—"

My eyebrows shot up.

"I was pretending to have tea," she explained. "Sandy was discussing real estate with his father and the brother-in-law. Sister and mother and I discussed shopping for the perfect dress, the horrors of vacuum cleaner repair, and renewing stained carpets."

"Are you saying that you contributed to this discussion?"

"The same as I had the tea." She thought a moment. "Mother wanted to know which eye makeup I prefer, Maybelline or Revlon."

I snorted. "What did you tell them?"

"I told the truth. I said that I've always felt that if I spend ten minutes applying the perfect eye makeup, I might improve myself. But if I spend ten minutes reading a good book, I might improve the world."

"Ooh. What did they say to that?"

"After an appropriate pause, the sister said that her clothes dryer was on the fritz and the mother said it was a good thing the weather reporters expect sunshine for a few days."

"Why didn't you just discuss real estate with Sandy and the guys?"

"They were on one side of the room, we were on the other. It just didn't seem—possible."

. . . Late bulletin regarding the alleged cocaine dealer released today on one-hundred-thousand-dollars' bail who claimed that a burglar got into his beachfront house and planted ten kilos of cocaine in his bedroom safe. Kamal Mihram and two of his aides were killed by a car bomb in the mid-Manhattan area. The names of the aides are being withheld pending notification of next of kin. Further details as they are available . . .

"Next of kin?"

"Rats, lizards." I turned the set off.

"You go back to bed," Jessica said. "I shouldn't have come here."

"Of course, you should have—"

"You're tired. And we've got a full day ahead of us."

"—that's why you've got a key. Full day?"

She nodded. "We have to deliver the rest of the tapes to those politicians. It isn't right to delay on this."

"They'll be happy to know that they're off the hook."

I leaned forward and circled her in a friendly hug. We held each other like that for a few minutes. It felt good.

"Why not settle it right now?"

"What do you mean?"

"Call him. Call Sandy now."

"I'll wake him."

"So what?"

Resolutely, she reached for the phone and dialed the eleven digits. She waited, counting the rings. I yawned, wanting another drink, not having the energy to get up and fetch it myself. I stretched out comfortably on the couch, my head in Jessica's lap, my feet reaching over the armrest. I could hear the rings, too—four, five. Jessica tucked the telephone receiver between her ear and her shoulder and idly played with my unkempt, slept-on hair. I settled comfortably in to receive her attentions. Six, sev—

"Hello? Sandy . . ."

If you have enjoyed this book and would like to receive details of other Walker Mystery-Suspense Novels please write to: